# Truth Lies Dying

Graeme Hampton was born in Paisley and grew up in Stirling. The Denning and Fisher crime thriller series is inspired by his time living in London in his twenties. He now lives in Hastings, East Sussex.

# Also by Graeme Hampton

## D.I Denning and D.S Fisher

*Know No Evil*
*Blood Family*
*The Darkness Within*
*Run For Cover*
*Shame the Devil*
*Truth Lies Dying*

# GRAEME HAMPTON

# TRUTH LIES DYING

hera

First published in the United Kingdom in 2023 by

Hera Books
Unit 9 (Canelo), 5th Floor
Cargo Works, 1–2 Hatfields
London SE1 9PG
United Kingdom

A CIP catalogue record for this book is available from the British Library.

Print ISBN 978 1 80436 542 7
Ebook ISBN 978 1 80436 541 0

Look for more great books at www.herabooks.com

Printed and bound in Great Britain by Clays Ltd, Elcograf S.p.A.

1

*Patricia Woodhouse AKA The Old Bag. Thanks for all your support and encouragement.*

# Prologue

It's another cold night. A biting chill burrows deep into the bones and stays there. It's the cold he hates the most. It stays with you, especially at night.

One of the younger lads has lit a brazier, stuffed it with debris and old bits of rubbish. It gives off some warmth, but it isn't enough. Some of the others have gathered round it, but he doesn't want to get too close. He's learned from experience that it often pays to keep your distance. If a fight were to break out, brought on by drink or drugs or cold or hunger, it could turn nasty very quickly.

The others are several feet away, and he's aware of the chattering coming from the group. Sometimes he's tempted to go over and join them: there is, after all, an argument for there being safety in numbers.

But, no, it's better to keep himself to himself.

Except for young Corey...

He thinks of his family, warm and loved in what was once his family home. He tries to blot out the pain but the tears come, as they always do whenever he thinks about what could have been.

He's lost track of the days and the months, which all seem to blend into a timeless nothingness now, but he feels Christmas is close.

Sometimes you can just sense certain things, like the changing seasons or stillness in the air that separates night from day, despite the constant hum of extraneous sound that is never too far away.

He thinks back to the Christmases of long ago, of happier times with family. Perhaps that is what he misses most. The comfort of having loved ones around him. To feel part of something loved and valued. What he has now is nothing. An emptiness. A hollow ache...

Even though he's wearing all the clothes he owns, he still can't escape the cold. He should be used to it by now. This is his second winter living rough; finding shelter and safety wherever he can. Keeping his head down and trying to remain unseen. In the summer it's just about bearable. But it's the winter they all fear. Unless they can find somewhere protected from the elements, the cold will finish them off. The older ones and the sick ones first.

In the cold half-light of their underground cavern, he spots a figure approaching him. At first, he assumes it's someone from the group by the fire; one of the younger ones come over to blag some money he doesn't have, or a smoke or booze. Generally, the others leave him alone.

As the figure grows closer, he can sense there's something familiar about him. He's wearing a heavy jacket with the hood pulled up and his face is obscured, but the way he walks reminds him of someone.

It must be someone from the group; no one else knows about this place. But this isn't one of them. This is someone else.

Someone dangerous.

The figure takes something out of an inside pocket. He can't see what it is, but there's a glint of the fire on metal.

It's only when the figure gets closer that he recognises him.

By then it's too late.

# Chapter One

Shoreditch Tube station. Or at least, what remained of it. Tucked away at the end of an unassuming alleyway off the lively throughfare of Brick Lane, the fringes of the financial heart of London, where the City slowly blends into the urban sprawl of East London.

The area had a rougher, less polished feel than nearby streets, with their glossy glass and metal office blocks and trendy café bar culture.

The chilly bite of winter was making itself felt in the frigid air.

DI Matthew Denning belonged to one of the Metropolitan Police's Major Investigation Teams that was part of the wider Homicide and Major Crime Command, and was familiar with the area. Though, to be fair, not this actual part of it. He and his wife, Sarah, lived in an attractive loft apartment in trendy Hoxton, not far from the depressing scene that greeted him now. Not far, and yet it could have been a million miles away. Hoxton had a nicer feel to it: less urban and more gentrified. But as gentrification slowly encroached on more and more of London's urban spaces, it rendered whole swathes of the city increasingly unaffordable for the people who lived there.

The exterior of the former station building now served as a canvas for local street artists, and was adorned with an eclectic wash of urban art. Some of it had merit, a budding Banksy developing their unique style, while some of it was just plain old graffiti.

Denning parked his Ford Focus at the top of the narrow street that led to the station, squeezing it between the numerous squad cars and two police vans that had already taken up most of the limited space.

After getting out the car, he pulled the collar of his coat up to protect against the chill wind blowing in from the east. The weather forecast that morning had said there was a chance of snow later that week, and he didn't doubt it.

'Is this it?' Denning asked a uniformed officer standing guard by the outer cordon, which stretched from the end of the alleyway where it met Brick Lane to the scrap of frost-hardened scrubland that edged the side of the old building; the blue-and-white police tape hung limp and saggy in the cold winter air. White-suited crime scene investigators were entering the old station building, advertising the fact this was now the scene of a serious crime.

''Fraid so,' came the reply. He nodded Denning through, explaining that the senior officer in charge was a man called Mike Jephcott. He pointed to a broad, bearded man standing by the entrance to the old station. Denning ducked under the police tape and approached.

There were several uniformed officers milling around the area immediately in front of the station, talking to what looked like a group of rough sleepers; grim-faced and belligerent, clearly resenting the presence of police officers on their patch. They were huddled together, trying to insulate themselves from the cold through grouped body heat.

'Inspector Jephcott?' Denning said, his gloved hand outstretched. Jephcott shot him a puzzled glance. 'DI Denning,' he added. 'East London Major Investigation Team.'

Jephcott's expression softened slightly. 'Thanks for coming out. This is probably small beer for you, but we have to be seen to be doing everything by the book, and this is technically your bag and ours.'

'Ours…?'

Jephcott gave Denning a dry smile. 'I'm with the Met's Territorial Support Group, but the local CID are doing the bulk of the grunt work. We're not exactly dealing with master criminals here.'

Denning looked over at the various rag-tag of rough sleepers, wary eyes flashing back at the uniformed officers who were speaking to them. 'What exactly happened here?'

Jephcott took him to one side as several CSIs exited the building. 'The old station was being used by a group of homeless people. We received an anonymous tip-off claiming the building was being used for drug dealing. So far, we've discovered a quantity of both Class A and B drugs. Mostly amphetamines, cannabis and ecstasy, but it's possible there are more. We won't know until the search resumes. Local uniforms are giving us a hand with it.'

Denning glanced over again at the rough sleepers. They didn't look to him like drug dealers, but what exactly did drug dealers look like? 'What are they saying?'

'Predictably, they're all denying all knowledge of any drugs. They claim they were planted.' Jephcott gave a dry chuckle. 'That's their story and they're sticking to it.'

'So why were we called in?' Denning asked. Drugs, however serious the damage they did and the ruthlessness of the people who benefitted from their supply and distribution, weren't his remit. Clearly, something more serious had happened here.

'While we were searching the premises,' Jephcott continued, 'we discovered one man, slightly separate to the others, who seemed to be asleep throughout the raid. When an officer approached him, he was found to be unresponsive. On closer examination we discovered he'd been fatally stabbed.'

'Any sign of a murder weapon?'

'The Crime Scene bods are searching now, but nothing's turned up so far, and we didn't discover anything when we searched the homeless people.'

'I presume our victim hasn't been ID'd?'

'Nobody seemed to know who he was.' Jephcott sniffed. 'Or at least, if they do know, they're not saying. In fact, they're not saying anything that's of much use.'

The group stood in an awkward huddle, throwing angry looks in Denning's direction. To them, he was just another police officer, even if he wasn't wearing a uniform. There would be as little incentive to help him as there would be to talk to Jephcott and his team. 'You think one of them is responsible?' Denning asked.

'That's why your lot are here. We can hold them here for a while, or take them all down the nearest nick if you want to interview them under caution. But to be honest with you, I doubt you'd get much more out of them than we have.'

'Will there be any arrests in relation to the drugs find?'

'We probably should arrest the lot of them for possession and distribution of controlled drugs. And if we were doing this strictly by the book, that's exactly what I'd do. But then I've got to ask myself if it's worth the hassle, not to mention the waste of resources. We'd have to try and link the drugs to the individuals and then go for "conspiracy to supply". And proving any of it is going to be all but impossible.' He glanced over at the group and shrugged. 'They're more likely to be treated as potential witnesses and vulnerable people.' He lowered his voice. 'Strictly off the record, Inspector Denning, if we thought this was part of something bigger we'd hand the whole thing over to Serious and Organised Crime Command, which would mean you'd be running your investigation in tandem with them. As it is, I'd put money on this being something low key. It's the big players behind this that matter, and I can't see our friends over there willingly offering any useful names.' Jephcott pointed to the derelict station. 'There's a murdered man in there, and right now I'd say that's everyone's main priority.'

Denning sighed. This was going to be a tricky case. No easy answers. Maybe no answers at all. But it still had to be investigated as thoroughly as any other murder scene, even if his team wasn't going to thank him for dumping this one on their desks. Nor his DCI for that matter... 'OK,' he said. 'I'd better take a look.'

# Chapter Two

There had originally been two entrances to the station: the larger one on the left had been boarded up and was now obscured by a mass of graffiti, while the smaller one to the right was open. Jephcott led him through it. It opened onto a steep metal staircase leading down to where the station's platform had been, and had probably served as an emergency exit when the station had still been in use. 'The station closed a few years back. This staircase was put in afterwards,' Jephcott said, reading his thoughts. 'Apparently the place was used as a pop-up cinema for a time shortly after closure, and there had been plans to turn it into an art gallery. All came to nothing, predictably enough, and the building's been derelict ever since.'

To the left was another door that presumably led to the station interior. It was secured by a couple of padlocks and an iron bar.

'The main part of the station is sealed off and is protected by an alarm system that was put in by the developers who bought the place a couple of years ago,' Jephcott continued as they descended the stairs. 'The lower part of the station wasn't so well secured – just a flimsy padlock – which is presumably how our homeless friends gained entry.'

Denning followed Jephcott, taking care as he did so. 'Developers? So, someone's bought the place?'

Jephcott offered a throaty laugh. 'It seems so. Some mug. We've tried to contact them, but no luck so far. I don't know what the fuck they planned to do with this place, but it's probably riddled with dry rot and Christ knows what else.'

'Presumably they had plans for it?'

'I suspect the building's listed, so it's unlikely they'll be allowed to do anything too drastic, but you know how these things work – grease the right palms and anything's possible.'

Denning knew all too well how these things worked. Property developers had an uncanny knack of getting their own way when it came to destroying parts of the city's heritage. The former station was part of London's history, even if it was in a dilapidated state.

What remained of the former platform area was now overgrown and littered with debris. On the abandoned track-bed, the dying embers of a fire flickered in an impromptu brazier that had been constructed from a couple of dustbins and an abandoned shopping trolley. The uniformed officers who'd conducted the search for drugs had erected several mobile arc lights, which illuminated the gloomy space. Despite this, dark shadows reached into far corners, giving the space a slightly eerie feel. One end of the station had been bricked off, while at the other end there was a steel security fence, beyond which trains trundled into and out of the nearby terminus at Liverpool Street. Overhead, rusting metal work and the ragged remains of old cabling hinted at the building's former purpose. But as Denning looked around the desperate scene, desolate and decayed, he found it hard to believe it had once been a busy railway station.

'Over there.' Jephcott pointed to a bustle of activity a few meters from the steel fence that separated the weed-encrusted track-bed from the still operational railway. There were several CSIs examining the scene, while the crime scene photographer took pictures. A shaft of wintery sunlight illuminated a short, exposed section of track-bed between the body and the fence.

Lying on the ground, staring up at the roof, was the body of what looked like an elderly man. His eyes glazed, a gaping wound in his chest. Sheila Gorton, the crime scene manager, nodded a greeting at Denning.

'Stabbed in the heart,' she said, lowering her face mask. 'Probably bled out quite quickly. Whilst death wouldn't have been instantaneous, it wouldn't have taken long. Particularly as I suspect, like most rough sleepers, he probably wasn't in the best of health to start with.'

'How many people were there down here?' Denning asked.

'We counted fifteen when we raided the place this morning,' Jephcott said. 'But it could be more or less than that on any given night. This place is reasonably safe and it offers shelter. Preferable to sleeping out in the open. Especially at this time of the year.'

'Plus there's safety in numbers,' Gorton added. 'A community like this will look out for each other.'

'Except someone clearly didn't.' Denning studied the victim. He looked like he was an old man, but Denning knew looks would be deceptive in this instance. Someone living rough with a poor diet and healthcare would be aged beyond their years.

Their victim had thin sandy hair, straggly and thinning. His skin was raggedy, with pock marks and a large, unsightly boil on one cheek. His lips had a bluey-purple tinge about them. A grey beard probably added several years to his age.

'We're assuming he was killed by a fellow rough sleeper,' Gorton said. It sounded like a statement but came across more as a question.

Jephcott chortled slightly. 'I'd say that was a fairly obvious assumption.'

Denning didn't say anything. Obvious or not, it was still an assumption, and in any murder investigation it was often dangerous to assume anything until you had all the facts.

'I take it even an approximate time of death is out of the question at this stage?' he asked Gorton.

She offered a wary smile. 'Blood has only just started clotting, so I'd say sometime in the last twenty-four to forty-eight hours. I'll ask the pathologist to fast-track the post-mortem, but it will be tomorrow at the earliest. I know they're as over-worked and under-staffed as the rest of us at the moment.'

Denning nodded. 'Tomorrow's fine. We need to ID him first.'

He looked at the scene around him. Beyond the perimeter fencing that separated the old station from the main London to East Anglia line, Denning could see trains trundling past, either slowing down as they came into London, or speeding up as they left it. Liverpool Street Station was less than a mile away. There would be trains in and out every few minutes. It was just possible to make the area out from the railway. In which case, perhaps someone had seen something.

'You've spoken to everyone who was living down here?' Denning asked Jephcott.

'Everyone who was present when we arrived. But as there's no official record of who does or doesn't doss down here, there's no way of knowing if the person responsible hadn't already legged it before we arrived on the scene.'

'What are the rough sleepers saying?'

He shrugged. 'Very little of any use. Naturally they're denying any knowledge of the drugs, and pleading total ignorance when it comes to the murder.'

'Understandable about the drugs, but you might have thought they'd be more helpful when it comes to one of their own being stabbed to death,' Denning said. 'What's your gut feeling on this?'

Jephcott shrugged again. 'If one of them did do it, then good luck getting any of that lot to talk.' He turned to Denning. 'But that's your call, mate, not mine.'

Denning rankled at the way he said "that lot" as though the unhoused community who called this derelict space home were little more than social flotsam whose lives somehow mattered less than others.

It was easy to judge, not so easy to empathise.

They headed back up to the station entrance.

Denning spotted DS Molly Fisher and DS Deepak Neeraj arriving together in Neeraj's Golf, parking it immediately behind his Focus. They waved their ID at the uniformed officer beside the outer cordon and headed over to Denning.

'What happened here then, boss?' Neeraj asked. As usual he was wearing his trademark leather jacket, his hair gelled to perfection. Molly Fisher was wearing a sensible fleece and scarf.

'A rough sleeper has been murdered.' He filled them in on what little he knew so far.

'A homeless bloke?' Neeraj said. 'Shit, boss, it could have been any one of them that killed him.' Neeraj was looking over at the rough sleepers who had gathered by the police van. They were still being interviewed by the uniformed coppers, though it was unlikely they were saying anything useful.

'We still need to find out who did it, Deep. He was still a person. And I believe the correct term is "unhoused" rather than homeless.'

His comment silenced Neeraj, though Denning suspected the DS rolled his eyes as soon as his back was turned.

Molly said, 'Have they been formally interviewed?'

'Not by us. Uniform have questioned them. Ostensibly about a quantity of drugs that were found on the premises, but it's down to us to ask about the murder, at least officially. So far, they're not being very cooperative.'

'Understandable under the circumstances,' Molly said. 'Do we have a name?'

'Not yet.' Denning rubbed a hand through his wavy hair. 'To be honest, there's not much to go on. I could hazard a guess at his age.'

'So what do you want us to do, boss?' Neeraj asked. He looked like he'd rather be somewhere else. Somewhere warm probably.

'Speak to them,' Denning said. 'Get as many statements as you can. One of them must have known something about our victim. A name, even a first name would be helpful at this stage.'

'What about the drugs?' Molly asked.

'Leave that to uniform and the regular CID.' He repeated what Jephcott had told him about the unlikelihood of any charges being brought regarding the drugs. 'Our interest is solely in the murder victim.'

Molly nodded while Neeraj still looked unconvinced this was worthy of their time and energy.

Denning knew Molly Fisher had worked for CID before she'd joined Homicide and Major Crimes eighteen months ago. He had heard a rumour CID was about to face yet another Met Police re-branding, and would subsequently be known as Non Specialist Serious/Complex Crimes Department. He shook his head at the thought. Sometimes it felt like the Met obsessed itself with and PR at the expense of actual policing. Not that it really mattered in the grand scheme of things: their priority now was finding a killer.

'Anything they can tell us would be useful.' But from the scowls he saw on the rough sleepers' faces, he wasn't holding out much hope.

# Chapter Three

Molly approached the nervous-looking group. They were huddled together against the cold and most looked like they could do with a decent meal as much as somewhere warm to sleep.

Her brother, Ben, had been homeless for a while. He'd spent time in a homeless shelter until he'd been kicked out of that for causing trouble. Trouble which he insisted hadn't been his fault. Ben was doing OK for himself now: working in a hotel in Newquay. He even had a girlfriend. The last time she'd spoken to him he'd seemed happy. But that was nearly six months ago, and a lot could change in that time.

They were a disparate group. Most of them looked like grizzled, world-hardened men in their fifties and sixties, possibly older. However, there were a few who looked to be younger: she guessed in their twenties or late teens. A young woman, who couldn't have been more than eighteens, was clinging to a man of around the same age. They were both smoking roll-ups, similar to the kind her ex-boyfriend used to smoke, though his were so often laced with dope.

'I'll talk to those two,' she said to Neeraj. 'Why don't you start with the older guys.' Neeraj flashed her a look that questioned why she should assume authority

– they were both of the same rank – but he nodded and approached the older men.

She smiled as she neared the girl and the young lad, but she sensed straightaway this was probably going to be a fruitless exercise. She was a police officer, even if she wasn't wearing the uniform, and for people on the fringes of society that usually meant trouble.

'I'm Detective Sergeant Molly Fisher,' she said. 'Is it OK to talk to you?'

'We've already told those coppers over there,' the girl said aggressively, 'we don't know nothing about the drugs.'

The girl had dyed green hair, though the dye was fading and her natural black was showing. She was dressed in a dark blue anorak with a black-and-grey scarf, faded jeans and a pair of well-scuffed Doc Marten boots. The lad beside her was wearing a bottle green bomber-style jacket and a black beanie hat. He had piercings all down his left ear, and a tattoo of a snake running from one side of his face and down his neck. His arm was around the girl's shoulders as though he was trying to protect her from some unseen threat, yet he seemed so young and vulnerable, it looked to Molly like he was the one in need of protecting.

'I'm not interested in the drugs,' Molly said. 'That's not why I'm here.'

They looked at each other and then at her. 'It was nothing to do with us anyway,' the boy said. 'They was planted.'

'Look, I really couldn't care less about the drugs. The chances are it won't be taken any further.' She was only repeating what Denning had told her, though technically she wasn't in a position to offer them reassurances she couldn't guarantee.

They looked at Molly with doubtful expressions.

'What are your names?' she asked.

Another exchange of looks passed between them. After a moment it was the boy who spoke. 'Corey,' he mumbled.

'Corey what?'

He shrugged. 'Just Corey.'

It was the best she was going to get. 'What about you?' She looked at the girl, who stared back defiantly. Eventually she gave in. 'Zella,' she said.

Molly made a mental note. There was a good chance neither had given her their real name, but at least she had something to call them. 'What about the man who was stabbed? Do you know his name?'

'Kept himself to himself,' Zella said. 'Wasn't exactly the sociable type.'

'He's dead, Zella,' Molly said. 'He must have had a family. Loved ones. They'll need to be informed. It would help if we knew who he was.'

Corey shuffled awkwardly. 'He said his name was John. I don't know any more than that.'

*John.* She suspected it was a made-up name too. 'Can you tell me anything about him? Did he ever mention any family? Or anyone he was close to?'

Another couple of shrugs.

'Anything you can tell me would be helpful.'

After a moment, Corey spoke. 'Like Zella said, he kept himself to himself. We never asked him any questions and he never bothered us.' He sniffed and rubbed his hand under his nose. 'I'm sorry he's dead though. He was an OK bloke.'

'OK…?'

She noticed Zella jab him in the ribs and he stared at the ground. 'I mean he never bothered anyone,' Corey added quietly. 'Not like some of the older geezers. Some of them can be a pain when they're pissed. Shouting and the like. But he just kept himself to himself.'

Molly couldn't not feel sorry for them. A group of people forced to survive together in desperate circumstances. People that society would prefer to ignore. Outsiders. She could relate to being an outsider, though she'd never had to experience homelessness first hand.

'Anything you can tell me, Corey... anything at all would be helpful. Did he ever mention anyone? Anyone he cared about?'

Molly was aware of Zella's eyes burning into him. If she could get Corey on his own, away from Zella... She had some kind of hold over him. Looking more closely at the two of them, Molly reckoned Zella was probably slightly older than Corey; maybe early-to-mid-twenties. Close up, Corey looked younger than she'd first thought. Probably still in his mid-teens. Did *they* have families, she wondered. Did anyone care that their children were living like this? Freezing in a derelict building only a few weeks before Christmas?

'I've told you all I know,' Corey said, glancing back at Zella. 'I didn't know him.'

Molly could sense she was fighting a losing battle. She decided to try a different approach. 'OK, have either of you seen anyone suspicious hanging around here recently? Anyone new, or anyone who seemed to take an interest in John?'

'People pitch up and then piss off all the time,' Corey said.

'But no one new?'

'I dunno. Maybe. Sometimes you see a face one day then you never see them again.'

'How did you two find out about this place?' Molly glanced over at the abandoned station: not the most salubrious of places, but protected from the elements, and with only one way in and out, probably fairly safe. She knew all about the difficulty of finding affordable accommodation in London from first-hand experience. She sympathised with their plight.

'Word gets out on the streets. If you're lucky, you hear about a squat going,' Zella told her. 'We had to move out of the last place we were staying after the owner turned up with a couple of big blokes with baseball bats. We didn't have a lot of choice but to move after that. Luckily someone knew about this place. We tried to get into the main station building but it's locked and bolted.' She gave Molly a withering look. 'I know what you're thinking, but it was better than nothing.'

Molly wanted to ask about their families, but she knew that was none of her business. Their life stories were only relevant in as much as they had something significant to add to the murder investigation. 'Where will you go now?'

Corey and Zella looked at each other. Zella spoke first: 'We'll find somewhere, don't worry about us.'

'I may need to speak to you again,' Molly said. She went to hand a card with her contact details to Zella, but she refused to take it. Molly handed it to Corey instead. She doubted he had a mobile phone or any actual means of contacting her and suspected the card would end up in the nearest bin anyway, but she had to do things by the book. 'Get in touch,' she said. 'If either of you do remember anything.'

Zella stared at her for a moment: she had a hard face, but not without a hint of compassion. 'What's the point? It's not as if you lot give a stuff about us.'

With that, she grabbed Corey by the elbow and herded him back towards the rest of the group.

# Chapter Four

The start of a murder investigation always saw a buzz of excitement pass between the team as they anticipated the direction the investigation would take. This time, however, the atmosphere seemed more subdued.

This was one of the smallest MITs in the Met. Their numbers had gradually been reducing as detectives had left and not been replaced. Denning knew there was no point complaining to his superiors about the lack of officers; it was the same story throughout the Met. The best he could expect would be sympathetic nodding and a timely reminder about cuts to the service overall.

The team were sitting at their desks, looking at Denning, waiting for him to begin. He could sense this was going to be a hard sell for them. A stabbing in London. Hardly a rarity these days. Things were made harder here by the anonymity of the victim. No grieving family snapping at their heels, urging them to find the culprit amidst tears and recriminations. At least, not yet.

There were photos of the crime scene pinned to the whiteboard, alongside various shots of the station building and the surrounding streets. The crime scene photos had been enlarged with arrows and other indicators added. Denning had written 'John…?' on the board, next to a post-mortem photo of their as yet unnamed victim.

'OK, team,' Denning said, starting the briefing. 'This is a tricky situation and one that calls for tact and respect at all times when dealing with the unhoused community who have now been displaced. None of them asked to end up in the situation they found themselves in and we need to remember that. Unfortunately, we don't have a great deal to work with here. Until the post-mortem results come in, we can only guess at our victim's exact age, but we're assuming it's around late fifties to early sixties. It's not known how long he's been sleeping rough for or where he originates from. But we do know he was stabbed to death sometime yesterday evening. Right now, we need an ID. I know this is going to feel like something of a long shot, but let's get on to Missing Persons and see if anyone fitting our victim's description has been reported missing. Dave, I'm handing that over to you.'

Dave Kinsella was an old school copper, broad about the shoulders and waist, with beefy arms, an impatient attitude. He said whatever was on his mind and didn't care who he offended. Despite this, Denning held a weird kind of affection for Kinsella: he was part of a dying breed, soon to be swept away by fast-tracked graduates who'd never had to fight their way to the top. Detectives like Denning. Kinsella had resented Denning's presence on the team at first, regarding him as an over-educated, bleeding-heart liberal. Over time, however, they had developed a kind of mutual respect for one another.

'I'll get on to them,' Kinsella said, 'but I wouldn't hold out much hope.'

'Once we know who he was,' Denning said, 'we'll have a fighting chance of finding out who killed him.'

'Aren't we assuming he was killed by another homeless bloke?' Neeraj said.

'I agree it's possible he was killed by a fellow rough sleeper,' Denning said, 'but at this stage, we don't assume anything, Deep.'

'That's where I'd stake the clever money,' Kinsella said. 'And I'd reckon whoever did it will have long since scarpered.' He sniffed and shook his head. 'If you want honest opinion, we're wasting our time on this one.'

'He's a murder victim, Dave,' Denning said calmly. 'As I've already made clear, we treat him with the same respect we treat any other victim. And let's not automatically assume he *was* killed by one of the other rough sleepers. Yes, it is a possibility, and we can't rule it out, but we keep our options open here. Don't let's allow prejudice to get in our way.' He was looking at Kinsella when he said this, though judging by the look on Kinsella's face, his words had been met by deaf ears.

'With respect, boss,' Neeraj offered, 'Dave's right. How can we justify making this a priority with so much other shit going on out there. At the end of the day, how much of a big deal is some homeless – sorry, "unhoused" – bloke getting stabbed to death?'

Even the usually open-minded Trudi Bell was looking doubtful. 'It's not like that kind of thing is a one-off,' she said. 'These guys are always going for each other. And the chances of us getting any of them to grass up one of their own isn't great.' She looked apologetically at Denning. 'I'm not saying it's right, but it's a fact of life.'

DC Trudi Bell was in her early thirties, the same age as, and good friends with, Molly Fisher. Both her father and her grandfather had been Met police officers, so it had felt like something of a family tradition for Trudi to join the police, though she was the first in her family to become a detective.

Denning waited until she'd finished speaking before he continued. 'I repeat what I just said, everyone. The victim's circumstances are irrelevant here. We don't know this man's background, and we don't know the reasons that led to him living in an abandoned Tube station in the middle of winter. This man could easily have been you or someone close to you. Remember that.'

Trudi nodded sheepishly. 'Fair comment, boss. Sorry.'

'All that is very admirable,' Kinsella said. 'Except for one thing: we don't know who the hell he is.' He looked around the room for support. Denning saw Neeraj shrug, while Molly Fisher stared impassively back at Kinsella, the only member of his team who was yet to offer an opinion.

'Molly,' Denning said, 'what's your take on all this?'

She gave a half-hearted shrug and looked at her colleagues. 'The boss is right. For all we know, this guy could have loved ones out there who are missing him. They have a right to justice. Same as any family. The day we get to pick and choose which crimes we take seriously is the day we know we're in the wrong business.'

The room fell silent. Eventually Kinsella spoke. 'OK, then, let's go for it. We ignore all the other murder cases out there – the kids who've been stabbed for the latest iPhone, the pensioners murdered in their own homes for a handful of valuables, not to mention the shootings that are now almost a daily occurrence – and we invest our sweat, blood and tears in finding out who killed this bloke. Where do we start?'

'The drugs angle is worth exploring,' Trudi said. 'How much did the Territorial Support boys find?'

'A sizeable amount, which suggests dealing rather than personal use,' Denning said. 'Though DI Jephcott said there have been no reports of drug dealing from that particular location. Of course, that doesn't mean that it wasn't going on, but the local Territorial Support Group usually has a pretty good idea of what's happening in their own patch.'

'Maybe our bloke was looking after them for someone,' Trudi suggested. 'That would give our killer a strong motive, assuming it was the drugs they were after.'

'Except why kill him and leave the drugs?' Molly said.

'Maybe it wasn't by choice. Maybe he refused to say where they were and that's why he was killed.' Neeraj shrugged, as though he was doing nothing more than throwing random ideas around the room.

'According to Jephcott,' Denning said, 'the drugs weren't that difficult to locate. They were stashed under some bricks near the bottom of the stairs. Anyone who was determined enough could have found them.'

'Could the drugs have been for personal use after all?' Trudi asked.

'What, a quantity of that size?' Kinsella retorted. 'And forgive me for making generalised assumptions here, but where would a bunch of homeless people find the money to buy a load of Class A drugs for their personal use?'

'Maybe it had nothing to do with them? Maybe someone was just storing the drugs there and our victim got shirty with whoever it was and ended up paying the price.' Trudi looked around the room only to be met by a sea of bemused faces.

'What do we make of this anonymous tip-off?' Molly Fisher asked. 'What would someone hope to gain by grassing up a bunch of rough sleepers who might have had drugs around?'

'Rival drug dealers?' Neeraj offered.

'I don't know, Deep. But personally I don't think this is to do with drugs.' Denning was working on little more than a gut feeling, but something told him the drugs issue was a distraction, and they were in danger of allowing themselves to pursue an angle that wasn't relevant.

However, he wrote the word 'drugs' on the whiteboard, drew a circle round it in red marker pen and put a large question mark above it.

'OK, let's move on from the drugs angle. Our priority right now is identifying our victim. I suggest we start with Missing Persons. I know that's going to be like searching for the proverbial needle in a haystack, but it's our best starting point.'

'We don't even know how old he is,' Neeraj complained.

'No, but if we look for anyone reported missing within the past few years who is aged anything from late-forties to late-sixties, it'll hopefully give us a starting point. We should have a clearer indication of our victim's age after the post-mortem tomorrow, but let's not wait until then. Start looking now, see if anything jumps out at us. Molly, Deep, any luck with the rough sleepers you spoke with earlier?'

Neeraj pulled a face. 'Nothing there, boss. They weren't in the mood for talking to us. Claimed they'd already spoken to the police. I tried to tell them that was uniform they spoke to and it was only about the drugs and we were investigating the murder. But they just clammed up.'

Denning suspected that Neeraj hadn't approached the task with much enthusiasm. He could tell that, like Kinsella, he still wasn't entirely convinced this investigation was worth their effort. He hoped to have better luck with DS Fisher. 'Molly…?'

She glanced at her notes, then shook her head. 'Same as Deep, unfortunately. Very little that was of any use to us.' She paused for a second. 'Except…'

'Go on, Molly. Anything to work with would be useful right now.'

'A young couple I spoke with – well, I *assume* they were a couple – I felt one of them knew more about our victim than he was letting on. I mean, I can't be certain. It is possible he was just nervous, or slightly overwhelmed by all the attention, but I got the impression he knew something.'

'Worth speaking to again?'

'I'd need to get him away from the girl. She was keen to make sure he stayed tight-lipped.' She shrugged. 'Mind you, even if I could find him and get him on his own, there's no guarantee he'd tell me anything.'

'It's worth a try, Molly. See if you can track him down and get him to talk. Anything he can tell you, obviously treated in the strictest confidence, etc. And emphasise again this has nothing to do with the drugs. We want to know who this guy was and why he was killed.'

Molly nodded. Denning looked at the whiteboard: there were several photographs of the former station building, as well as the derelict area underneath where the trains had once run. 'Right, what do we know about the station itself? Have we spoken to the railway authorities?'

'Bit more luck there, boss,' Trudi said. 'I checked out a website called *Abandoned London*. The station closed in 2006 when the old East London Line was rerouted to form part of the new London Overground network. It seems the building changed hands a few times since then; various plans have been submitted over the years to convert it into everything from an art gallery to the inevitable luxury apartment block. The plans were turned down for whatever reasons and the building eventually became derelict. That is until about eight months ago when it was bought by a property development company with a reputation for high-end commercial projects.'

'Any idea what their plans were for the building?'

Trudi checked her notes. 'It doesn't say. But I imagine the building was becoming a bit of an eyesore. And if it *was* being used for drug dealing, then all the more reason to do something with it.'

'Do we know the name of the property developers?'

'Excelsior Developments. They're based in Islington, but that's all I've managed to find out about them so far.'

'OK, I'll speak to them. At the very least we should be liaising with them as owners of the property during the course of our investigation.'

He thought about it. Presumably someone had plans for the station. This was London after all, and empty buildings on prime sites tended not to stay empty for too long.

'Do you think the developers knew about the rough sleepers living there?' Molly asked.

It was a good question. If they did know, then how did the homeless community fit in with their plans? 'I think that's something we need to ask them,' Denning said.

'There is one possibility we seem to be overlooking,' Kinsella said, his arms folded across his barrel of a chest. 'Something we'd probably rather not all think about.'

'Go on, Dave,' Denning said, humouring him.

'There could be a nutter out there targeting homeless people.'

'OK, that's something we have to consider,' Denning said. 'But why go into a community to kill our victim? Why not target someone living somewhere more open?'

'Lack of CCTV?' Kinsella suggested. 'Lack of credible witnesses? Who knows. But it's a possibility.'

It was an angle Denning was reluctant to consider, even though it was something they couldn't entirely rule out at this stage. 'If that is the case, then we really do need to find this individual, as there's a real chance this victim won't be the last.'

# Chapter Five

Denning sat opposite DCI Elizabeth McKenna, who was sitting on the other side of the large desk in her small office, which was separated from the main MIT space by a glass-walled partition. She'd allowed Denning to take the lead as senior investigating officer without visibly breathing down his neck.

That was the good thing about McKenna: she'd give her officers the responsibility and let them direct the course of an investigation by whatever means they felt appropriate. But if they screwed up, she'd be down on them like the angry brother of their worst enemy.

Born and brought up in Motherwell, near Glasgow, McKenna had worked her way through the ranks, rising from PC to detective chief inspector, dodging bullets both literal and metaphorical along the way. At some point in her career, she had earned the nickname Betty Taggart, a sobriquet that was only ever uttered out of earshot.

Despite getting off to something of a rocky start, she and Denning had developed a comfortable working relationship based on mutual respect, if not actual fondness.

Now, she fixed him with one of her gimlet stares.

'I've read DI Jephcott's report,' she said. 'Do you believe there's any connection between the drugs bust and the murder?'

Denning knew that however difficult it had been to convince his team that the murder of a homeless man should take as much priority as any other murder, it was going to be ten times harder to convince his DCI. He could already sense from the stony look on McKenna's face that he was going to have to go for the hard sell approach if he was to have any hope of persuading her to invest the time and resources necessary to solve this murder.

'I can't say for certain at this stage,' he said. 'But I'm not convinced the drug connection is directly relevant.'

'No?' She raised an eyebrow.

He tried not to shuffle uncomfortably in his chair. 'Unless we can find a direct connection between our victim and drugs – either dealing or using – then I think we should leave the Territorial Support Team and local CID to explore the drugs connection. If we do go down that avenue, I think it might end up being a distraction for us.' The truth was, he didn't know for certain. But the drugs *felt* like a distraction: the anonymous tip-off, the ease with which they were found. It all felt a little bit too convenient.

'Hmm.' He could almost see the cogs turning in McKenna's head. 'OK, Matt, where do you want to go with this?'

He'd formulated a ready answer in his head before he'd followed her into her office a few minutes ago. Now his mind wasn't as certain as it had been during the briefing. McKenna had a habit of undermining his theories with just one withering look. But he decided to go for it anyway. 'I don't think our victim had anything to do with drugs. I'm not even certain at this stage that what happened even involved the unhoused community living there. I think both could turn out to be circumstantial here. Considering the only people who knew about how to get down there were other homeless people, that does suggest he's been targeted deliberately.'

'We don't want to overthink this case, Matt, and go looking for things that aren't there.'

'Equally, we don't want to overlook something just because it doesn't fit a particular narrative,' he said.

McKenna thought for a moment. 'OK, so let's not assume the obvious. What is it about this case that's ringing alarm bells with you?'

He couldn't say. At least not just yet. 'If this was a question of rough sleepers falling out over drugs or money or whatever, it would have been messier, more vicious. The death would have been the result of a fight, but that wasn't the case here.'

'We don't have the full picture yet. The post–mortem might throw up something about his death that we don't know.'

'True. And until we have the PM results, there's probably not too much point in speculating.'

'What does your team think?'

He repeated the concerns raised by Kinsella and Neeraj, but reiterated his argument about their victim being as deserving of justice as anyone else. Judging by the look on her face, McKenna was still in need of some convincing.

'I hear what you're saying, Matt. And it's terribly laudable.' She paused, steepling her fingers under her chin. 'And whilst I don't share the unenlightened approach of DS Neeraj and DS Kinsella, I do share their concerns about prioritising our resources. You know how much scrutiny the Met is under at the moment. The media are just panting to find yet another damaging story to run with. And with every negative headline, morale shrinks ever lower.' She offered him a smile that didn't quite reach her eyes. 'Whether we like it or not, it's the high-profile cases that people are interested in. And even though none of us would ever admit this, it's the victims that command the most sympathy which get the public onside. A homeless man, with possible drug connections – and it's not me thinking this, it's the media who will slant the story in that direction – is unlikely to tug on too many heart strings. Added to that, assuming this gets as far as court, a group of homeless people are unlikely to make the most reliable of witnesses.'

'Are you saying we should drop the investigation?'

She shook her head. 'Of course not. A man has been murdered. It's our job to investigate. All I am saying is that this investigation needs to be time limited. Either find a quick resolution to the case or drop it. If this does turn out to be a fight between a couple of rough sleepers that got out of hand, then persuading the CPS to take it further is going to be an uphill struggle. If you haven't got a reasonable breakthrough by this time next week, we file this under "unsolved", got it?'

He understood where she was coming from. She was the one who would ultimately carry the can for this investigation. Whilst she was right to say it wasn't going to be a straightforward investigation, that didn't mean they should cut corners.

'It was my intention to give this investigation the same level of focus I would give to any other investigation. I can't guarantee a quick turnaround.'

A heavy silence grew in the room. McKenna tapped her chin with her steepled fingers. 'Matt, you've probably heard the rumours.' She paused, making sure she had his full attention. 'I'm due to retire next year, and between you and me, I'm counting the days. Literally. It does mean this chair is going to be empty. Until they can find someone suitable to fill it. Now, you've got an excellent track record – you get results and you play by the rules, most of the time – and this has been noticed by our elders and betters in senior management.' Another pause, lengthier and heavier than before, just to make sure he got the point. 'However, you haven't been a DI for long, and there's no guarantee the job won't be offered to someone outside this team. And that brings me to my next point. Something that hasn't reached the rumour mill yet and has to remain within these four walls.'

'I'm not in the habit of gossiping.'

She gave him a look, then continued. 'There's a very real chance this particular MIT will be disbanded after I leave.'

'Disbanded?' He couldn't believe what he was hearing. No one had even hinted at this. 'Why? We're a good team. You said it yourself – we get results.'

'OK, perhaps "disbanded" was the wrong word. In reality, the team will probably be merged with another of the smaller MITs, but I can't promise that will be the case. You know the score. The Met is as much about cost efficiency as it is about accountability at the moment. This is – and has been for some time now – one of the smaller units operating within Homicide Command. Granted, we're small but effective, however, we have on occasions had to call in support from other teams, and that takes them away from the cases they're working on. Yes, I know it's a quid pro quo arrangement, and we've helped other teams out in the past. Unfortunately, the cold, hard reality is that there just aren't enough murder squad detectives to go around, and despite government promises about recruitment drives, the reality is that more detectives are leaving the Met than there are joining.'

'You're seriously saying that there's a chance this team could be broken up?'

'There's no certainty all the members could be taken on by the same MIT. I mean, Dave Kinsella is OK, he's not got long until retirement. Neeraj is way overdue for promotion and would stand a better chance in another, larger, team. Similarly, DS Fisher has shown that she has leadership potential on occasions.' She paused. 'Then there's you. If you were to get the DCI post, you'd stand a better chance of keeping this MIT going, at least in the short term. Failing that, your chances of moving somewhere else and remaining in a senior role would be greater if you were at least being considered for a DCI's position. And that means playing the game. The one thing going against you – if I'm allowed to be completely honest with you, Matt – is your unwillingness to take the politics of Met policing seriously. This job is as much about keeping your nose clean as it is about catching killers. More so sometimes.'

Denning felt like he'd been poleaxed. This was emotional blackmail: don't rock the boat and keep his team together, or make waves and it could spell the end for them. He hadn't been there for long, but in that time he'd bonded with them. They respected him, even if they didn't always like him. He owed it to them to keep the team going. But McKenna had a point: policing for him had always been about criminals and justice. He knew that to get anywhere in the police force of the twenty-first century you needed to know how to make all the right noises, and this was something he neither enjoyed doing, nor was he any good at it. But if it meant the end of his team, then perhaps it was time he learned how to play the game, for their sake.

'Give me a week,' he said. 'I can't promise anything, but at least we'll know if we've got a cat-in-hell's chance of solving this crime.'

He only wished he felt as confident as he sounded.

# Chapter Six

Molly wasn't even sure what she was looking for. Denning had suggested taking Neeraj with her, but she knew that if she did have any luck tracking down the boy who called himself Corey, or his strange, spiky girlfriend, she stood a much better chance of getting them to talk if she was by herself. Despite being a decent bloke once you got to know him, Deepak Neeraj could sometimes come across as a bit of a prat. He meant well, but he lacked tact and diplomacy, and this situation called for bucketloads of both.

She shivered slightly as she approached the abandoned station. The temperature was dropping and there was a noticeable chill in the air. She couldn't recall if the weather forecast had said there was snow heading their way, but she wouldn't be surprised if it made an appearance.

The area in front of the station was still awash with police and forensic teams, though they were starting to dial things back now. There was just the one police van parked at the top of the approach road. The blue-and-white police tape still hung around the outer protective cordon, a bored-looking young officer standing beside it, his eyes fixed on nothing in particular.

Molly could sense Denning's frustration at the team's general lack of enthusiasm for this case. But equally she could understand the team's unwillingness to spend time and energy on something that might yet turn out to be little more than a falling out between a bunch of rough sleepers. Even now she wondered what the point was in trying to track down someone who had made it perfectly clear to her the last time they spoke that he didn't have anything to say to her. But she agreed with Denning. This was a murder case, and the victim was as deserving of justice as anyone. She pulled the collar of her fleece up against the chill wind and approached the uniformed officer guarding the cordon. He looked cold even in his protective jacket, shuffling from foot to foot when he thought no one was looking.

She showed him her ID and he nodded his acknowledgement. 'Where have they gone?' she asked. 'The people who were staying here?'

'You mean that homeless lot?' He looked about fifteen, though she suspected he was at least in his early-to-mid-twenties. 'They're milling around somewhere. Apparently most of them wanted to go back in there when we've finished. Can you believe that? They actually want to go back into that shitty hole?'

'I can believe it,' Molly said quietly, 'if they've got nowhere else to go. That's their home in there. Or at least it was.'

He gave a disdainful snort. 'Someone from the council came down and spoke to them. Offered them temporary accommodation over Christmas. She said they didn't want to know. Well, maybe one or two of them did, but the rest, they either don't care or they're too off their tits on drink or drugs. Or they're just plain headcases.'

'They still need somewhere to live,' Molly said, 'like the rest of us.'

He looked blankly at her for a second, then sniffed and said, 'Right enough. Not our problem though.'

She looked at him for a few seconds, then smiled, still holding the stare. 'I'm sorry, I didn't get your name.'

'PC Simmons. Aaron Simmons.' He looked like he was going to offer her a handshake for a second then thought better of it.

'Well, PC Simmons,' Molly said coldly, 'we join the police to protect the public, irrespective of their personal circumstances. These people are as much in need of our protection as anyone else. Perhaps more so.' She offered the young PC another smile. 'Any one of us could end up homeless. For reasons that are beyond our control.' She was thinking about a documentary she'd seen not that long ago: an ex-marine who'd served in Iraq and Afghanistan had ended up sleeping rough after leaving the army. He'd been found dead from hypothermia in a shop doorway. A combination of alcoholism and mental health issues had seen him fall through the net. It was easy to look down on people who had been handed the shitty stick in life.

The young constable nodded and avoided eye contact, trying to hide his embarrassment.

'I need to speak to a young lad. Early twenties, dirty blond hair, wearing a black anorak over a grey hoodie. A beanie hat… He might have a young girl with him of a similar age.' She described Zella, though she hoped she wasn't around.

The uniformed officer shrugged. 'He might have been one of them that took up the offer of free accommodation.' He looked at Molly, trying to appear sympathetic. 'Sorry, I dunno more than that. Your lot all took statements from them after the CID boys spoke to them. I don't suppose there was much point in asking them for their contact details.' He gave a half-smile at this comment, but Molly let her expression warn him his humour wasn't finding an appreciative audience. Perhaps sensing an official reprimand might be on the cards if she decided to put in a formal complaint, he changed his tone. 'Look, I don't know where they've gone, but like I said, I expect most of them will wander back here when forensics have finished in there, which shouldn't be too long by the look of it. Maybe if you come back tonight?'

But she didn't have time to come back later. If they didn't make some progress with this case soon then the team really would start to regard it as a lost cause.

Despite the young PC's claim about the community having drifted away, there was still a small group of about half a dozen hanging round the scrub of park near the station. They were sitting on benches, either drinking from cans or smoking, or both. One of them had a little dog wrapped in what looked like a knitted jacket. They were milling around, presumably hoping they could return to the station once the police and forensics had finished in there. There was little chance of that happening.

The park had a desolate feel about it. In summer, at this time of the day, it would probably have been cheery and alive with dog walkers and children playing. But on a grey, dull day in December it looked cold and unwelcoming.

As she approached the group, Molly could sense their wary eyes burning into her. Even the dog seemed to eye her warily. 'Copper,' she heard one of them say once she was within earshot. The group shuffled awkwardly, eyes now anywhere but on her.

She recognised one of the group from earlier. He looked to be close enough in age to Corey and Zella to at least be passingly familiar with them. 'I'm looking for Corey,' she said. 'Does anyone know where I can find them?'

Her question was met with a general shaking of heads. Their reticence was understandable: she was police and part of the reason they were now huddled together in a park rather than safe in their own space. 'It's important,' she added, hoping that might prompt a more positive response.

One of the men flashed a glance in her direction. She could smell stale cigarette smoke and booze coming off him in waves. Just like being back with Jon, she thought. Was this where her ex-boyfriend was destined to end up? Homeless and desperate without someone there to look after him? Perhaps she was being unfair...

'It is important,' she repeated.

The man looked at her again. There was stubble round his chin, but not enough to form a beard. His dark grey eyes contained a sadness she could only guess at.

'You could try the church hall near the old cinema,' one of them said.

'The church hall...?' She hoped they weren't about to send her on a wild goose chase.

'They have a soup kitchen there,' another man replied. 'They go there sometimes.'

She asked for directions and she made a mental note.

St Barnabas Church Hall was just off Whitechapel Road. Outside was a large, elegantly painted sign saying 'WUTH: Warming Up the Homeless'. It was run by a retired couple who told Molly they knew Corey and Zella by sight, but neither had been in that day. Molly asked if either of them knew where she could find Corey, or suggest a good place to look for him.

'I think they were sleeping rough in an old railway station,' the woman said. 'But we don't like to ask too many questions when they're here. We want them to see this as a safe place where they won't feel pressurised.'

Molly thanked them for their help and headed back outside.

It had been very warm in the hall and she felt the sharp contrast in temperature as soon as she was out the door.

This was turning out as she'd suspected it would. Trying to find someone who didn't want to be found and was skilled at staying off the radar. Corey was always going to be something of a longshot. Without a surname, and only a vague description, trying to track him down would be near impossible. The difficult bit was having to tell Denning that she'd failed.

The closest thing they had to a semi-reliable witness had vanished.

## Chapter Seven

Denning never felt comfortable in the company of property developers. It wasn't just because his ex-wife had recently been involved with one who had turned out to be a serial killer and then took Denning's ex-wife and son hostage, threatening to kill them... There was also the fact he just didn't like what they did for a living: converting swathes of London's history into overpriced carbuncles that mostly stood empty while other people slept in abandoned Tube stations.

The offices of Excelsior Properties were atop a converted pub on Upper Street, roughly halfway between Duncan Street and Charlton Place. The ground floor of the building was now an airy-looking Thai restaurant, while a side entrance led up to the offices above.

Steven Hodge was a senior partner in Excelsior Properties. He greeted Denning with an enthusiastic handshake and led him into a well-appointed office with quirky artwork and windows that overlooked busy Upper Street. Hodge gestured towards a pair of cream leather sofas that sat either side of a glass-topped coffee table in a corner of the room.

'Take a seat. Can I get you a tea or a coffee?' A hint of an East London accent that lurked beneath the smartly polished vowels. It was difficult to gauge Hodge's age, but Denning reckoned he was in his late forties. He wore a pair of skinny designer jeans with a beige linen jacket over an open-necked white shirt. Denning caught a glimpse of a thick gold chain underneath one of his cuffs. His after-shave smelt expensive: *Sauvage Elixir* by Dior, Denning reckoned, or something similar.

There was sharpness about Steven Hodge that suggested he was a man who worked hard at cultivating an image of effortless success.

'No thank you, Mr Hodge. I'd rather just ask you a few questions, if that's OK?'

Hodge smiled and waved his hand. 'Sure. Though, you said this was about a murder, so I'm not sure how much help I can be.'

'You recently bought the former Shoreditch Underground station just off Brick Lane, is that correct?'

He nodded. 'Well, my company did. We've got big plans for the site.' Hodge got up from the sofa and walked over to his desk. He rummaged in a drawer for a few seconds then took out an impressive-looking glossy brochure, which he handed to Denning.

There was a picture of the old station on the front, but not as Denning had seen it earlier that day – derelict and smothered in urban art. Instead, a computer-generated image showed a sleek and trendy restaurant, complete with white walls and pale grey slate flooring; a wide, open space on the ground floor and a mezzanine level that looked like it had been seamlessly slotted into the roof area. A solid wooden spiral staircase connected the two floors.

'A restaurant and café bar at street level,' Hodge said with some excitement, 'and a nightclub in the basement. The nightclub will have its own entrance leading directly down to the lower level. Two bars, plus a VIP area.'

Denning opened the brochure and glanced at the proposed plans for the building: the nightclub was going to incorporate a lot of the station's original architecture, including the Victorian brick arches and metalwork, all tastefully painted in subtle tones. Denning tossed the brochure onto the glass coffee table. 'Very impressive, Mr Hodge. Were you aware there was an unhoused community living there when you bought the building?'

'How could I have known that? They didn't exactly advertise their presence when we purchased the site.'

'But their presence must have been an inconvenience you could have done without?'

Hodge shuffled uncomfortably on the sofa, but quickly resumed his confident charm. 'They were trespassing on private property, Inspector. And besides, it's hardly a healthy place for people to live. The site is prone to flooding, and there are rats and God-only-knows what else down there.'

Denning wanted to point out it wasn't as though any of them were living there by choice, but such a comment was unlikely to provoke a nod of sympathy from someone like Hodge, whose sole concern was the building's potential for development.

'A restaurant and a nightclub.' Denning lifted the brochure from the coffee table and flicked through the glossy pages again. He imagined it would be the kind of place that would appeal to his wife and her colleagues: overpriced and pretentious. 'It's certainly ambitious,' he said.

Hodge's face broke into a wide smile. 'It's the perfect location. Just minutes from the City. And then there's the trendy Shoreditch crowd – they're always eager to try somewhere new and upmarket. We were lucky to get the site so cheaply.'

An unhoused community living in the basement probably helped lower the price, Denning thought. He suspected Hodge was fully aware that the building hadn't come with vacant possession when he'd bought it, despite his claim to the contrary.

'Did you ever visit the station?'

'Twice. Once with my architect and another time with a quantity surveyor and a structural engineer to check the integrity of the site. The planning consent stipulates that we can't alter the exterior of the building, so we have to work within the limitations of what's already there, but it's a surprisingly large space. A team of engineers is due to go in there early in the New Year prior to any remedial being carried out. Now that we've successfully secured the site, that should be able to go ahead as planned.'

'So you'll be starting work almost straightaway?'

'There's no point wasting any more time. We're aiming to have the restaurant open later next year, and then the nightclub soon afterwards.'

'It's all worked out well for you?,' Denning said. 'Now the unhoused community has been moved on after those drugs were found.'

'Yes, I won't deny that has made things easier. But as I said, these people had no legal right to be there. We would have had them evicted eventually. And I don't know anything about the drugs.' He stared back at Denning, defiantly. The rictus smile was still fixed on his face but any warmth it may have had was now gone. 'It's very unfortunate that a man has been murdered on the site, and we could really do without that kind of bad publicity, but I'm afraid I don't see how I can be of any help with your investigation, Inspector. I only heard about the murder this morning. I don't know who the victim was or why he was killed. Apart from owning the property where it happened, this has got nothing to do with me or my company.'

Denning nodded and placed the brochure back on the coffee table.

'Just one last question, Mr Hodge.' Denning reached into his jacket pocket and removed a photograph of the victim. He passed it over to Hodge. 'Do you recognise this man?'

Hodge looked at the picture for a moment then shook his head. 'No. I've never seen him before. Who is he?'

'That's what we're hoping to find out, Mr Hodge,' Denning said. 'And then once we've identified him, hopefully we can find out who killed him.'

# Chapter Eight

Molly was already looking forward to home time: eating something stodgy and microwavable for dinner, followed by zoning out in front of some rubbish on the telly. There were days when the job she loved felt more like a thankless exercise in crime management than something worthwhile. Denning had landed them with a thorny case that wasn't going to come with any easy answers.

She turned into the quiet street where she'd only been living for a few months. She was still getting used to calling her tiny flat home. The flat occupied the ground floor of a converted Victorian house in Stratford, East London. Despite its pokiness and unpretentious location, the rent took up a sizeable chunk of her salary.

It was already dark as she approached the flat; the wintery gloom casting long shadows in the streetlight. She could sense the temperatures were going to take another tumble that night, and there was a noticeable chill in the air. Hang the cost, she thought to herself, she would turn the central heating up a notch this evening.

Suddenly she stopped in her tracks. There was something scrawled on the glass of the communal front door.

She shuddered slightly when she realised what it was. The words 'You're Next' had been spray-painted onto the glass panel in red lettering. Instinctively, she looked up and down the street in case whoever had done it was still hanging around, taking sick pleasure from her reaction.

Molly stared at the words for a minute or so, suddenly oblivious to the gathering chill.

*You're Next.*

It was both disarmingly ambiguous and yet creepily sinister. Someone's idea of a joke, she thought...?

She unlocked the door and checked for any signs of a break-in, but apart from the bizarre graffiti on the front door, everything seemed normal. Quiet. A heavy silence filled the communal hallway. She thought about knocking on the door to the upstairs flat, but the middle-aged man who lived there – with whom she had only ever exchanged a couple of hurried pleasantries since she'd moved in – was rarely at home. She assumed he worked away from home most of the time, though she had yet to ascertain what he did for a living, or perhaps had a partner who lived elsewhere, and he only used the flat as somewhere to crash whenever he wanted time to himself. She hadn't seen or heard him for a few days, and as the glass fanlight above the door to his flat was dark, it was safe to assume he wasn't around at the moment. She could wander the street knocking on neighbours' doors asking if anyone had seen anything, but she was tired and there was a good chance the graffiti was just some sick bastard's depraved reference to what had happened to the flat's previous occupant.

She let herself into her flat and switched on the light in the narrow corridor that led to the kitchen and bathroom at the back of the flat. She entered the living room and sat on the sofa. Perhaps it was the cold or perhaps she was letting the words on the front door get to her, but she felt herself shiver.

The flat came with a history, which partly explained its affordability. Only a few months before, it had been the scene of a murder: a young father had been fatally stabbed on the doorstep while his partner and child were inside. The person responsible was now serving time in a psychiatric unit. The victim's widow and their young child had moved out, and as Molly had needed to find somewhere to stay after separating from her boyfriend, she had decided to rent the flat, in spite of what had happened in it.

At first, Molly had felt awkward about benefitting from someone's misfortune, but if she hadn't taken it, the flat would simply have been let to someone else.

Despite her refusal to let what had happened affect her, every time she opened the front door she thought about Kieran Judd bleeding to death in the hallway. She tried to blank it out of her mind most of the time, but that was easier said than done. The blood had been cleaned away but the memories still lingered.

She regained her composure and headed into the kitchen. She turned on the kettle, made herself a cup of tea and went back into the living room.

Although she tried to reassure herself the writing on the door was nothing to worry about, she felt disconcerted. She'd had an unsettling feeling for a while now; nothing specific, just silly little things that had put her mind on edge. There had been a couple of silent phone calls from an unknown number recently. A wrong number probably, but it had unsettled her. She was certain there had been someone on the other end of the line, but no one spoke. Then a couple of nights ago, as she was drawing the living room curtains, she thought she'd spotted someone on the other side of the street staring over at her flat. It had been no more than a figure lurking behind a van, and a moment later they were gone.

The flat had been the scene of a murder, so it was inevitable it would attract attention from ghouls from time to time. People were always going to be intrigued by a property with a macabre history.

But there was a niggling voice inside her that kept asking if it could be something else? Jon had been behaving strangely recently: the odd text message asking to meet up. Offers to help her move in or to decorate her new flat. He kept insisting he wanted nothing more than friendship, but could he really be after something more? There was no chance of them getting back together – too much water had passed under too many bridges for that to be a possibility. But Jon was never someone who liked taking no for an answer.

All this combined was putting her on edge.

She switched on the telly and turned to the BBC News. There was no point letting her mind wander on what might have been. Instead, she thought about Corey and the rest of the rough sleepers. Whatever the limitations of her flat, at least she had somewhere comfortable to sleep at night. She was certain Corey was going to say something about their victim when she'd spoken to him and Zella. If she could get another chance to speak to him…

She suddenly heard a noise outside: a clattering, like a tin can being kicked down the street. She climbed off the sofa and went to over the window, peering through the narrow gap where the curtains met, but the street was still quiet. A thin sheen of frost was glistening on the pavement, and the warm glow of domesticity emanated from her neighbours' windows. Everything looked normal and reassuring, so why couldn't she shake the feeling of dread that was building inside her...?

## Chapter Nine

Home for Matthew and Sarah Denning was an expensive loft apartment that occupied the top two floors of a converted factory-cum-warehouse in Shoreditch.

Denning was constantly aware that the only reason they could afford to live there was down to his wife's job as a hedge fund manager for a City bank, where she earned the kind of salary he could never hope to match, even if he took all the overtime the Met could throw at him.

The apartment was tastefully decorated, and had impressive views towards East London. It was also less than half a mile from the former Shoreditch Tube station.

Sarah was stretched out on one of the two large linen sofas that faced each other in the middle of the vast living room. She was leafing through some work papers; a glass of Chablis on the table beside the sofa; a gentle Mozart quintet playing on Classic FM.

'How was your day?' Denning asked, kissing her on the cheek.

'Same as usual.' She took a sip of Chablis. 'You?'

'Same as usual too.'

He would have told her about the murder, but there wouldn't be much point. Sarah tended not to take too much of an interest in his work, especially the gorier aspects of a murder investigation. In all fairness, he had never really paid too much attention to the finer details of her job either. Until recently. Until she had begun to make it clear she thinking about changing her job.

He headed up to the master bedroom on the mezzanine level, went into the marble-tiled ensuite, and turned on the shower.

As he undressed, he thought about his domestic situation. So often work dominated his thoughts, and life with Sarah just somehow went on around him. Both of them had always seemed reasonably contented in their jobs: they were both ambitious and not shy in chasing after promotion when it came along. They were financially comfortable and secure enough in their relationship that the work/life balance issues that affected so many of their friends had never been a problem for them.

Once in the shower, he let the jet of warm water pummel his body.

Sarah had recently turned down a job in New York, heading up her bank's US investment portfolios. One of the main reasons she'd turned the job down was for his benefit. His and Jake's. Jake was ten now; his son from his first marriage. He lived with Denning's ex-wife in a comfortable house in Surrey Quays, and father and son spent every other weekend together. Holidays and rare days off too, but, as so often happened, work took priority, and time with Jake had become something Denning treasured and valued and never dared to take for granted.

Whilst he had secretly been pleased with Sarah's decision to turn down the job, he was now plagued by guilt at the thought of having potentially held her back in her career. He knew Sarah hadn't been happy for some time and he was, albeit indirectly, at least partially to blame. Part of him wished he'd tried harder to persuade

Sarah to take the job, despite the potential disruption to his family life. Moving to New York would have been a massive step for both of them, even though he would have been the one making the greater sacrifice.

And then there was the work situation.

He thought back to his conversation with McKenna earlier that afternoon. If it was true about the team being disbanded, then his future looked uncertain. If that were the case, then their options would change; there could be a real possibility that they would be more dependent than ever on Sarah's career.

He turned off the shower, got out and dried himself. He changed into casual clothes, scruffy jeans and an old rugby top, and went downstairs to the living room. He and Sarah always took it in turn to cook dinner, and it was his turn tonight, even though he wasn't in the mood.

Sarah was still lying on the sofa. She had opened her laptop now and was writing what looked like a lengthy email.

'Why don't we go house-hunting this weekend,' he suggested. They had been talking about buying a house for some time, but it had never progressed beyond the looking-at-properties-online stage, and the whole thing had slightly been put on ice in recent months.

'What brought this on?' she asked.

'Well, we always said we never intended to stay here forever, and we could probably do with a change of scene.'

She gave a little chuckle. 'I thought you were against the idea of moving?'

'I wasn't exactly against it. I just didn't want us to feel pressurised into buying somewhere simply for the sake of it. And I'm only suggesting we look at places. We don't have to commit ourselves to anything.'

She finished writing her email, then closed the laptop. 'OK. I can have a look on some of the property websites, if you like. Where do we want to go? North or south of the river? Or out of London altogether? As long as there are good transport links, we could even think about Hertfordshire or Surrey?'

In truth he didn't really care. South meant being closer to Jake and his ex-wife, Claire, though there was a good chance they might move if her new relationship worked out.

They had friends who lived in a pleasant semi-detached house in Richmond, overlooking the river but that might be beyond their financial reach, even with their combined salaries.

He went into the kitchen and returned with a wine-glass. He poured himself some Chablis after topping up Sarah's glass.

He sat on the opposite sofa and sipped the wine. Sarah had opened her laptop up again and was presumably checking out property websites. As he watched her, his thoughts turned to their victim. The kind of places Sarah would be looking at would be selling for around a million. A luxury lifestyle that was a world away from that of their victim. Living rough, cold, and probably scared. How had he ended up in that situation? And why...? Denning couldn't help thinking the *why* was the key here.

Somehow he got the impression Steven Hodge *had* recognised their victim. Well, perhaps not exactly *recognised*, but at least had an idea of who he was.

This was going to be a tricky case. He was very aware of McKenna's words: *this investigation needs to be time limited. Either find a quick resolution to the case or drop it.*

That was easier for her to say than for him to do. Whichever way he looked at it, he couldn't help feeling sorry for their victim. *There but for the grace of God go I...* It was true. He glanced around the spacious flat, with its tasteful décor and expensive furniture. He took it all for granted, but it could all so easily disappear. If he and Sarah split up... if he lost his job... if he became seriously ill and could no longer work...

Potentially, it wouldn't take much for him to end up living rough in a derelict building in the middle of winter.

He took another sip of Chablis. It was difficult to ignore the fact he led a comfortable and privileged life compared with a lot of people. Did that mean he was out of touch with the people he was tasked with looking after? Did people living on the fringes of society regard him as part of the problem rather than the solution?

He had joined the police to help people.

If he were to meet the same fate as their victim, he would want someone to care enough to find out who killed him.

But there was so much that wasn't making sense here. Had their victim been deliberately targeted? If so, how did the killer know where to find him? Why kill him with so many other people around, when there was a real danger the killer could have been spotted? But would the other rough sleepers have done anything anyway? Despite the wall of silence from the homeless community, they had the impression their victim was something of a loner. Perhaps that had isolated him from the very community that should have been protecting him?

And how – if at all – did the drugs fit into it?

The more Denning thought about it, the more he was sure the drugs weren't the answer.

Whatever the case, they had a murderer who had killed someone who had little in life, and a victim who had chosen anonymity. And yet, someone out there must be missing him.

## Chapter Ten

Bethnal Green Police Station wasn't exactly high on Molly's list of places to visit that evening, but the officer on the other end of the line had been insistent that she was the person who had been asked for. And despite her misgivings, this was important.

She'd taken a taxi from the flat to the station, asking for a receipt in the vain hope that she might be able to claim the taxi fare back on expenses. This was, after all, police business.

The police station was an austere, modern-looking brick building that had been designed to look older, but ended up being both characterless and charmless at the same time.

The entrance doors slid open as she walked up the steps. She showed her warrant card to the civilian support officer on the front desk, explaining why she was there. He smiled noncommittally and buzzed her in, directing her down a long, grey-walled corridor to the custody suite at the rear of the station.

A burly uniformed desk sergeant checked her warrant card and sighed. 'I dunno why he asked for you. This isn't exactly a matter for the big boys.' He looked at Molly and grinned. 'Or girls…'

'I'm not entirely sure either,' Molly replied. 'Perhaps all will become clearer after I've spoken to him.'

The desk sergeant nodded slowly. She wasn't sure if that meant he agreed with her, or thought she was an idealistic idiot and was simply humouring her. He asked her to take a seat while he marched off in the direction of the cells. She heard him unlock a cell door and a couple of minutes later the bedraggled form of Corey ambled towards her.

'Shoplifting,' the desk sergeant said, shaking his head. 'And not the first time, is it?' He gave Corey a pitiful look.

'And you were going to keep him in overnight for shoplifting?' Molly said.

'He claims he's got nowhere to go. We gave him something to eat and a mug of tea. We were going to charge him, then he asked to speak to you. We found your card crumpled up in his jacket pocket.' He gave a little snort that could have almost passed for an attempt at a laugh. 'We did think that was a bit strange.'

'Are you going to charge him?' Molly asked.

'There's not much point, is there? If it goes to court he'll probably get a fine, which he won't be able to pay. And then it's more paperwork for us.' Another snort. 'Now he's got his fairy godmother to bail him out... Maybe you could try and knock some sense into him?'

Corey looked slightly pathetic but otherwise OK. A night in a police cell with a mug of tea and something to eat was probably a better offer than whatever alternative living conditions he was now experiencing. At least it was warm in the custody suite.

'I'll take him off your hands then,' Molly said. In truth, she still didn't know why Corey had asked for her. What exactly did he think she could do for him in the face of a shoplifting charge? But there would be little point in trying to explain the intricacies of the Metropolitan Police's operational structures: as far as Corey was

60

concerned, she was a copper, and murder, shoplifting and anything else they could arrest you for all came under the same umbrella of 'crime'.

After signing the paperwork, the desk sergeant handed over Corey's meagre belongings and buzzed the pair of them out of the custody suite. Once they were outside, the brittle air stung Molly in the face. 'So what's this about, Corey? I should be at home right now, curled up on my sofa watching *Emmerdale*.'

'I was going to do a deal with you,' he said. 'If I told you stuff, you'd persuade them to let me go.'

Molly briefly wondered if, perhaps, it had been a mistake to give Corey her card. But she needed to speak to him, and at least this way she wasn't going to have to try and track him down.

'Well now they have let you go, why don't you tell me what you know?'

'It probably wasn't important anyway.'

'If you mess me around, Corey, I'll march you back into that station and have you charged with shoplifting. Not to mention withholding information about a murder.'

The expression on her face told him she wasn't joking. She'd been dragged out in the middle of a cold night; she was damn sure this was going to be a worth it.

'I wouldn't mind something to eat,' he said. 'The food they give in there is rubbish.'

She took them to a nearby McDonald's and ordered a burger and fries for Corey and a black coffee for herself. They found a table upstairs, where it was quieter.

Corey ate like it was the first proper food he'd seen in days, which, with the exception of the sandwich at the police station, it quite possibly was. She couldn't help feeling sympathy for him. He seemed so young, and painfully thin. She wanted to ask him about his family, but it was none of her business.

'Where are you living now?' she asked.

'We've got a squat,' he said. 'Not far from here.'

'Whereabouts?' Corey remained tight-lipped. 'I might need to speak to you again. And then there's always the chance you might need another favour if you're arrested again…'

'Kempton Way,' he said after a moment. 'One of the old council flats.'

She made a note. She had no idea where Kempton Way was, but she'd check it on Google Maps later, just to make sure. That was, of course, assuming Corey was telling her the truth. After giving the lad a few minutes to eat, she said, 'The man who was stabbed, Corey. What do you know about what happened? And bear in mind I've been around long enough to know bullshit when I hear it.' She leaned in closer to him. She could smell the unwashed feral stench that emanated from him. 'I only want to know who killed him, Corey.'

He ate more of his burger, munching eagerly, flicking the occasional look in Molly's direction. There was a petulant look on his face, like a sulky child who had been told off for something he hadn't done. When he'd finished his mouthful, he said, 'He was OK, except when he was pissed. He would turn into a crazy man then. And then other times, he would just cry for no reason.'

'Cry?'

'Yeah. He tried to hug me once. I told him to piss off.' He took another bite of his burger. 'I'm not like that. He kept himself to himself. Nobody really knew much about him. When me and Zella pitched up, he was already there.

He would just sit in the corner keeping himself to himself. He never used to go out begging like the rest of us either.'

'What else?'

'I think he was a posh bloke.'

'Posh? What makes you think that?'

He shrugged. 'He never spoke much, but when he did, he sounded… well, posh. You know, like people who read the news on the telly speak. And he had a nice watch. It looked expensive.' He stopped talking and looked at the floor, worried that he'd said too much.

'What happened to the watch?' Molly asked.

He shrugged. 'How would I know?'

He was defensive and Molly wondered if he'd regretted telling her about the watch. But she was intrigued by what he meant by posh. 'He never said what he did before he was homeless? Did he ever mention a family?'

Corey shook his head. 'He could be a bit weird.'

'Weird? How?'

'He used to call me by another name sometimes. I mean, he knew what my name was, but sometimes he'd call me Leo or Theo. At least that's what it sounded like.'

Molly made a mental note. It was possible this could be significant. 'You said he was posh. Was that because of something he told you? Something about his life before he was homeless?'

Corey grabbed a handful of fries, stuffing them into his mouth. She wondered when he last had a decent meal; one that didn't consist of junk food.

'He had a family, but he didn't speak about them much. Except if he had been drinking.'

'Did he say anything about his family?'

A shake of the head. 'But I think he had a son. He used to say something about "my boy".'

'A son?' She pondered on the relevance of this. 'Anything else?'

He shook his head.

Molly wondered how much of what he'd just told her was actually true.

She sat in silence while he finished his burger. She couldn't help but feel sorry for him. He was a nice lad who had clearly been through some shit in his life to have ended up falling through the cracks. She remembered something Jon had said to her once about how she liked to collect waifs and strays: there had been Colin, a victim of sexual abuse that she'd befriended during an investigation into the murder of a former police officer. And then there was Paul Chitterly, a petty criminal whose girlfriend had been murdered back in the summer after becoming involved with a dangerous gang. Then there was Bex… She hadn't thought about Bex for a while. She tried hard not to think about Bex; the memories were still too difficult…

'OK, so tell me about you and our victim.' Molly chose her words with care. 'He was fond of you…?'

Corey picked at the detritus of fries in the box on the table. 'What are you saying? It was nothing like—'

'I'm not suggesting it was anything improper,' she said. 'He called you Leo. Could that have been his son?'

Corey shrugged. 'I don't know. He only said it when he'd had a skinful.'

'And how often was that?'

'Whenever he could get hold of booze.'

'What about drugs? Did he ever touch them?'

He finished the fries and shook the empty box just in case any more should magically appear. 'I told you, I don't know anything about any drugs.'

'I'm not accusing you of anything, Corey, and I really couldn't care less about the drugs. I want to know what happened the night our victim was killed, and I think you know more than you're letting on.' She paused, letting her words sink in. 'Did you see anyone talking to him? Or anyone strange hanging round the station? Any new faces?'

'Like I told you when you asked us before, people come and go all the time,' he said.

'What about someone who looked like they didn't belong there?'

'There have been a couple of strange men hanging around recently, but I don't think they had anything to do with what happened.'

'Strange men. Can you describe them?'

'It was a few weeks ago,' he said. 'Sharp suits. We thought they might be police, come to chuck us out, but they just ignored us.'

'What did they want?'

'They just looked around the place. Didn't speak. They had torches.'

'How old were they?' Molly asked.

'I don't know. I couldn't really see them. Forties. Smartly dressed. They were wearing heavy coats, even though it wasn't all that cold then, not like now.'

The developers, Molly thought, checking on their investment. They would need to confirm that.

'Anyone else been round recently? Anyone you didn't recognise?'

He shook his head. A moment later he met Molly's gaze. 'Well, there was one bloke. I wasn't sure. We'd all had a bit of a smoke...' His face fell and he closed his mouth, already having told her more then he wanted to.

'I told you I couldn't give a stuff about drugs, Corey. This is more important.'

'There was a slick geezer who was hanging around,' he said after a moment. 'I saw him speaking to John.'

'When was this?'

'A few days ago. Maybe a week. I can't be sure because I was out of it, but I saw a bloke talking to him.'

'Was it one of the same men from before?'

He screwed his face up in thought. 'I dunno… maybe. I don't think so…' A look of embarrassment spread across his face. 'I was out of it. I don't even know if it happened or if I imagined it.'

'What happened, Corey? This could be important.'

'The bloke handed him something. I think they might have been arguing. It was dark and we was a good bit away. But it looked like the bloke handed something to him.'

'What was it?'

'An envelope. A large one.'

'Did you see what was in it?'

'No.'

She didn't believe him. 'Corey, it's very important. What was in the envelope?'

'It looked like money. Lots of money.'

## Chapter Eleven

Molly and Corey parted company outside McDonald's. She wasn't sure if she should offer him money or if he'd just spend it on booze or drugs, and if he did that was his choice and not for her to judge. What Corey really needed was a roof over his head and stability. And she wasn't in a position to offer that.

She asked him to get in touch if he could think of anything, or remember what the mystery man with the envelope looked like.

That was assuming the man and the envelope even existed.

It was possible Corey had been stringing her along. So far he'd got a free meal out of her just for telling her what he thought she wanted to hear.

Could she even trust him?

The stuff about their victim having a family rang true, but the mysterious man with the money... Why would a stranger hand a homeless man money? She'd asked Corey to describe the cash, but he didn't know how much it was. He couldn't even approximate how much it might have been, but he reckoned it was a lot. A huge wad, he'd said.

He'd been vague when she'd pressed him about what happened to the cash. He claimed the stranger left, taking the envelope with him. It seemed Corey hadn't asked their victim about the money, or who the man was. According to Corey there was no point, he would have told Corey to piss off, or worse, depending on how much booze he'd had.

So what had happened to the money?

For a second, she wondered if Corey and Zella had taken it. Could they have stabbed the victim in exchange for an envelope full of cash? It was certainly possible. But they would have surely used the money to feed themselves, or even find a decent place to live if there had been enough of it.

It was just possible this had something to do with the property developer, Steven Hodge, paying the rough sleepers to vacate the premises. But if that was the case, why give it to their victim?

She headed towards Bethnal Green Tube station, which was only a five-minute walk away. If the Central Line was running OK, she'd be home in less than twenty minutes. As she walked along Cambridge Heath Road she thought she caught sight of someone following her. She glanced over her shoulder, but there was just the usual throng of people making their way home from an evening out drinking or whatever post-work relaxation they'd engaged in. She knew she had to stop with this paranoia before it got out of hand. She saw the Tube station just up ahead. She hurried down the steps to the subway and turned into the station's booking office, tapped her Oyster card and passed through the barriers, following the signs for the platforms.

Bethnal Green Tube station had been the scene of an horrific disaster in the early 1940s. Jon had written an article about it a few years back. The partially built station had been used as an air-raid shelter during the Second

World War, and over a hundred people had been crushed to death one evening when panic had sent many people down the station entrance, resulting in a stampede. Molly shuddered as she thought of what those people must have felt as panic engulfed them when they realised there was no means of escape.

She glanced over her shoulder again: there was a young man in a baseball cap several steps behind her, the peak of the cap pulled down so she couldn't see his face clearly. She thought it might have been one of Corey's friends following her to ask her why she wanted to speak to Corey, but could that be the same man she'd glimpsed watching her flat the other night? Molly stopped to watch what he did next, but he ducked out of sight. Was he really following her? She headed down to the eastbound platform, but with another glance over her shoulder she saw the man in the cap was only a few paces behind her again.

The platform was busy: people were heading home from an evening out. Why should this man be any different?

As she approached the platform, she heard a train approaching. The man in the cap was standing a few feet away, further along the platform. As she glanced over her shoulder, he turned his head away. He was of slight build, but his shoulders suggested he worked out. Casually dressed, but not scruffy, so probably not someone from the homeless community. As the train pulled in, she made sure she was close to the doors. The doors opened and she hopped on. She watched as the man got on too. Just when the doors were about to close, she quickly hopped back off the carriage, as the doors slid shut behind her. A moment later the train pulled out of the station and headed east.

She couldn't see the man who had been following her, but he had to still be on the train.

She could see more passengers heading down the stairs onto the platform. The indicator board said the next east-bound train was two minutes away.

Molly pressed herself against a metal pillar and breathed slowly. She knew she was overreacting. There were lots of people on the platform now: most dressed in suits and the smart/casual clothing of office workers returning from an evening at a bar or restaurant. Others were scruffier: students, or people who worked in shops or cafés nearby. The man who'd got on the same train as her was probably just another one of the crowd. She took her phone out of her bag and checked for any messages or calls, but there weren't any.

Another glance at the indicator board told her the next train was now only a minute away. She waited until her heartbeat had returned to normal, but she was suddenly aware that her legs were shaking.

She had to pull herself together; paranoia and jumping at shadows was not going to help her. She needed to stay calm. She walked to the end of the platform, making sure her legs were steadier now. Once she saw the train pull into the platform, she relaxed slightly. There was no one watching her.

The train drew to a halt and the doors slid open. Molly boarded the train and took one of the remaining available seats. The other passengers in the carriage were either looking at their phones, listening to music or absorbed in a newspaper or book. No one seemed interested in her. And why would they be? She was just another lone woman travelling home by Tube.

## Chapter Twelve

The next morning, Denning parked his as close as he could to the mortuary entrance at Charing Cross Hospital.

It was still early and he hadn't slept well. At least, not well enough to feel he could face the day with any real enthusiasm without a strong black coffee or two. He knew he had to shake himself out of this feeling of stupor; he had a murder investigation to lead, and a team that would be looking to him to guide them. Not to mention an impatient DCI who wanted quick and easy answers so she could face her retirement with nothing nasty hanging over her.

He pushed open the heavy glass door that led to the main mortuary suite and sought out the pathologist who had conducted the post-mortem on their victim. Dr Baker was already in his office waiting for Denning. Denning was secretly relieved that Baker had already completed the post-mortem. It wasn't that he was squeamish about post-mortems – he'd been a detective for too long to feel uncomfortable at the sight of a dead body being cut and sliced on a mortuary slab – it was just that he found the whole process time consuming and unnecessary. Technically both he, as senior investigating officer, and Sheila Gorton as crime scene manager, should have attended the actual post-mortem, but with budgets being slashed and workloads being prioritised, it was difficult for them to justify their joint presence. Baker would let him know in his report if he had discovered anything of note.

'Matt,' Baker said with a smile, indicating Denning should take a seat in the uncomfortably small office. 'How's things?'

Baker was a florid, bearded man in his fifties, with a mop of thick greying hair that was always trying its best to escape from his mortuary cap.

Denning smiled and sat down opposite him. 'I'm hoping you've got something positive to tell me.'

Baker sipped his tea from a chipped china mug with 'World's Best Butcher' emblazoned on the side. 'Would you like a cup, by the way?'

Denning shook his head. 'I'd rather crack on if you don't mind.'

Baker coughed, then sat back on his chair. 'Obviously I'll email you the full report once I've typed it up, but in the meantime, I can confirm that our victim was killed by a single stab wound to the heart. Neat and precise, and I would say carried out with some force. A non-serrated blade about six inches in length. There are no signs of defensive wounds, so it's possible our victim was asleep when he was killed, though that's just supposition on my part. I would say he's been dead for less than forty-eight hours, but more than twenty-four, therefore approximating the time of death as being the early hours of Monday morning, possibly very late Sunday night.'

'What can you tell me about the victim himself?'

Baker took another sip of tea. 'Age, early fifties, or at least somewhere between late forties and mid-fifties. Not in the best of health – there's evidence of significant liver damage, probably the result of heavy alcohol consumption. Evidence too of poor diet, which is to be expected under the circumstances. I'd say the alcohol damage stretched back some time, judging by the state of his liver.'

'So, liver damage and poor diet would suggest he'd been living rough for a while?'

A shrug from Baker. 'I wouldn't like to say how long he's been sleeping rough for, but the liver damage would definitely indicate long-term alcohol consumption.' Baker pawed at his beard. 'There was one thing I did find interesting.' He paused, looking up at Denning. 'There's evidence of expensive dental work. A couple of implants and some ceramic fillings. The implants are around ten to fifteen years old, so not recent. A bit trickier to date the fillings, but probably no older than twenty years. I don't want to jump to any conclusions here, but I would surmise the work was carried out before he began sleeping rough.'

'Expensive?'

'Oh, I would say the cost of this kind of dental work would cost in the thousands, and almost certainly carried out by a private dentist. Suggesting that at some point in his life our man had money, or at least access to money.'

'Interesting. What are the chances of tracing the dentist who did the work?'

'I have a friend who works for a practice in Harley Street. I can email him the details and see what he says.'

Denning allowed himself a smile. It felt like there was a good chance they were finally about to start getting somewhere. He thought about the murder itself. 'When you say the knife wound was "neat and precise", that suggests it wasn't a frenzied attack.' Denning was thinking out loud rather than asking a specific question. If this had been the result of an argument between two people from the homeless community, would it have been so level-headed?

'That, taken alongside the lack of defence wounds, would suggest this was deliberate. Maybe not planned exactly, but it does suggest this wasn't the result of a fight that got out of hand.'

'Can we draw any kind of inference from that?' Denning asked.

Baker gave a thin smile. 'That's your job, Matt. Mine is to give you the cold, hard facts about our victim and the manner of his death. All I can say is that there are no wounds beyond the fatal stabbing to the heart. As to what that does or doesn't prove...' He shrugged and took another sip of his tea.

Denning was still thinking, trying to kickstart his brain into functioning at something close to full capacity. 'Was there anything else about our victim that you think is noteworthy?'

Baker slurped down the rest of his tea, then placed the mug on his desk. 'His skin and hair were in a poor condition. As were his fingernails. Evidence of significant vitamin deficiency, which all corresponds with what I said about poor diet. However, with the exception of his liver and to a lesser extent his kidneys, his internal organs appeared to be in a reasonably good condition. My professional opinion would say that suggests this was someone who was in basically good health until recently. I've had people his age on the slab who've been in a much worse condition.'

'Meaning what? He hadn't been sleeping rough for long?'

'It would suggest he lived comfortably at some point in his life. Beyond that, I wouldn't like to speculate.'

Denning pondered this. This seemed to point to their victim having only recently become homeless – within the last few years at most. So what did he do before he ended up sleeping rough?

'Can you let me know about the dental work?' Denning said. 'It's looking like this could be our best chance of identifying him.'

'I'll get onto it straightaway. Well, as soon as I've had another cuppa.'

# Chapter Thirteen

Denning was sitting at his desk, waiting for a call from Jephcott to update him on the outcome of the drugs find. He was reading over the forensic report from Sheila Gorton. The blood splatter at the crime scene confirmed what they already suspected: their victim had been killed where he was found.

Now that the post-mortem was complete, arrangements would need to be made for the funeral. Arrangements that would be best made by the victim's family.

An email pinged into his inbox from Baker: he'd heard back from his friend regarding their victim's dental work. A dentist in West London had confirmed that the work had been carried out by their practice just over a decade ago. The patient's name was Raymond John Bowden.

There was something familiar about the name. Denning tried to focus: Ray Bowden. It had been something big, but he couldn't remember the details off the top of his head.

He logged on to the Police National Computer database, entered his authorisation code and typed the name Raymond Bowden.

There was a match. The date of birth give their victim's age as fifty-two, and there was an address in West London. Then the information came up on the screen, and Denning remembered why the name was familiar. A property scam, where gullible investors had been conned out of several million pounds after being advised to invest in a proposed marina and housing development on the south coast. The development never happened – even though planning permission had been applied for with the relevant local authority. The main players had disappeared as soon as it became clear no building work was going to materialise, and twitchy investors had started asking awkward questions.

According to the PNC, Bowden had acted as an intermediary: he ran an investment company at the time, alongside his business partner, Malcolm Carver. Carver had claimed he knew nothing about his partner's involvement in the scam, and was himself as much a victim as the investors who lost money.

Bowden had pleaded Not Guilty in court, but the jury had been unconvinced by his claims of innocence. He was sentenced to seven years for fraud. He'd initially appealed the sentence but had lost the appeal. There had been no subsequent appeals.

Doing the maths in his head, Denning worked out that assuming he had served around half his sentence, Bowden would have been released just over a year ago. He must have been sleeping rough since then. Denning wondered how and why he ended up on the streets. Bowden had a home, a family and a successful career before he'd been sent down. Yes, there was the shame and embarrassment of the trial and subsequent conviction, but at the end of the day it was a fraud case, not murder or child abuse. Even in those circumstances, Denning had known families forgive the perpetrator and allow them to return to the fold.

Why hadn't Bowden's family reported him missing?

He thought back to the case. He hadn't been involved in the investigation himself, and these days cases like this would be handled by the National Crime Agency.

Denning was thinking things over in his head. A property scam. The old station where Bowden had been sleeping had just been bought by a property developer. Property developers owned so much empty property in London it was hardly unusual, but it was still a strange coincidence.

Then there was the fraud case itself. The information on the police database covered the basics, but it was light on specifics. It didn't say exactly how many investors had lost money, or exactly how much each investor had lost, but the overall fraud came to several million.

Had one of those disgruntled investors heard that Bowden had been released from prison and wanted to exact their revenge? It was extreme but these things happened.

Denning had a friend who now worked for the NCA and had been a DC working for West London CID at the time of the fraud case. He might remember more details.

He looked over at McKenna's office door. He now felt like he had enough to make her start taking the case more seriously. Or at least to take the pressure off for the time being.

# Chapter Fourteen

'We have a name,' Denning said, addressing the room at the start of the next briefing. He wrote 'RAYMOND JOHN BOWDEN' on the whiteboard. 'Ray Bowden served time for property fraud a few years ago,' he said. Molly watched as their DI looked round the team as though he was trying to read the room for a reaction. Now they had a name for their victim, he was no longer an anonymous corpse in an abandoned Tube station. Molly wondered if the fact he'd had a criminal record would influence her colleagues' opinion. 'He was released just over a year ago,' Denning continued. 'It looks as though he's been living rough since then.'

'What about the drugs?' Kinsella asked.

'There's nothing to prove the rough sleepers even knew about them.' Denning said. 'I spoke to DI Jephcott this morning, and he is now convinced the drugs were only being stashed there.'

'Cuckooing?' Molly suggested. He looked at the rest of the team. 'It's possible, isn't it? Vulnerable people. They're probably not going to kick up a fuss if anyone comes on heavy, are they?'

Cuckooing, Molly knew, was when dealers took over the home of someone vulnerable and used their home to stash drugs or cash, and as a base for dealing. Sometimes weapons. Or even just to use a place for doing deals. It was more common than people thought, and it was becoming more so. Was that the case here?

'I don't think so, Molly,' Denning said. 'I think at most this was just somewhere to keep the drugs out of the way until they were needed and then they'd either be moved on to some other storage site, or divided up for distribution.' He paused. 'Or it's something else entirely.'

Molly could sense Denning was thinking about something he was reluctant to share with the team until he'd fully poked and prodded his theory to breaking point. But she was curious. She had her own theory about the drugs and wanted to know if they were on the same wavelength.

'Deep, any luck with CCTV?'

Neeraj shook his head. 'There were a couple of cameras near the alleyway on Brick Lane, but nothing useful. Despite the cold weather, there were a lot of people around, so it's going to take a lot of time to sift through the footage to find anyone who stands out.'

'Right, keep looking. Everything from the past forty-eight hours. Anything that stands out, or looks out of place.'

Neeraj nodded, aware he was stuck with a thankless task.

'What about forensics, Trudi? Anything to report?'

'No sign yet of the murder weapon. There are no useable prints either.'

'OK,' Denning said. 'Keep going. Once we've identified our victim, there's a good chance this case will start to gain some traction.'

He turned to Molly. 'Molly, you've spoken to the young homeless lad again. Did he have anything useful to add this time?'

She told them what Corey had said about their victim and the mysterious visit from the man with the envelope full of money. 'The only problem is, Corey isn't sure of the details. He can't swear it even happened as he was stoned at the time.'

'Great,' Kinsella said. 'An already unreliable witness just became even more unreliable.'

'There's something else,' Molly said. She mentioned what Corey had said about their victim calling him Leo or Theo. 'Again, Corey couldn't be specific.'

'That feels a bit fishy to me,' Kinsella said. 'Him and this young lad. That has to be suspicious.'

'No,' Molly said, 'I don't think it's anything like that.' She was thinking about what Corey had said. It didn't *feel* like it had been a sexual thing... rather, something else. 'I'm pretty certain his relationship with Corey was more a kind of paternal thing.'

'Seriously?' The look on Kinsella's face suggested he didn't share Molly's thinking.

'I think his relationship was an attempt to replicate what he'd had with his son.'

'Personally, I'm not convinced...' Kinsella shook his head and folded his beefy arms across his chest, a sign that he had nothing further to add to the general discourse.

'OK,' Denning said. 'I'd like you to speak to this guy, Corey, again. I get the impression he knows more than he's telling, and I still reckon he's our best bet at identifying our killer.'

'Did the PM throw up anything useful?' Neeraj asked.

'Cause of death was confirmed as a single stab wound through the heart. Neat and precise. It suggests someone knew what they were doing.'

'It *has* to be one of the homeless blokes,' Kinsella insisted. 'What do we think?'

There was a general shrugging of shoulders.

'Until we know for certain,' Trudi said, 'we shouldn't make assumptions about them just because of how they live.'

'So what *do* we know?' Kinsella asked.

'I spoke to Steven Hodge, the property developer who has bought the site,' Denning said. 'He was aware of the rough sleepers, but didn't recognise our victim when I showed him a photograph. Or at least, he said he didn't recognise him. I got the impression he wasn't being entirely honest.'

'Corey mentioned a couple of smartly dressed men visiting the station a few weeks ago. Description was vague, but one of them could easily have been Steven Hodge.'

'If he visited the site,' Kinsella said, 'then he must have seen the victim. Perhaps he did recognise him?'

'There were at least a dozen homeless men down there,' Trudi said. 'It would have needed a bloody good memory to have remembered what any of them looked like.'

'You think he's hiding something?' Molly asked.

'I don't think it would do any harm to look into his background,' Denning said. 'This situation has certainly worked out well for him. Now the unhoused community has gone, he can go ahead with the redevelopment.'

'It gives him a motive,' Trudi Bell said. 'Even if it is a bit drastic – killing someone just to get rid of some homeless people. Mind you, these property developers are ruthless.'

'Obviously we can't rule him out at this stage of the investigation,' Denning said, 'but I don't think he's our killer. I think murder might be a step too far, even for someone like Steven Hodge.' Denning wrote his name on the board: 'Steven Hodge'. He put a question mark next to the name. 'I think we need to keep everything on the table at this stage. But I can't help feeling that this was not a random killing. I think our victim knew his killer.'

'How come?' Kinsella didn't seem to share Denning's opinion. 'No offence, boss, but homeless people get killed all the time, and very often by other homeless people. Why should this one be any different just because he was once some rich bloke?'

'Now we know more about Bowden's background, it raises the possibility this is about something else,' Denning said. 'We need to look into his life, and find out if he had any enemies we should know about. I don't think this was a random killing. The post-mortem didn't show any evidence of violence before the murder, which suggests somebody deliberately killed our victim. And they did it for a reason. We need to discover that reason.'

# Chapter Fifteen

McKenna was sitting behind her desk when Denning entered her office. She was scribbling something on a notepad and placed her pen on the desk when she saw him in the doorway.

'Come in, Matt. Take a seat. I hope this is a progress report. I could do with hearing some good news.'

He sat opposite her and filled her in on what they'd discovered so far. 'We've ID'd our victim.'

She looked directly at him, arching an eyebrow. 'Well, that's progress. Is this a positive ID?'

'Not until we've spoken to the victim's family to have it confirmed officially, but it's solid enough. The victim's details came up on the system. He's done time.' Denning looked at McKenna, making sure he had her full attention before he delivered the punchline. 'Ray Bowden. He was part of an elaborate property scam a few years ago. This can't be a coincidence.'

If there was any flicker of recognition at the name it didn't show on her face. 'OK,' she said. 'Inform the family, offer our condolences and tell them not to hold out too much hope of getting a conviction.' She gave him a withering smile. 'Naturally, you'll sugar-coat that last bit.'

'I think the fraud may be significant.'

'You're not suggesting one of those angry investors somehow tracked him down and knifed him in revenge for stealing their money?'

'That's something we should at the very least consider.'

'OK, it's a possibility at this stage, but let's not focus on it too much. What else have you got?'

'The post-mortem results will be emailed through this afternoon, which will confirm what we already know,' he said, 'but according to the pathologist, Bowden's death was the result of a single stab wound.'

McKenna sat back in her chair, steepling her fingers and observing him as he spoke. He often wondered what thoughts were going through her mind at times like these. Was she trying to second-guess what he was going to say next? Or was she trying to work out their next step before he'd even finished telling her what they knew? McKenna was a cool customer, and never the easiest of people to read at the best of times.

'Thanks, Matt. Identification at least gives us something to work with. Speak to his family, see why he ended up living rough. It may lead us somewhere.' She paused. Leaned forward in her chair and placed her arms on her desk. 'What I really wanted to talk to you about was more of a personal matter.' For a moment he thought she looked embarrassed. Was she going to say she'd written a gushing recommendation for him to replace her as DCI? It seemed unlikely...

'It's Daniel Placzek,' she said.

Her words hit him like a boxer's punch. As far as Denning was concerned, Daniel Placzek had been consigned to history.

'What about him?'

'He has been attacked in prison. Last night. The prison authorities notified me this morning. They're being light on details. It seems he won't talk. Well, it's more of a case that he *can't* talk – his jaw's broken.'

'Attacked? Who by?'

'Another prisoner. I mean, no one has owned up to it but that's the assumption they're working on. Naturally there will be a full inquiry, but with these things there's no certainty that anything will come of it.'

'Any idea why he was attacked?'

'You know how it goes. Sometimes high-profile prisoners find themselves being targeted simply because of who they are. It's possible another prisoner did it in the hope of gaining notoriety and revelling in some kind of sick celebrity status – some little shit of a thug trying to make a name for himself.' McKenna paused, looked at her desk for a moment in an uncharacteristic gesture of awkwardness, then continued. 'But the prison has to look into the possibility that whoever did it had been put up to it.'

'Put up to it? Why? As in paid to attack him?' Why was McKenna telling Denning this? Then he made the connection. She looked him in the eye, clearly reading his thought.

'Obviously no one thinks that you were in any way responsible, Matt. But it's a question that has to be asked. If we were in their shoes, we'd be asking the same questions – who has a motive? And no one can be conclusively ruled out.'

'Me?' He should have tried harder to keep the incredulity out of his voice. 'They think I could have paid someone to harm Placzek? I wouldn't waste my energy.'

'I know that. And, to be fair, the prison authorities aren't seriously thinking you had anything to do with it. But as well as murdering several women, he did take your wife and son hostage. Threatened to kill them. And you, come to that. It was only down to good luck and good timing that he didn't succeed.'

'Ex-wife,' Denning said lamely. He was struggling to believe his DCI was taking this nonsense seriously. 'Claire and I are divorced.'

If his correction registered with her, she didn't let it show. 'Whatever the case, it could be seen as giving you a motive, albeit a very flimsy one.'

'What do you want me to do? Offer up my bank statements to prove I haven't paid some thug to beat up the man who nearly destroyed my family?'

McKenna laughed. 'No one is suggesting anything like that. This is all just FYI at this stage. I'm simply making you aware of the situation. If you are putting in for my job, they'll be going over your background with a very fine-tooth comb. You need to be aware. Something like this… it's bound to be mentioned in passing at the very least.'

'But nobody with half a brain would think I was in any way responsible.'

She threw him a wintry smile. 'Nobody who knows you would. Like I said – FYI.'

'Thanks for the heads-up. And I still haven't made up my mind about going for the DCI's post. At least not yet.' He paused. 'Besides, even if I did, there's no guarantee I'd get it, despite your optimism.'

McKenna shrugged. 'Your call, Matt. But you know you've got my backing.'

Denning nodded politely. 'Thanks. That's good to know.' He rose from the chair and headed towards the door. 'I'll let you know as soon as we confirm the ID on our victim. Until then, I've got a few leads that need to be followed up.'

With that, he closed the door and returned to his desk.

Daniel Placzek. Part of Denning wished the bastard had suffered, but that was such a dangerous road to go down. The damage that man had inflicted on his family, especially Jake. Even though he was resilient, Denning knew his son had struggled to come to terms with what Placzek had done. And now there was someone new in Jake's life, meaning he was going to have to learn to trust someone all over again.

He quickly googled Placzek's name, but there was nothing on any of the major news sites about the attack. They were obviously trying to keep it out of the media. But it would leak. Placzek's name would be out there again and the pain would come back. It would mean not only his name in the public eye again, but Jake's and Claire's too.

# Chapter Sixteen

Denning and Neeraj pulled up outside an elegant three-storey townhouse on a smart street in Holland Park. The street was lined with 4x4s and other cars that were unnecessarily large for central London. Luckily there was a parking space at the end of the street, beside a pretty Victorian church.

'Very nice,' Neeraj said. 'Must be worth a couple of million.'

'At least,' Denning said. 'Probably more.' Sarah had emailed him the details of a couple of properties she liked the look of. He now had a pretty accurate idea of how much houses in certain parts of London were selling for these days. Some areas were considerably more overpriced than others. Holland Park fell comfortably into that category.

They rang the doorbell of number twenty-two and waited for an answer. After a couple of minutes, a middle-aged woman in a smart cream trouser suit opened the door and looked quizzically at them. 'Yes?' she said coldly.

They showed her their IDs. 'We're here about Raymond Bowden,' Denning said. 'I wonder if we could talk to you.'

For a moment it looked like she was going to tell them she'd never heard of Raymond Bowden. Then she sighed, pulled open the door and said, 'I suppose you'd better come in, though I did speak to a couple of uniformed officers this morning.'

The interior of the house was as plush as the exterior suggested. They were shown in to a beautifully-furnished sitting room, with a pale sofa against one wall and a pair of well-padded armchairs arranged either side of a marble fireplace. A beautiful gilded mirror hung over the fireplace, and various pieces of solid-looking ceramic sculptures were dotted around the room.

The woman introduced herself as Andrea Bowden, and gestured for them to take a seat.

Denning and Neeraj sat on the sofa, while Bowden's widow sat on one of the armchairs. She eyed the two officers with suspicion. There was no offer of tea or coffee.

'I have to be honest,' she said, 'I haven't seen or spoken with my ex-husband for some time.' She looked at them as though she expected them to know what she meant by that. After neither detective spoke, she continued. 'Ray and I divorced shortly after he was sent to prison. He made it clear he wanted to sever all contact with us after he was sentenced. I had no option but to go along with his wishes.'

'So you haven't spoken to Ray for the past five years?' Denning asked.

'No.' She shook her head slowly. 'And that was his choice.'

'But you still use his name?'

'I've use the name Bowden professionally, so it was easier just to keep it.'

'What is it you do?' Neeraj asked.

'I'm a sculptor,' she replied coolly, as though she had expected them to already know this. 'I co-own a gallery in Knightsbridge. The Bowden & Sillars Gallery in Beauchamp Place.'

Denning had never heard of them, but he knew Sarah was very into her art, so there was a good chance she was familiar with their work.

Andrea Bowden nodded towards an intricately-painted ceramic vase that was sitting on a side-table. The picture on it looked like a golden mermaid holding a fish. 'That's one of mine,' she said. 'They sell for around four figures, so you can see why it was easier for me to keep the name Bowden.'

Denning nodded. He looked around at the sumptuous room. The luxury of her home contrasted so sharply with where Ray Bowden had spent his final days. 'He didn't try and contact you after he was released from prison?'

Her face hardened. 'Until I was informed of his death this morning, I was unaware that he had even been released from prison. I understood he'd been sentenced to seven years for his part in the property fraud. That was just over four years ago.'

Denning explained about Bowden having been released early, presumably for being a model prisoner, although until they'd officially spoken to the prison, this couldn't be confirmed. 'He didn't try and get in touch with you? He had to give the probation office an address when he was released, and according to the information we have, this was the address he gave them.'

She pulled an indifferent face. 'No one from the prison services contacted me, either to inform me he'd been released or to confirm that he had provided this address. He obviously hasn't lived here for the past five years, and I'm not sure he would have wanted to return, especially as our marriage was over.' Despite the fact she seemed to be doing her best to appear unaffected, Denning could sense a rawness in her voice, as though despite years of trying to bury the pain of Bowden's arrest and conviction, she hadn't entirely succeeded in erasing all traces of him from her life.

'He was living in a derelict Tube station,' Neeraj said. 'With a load of homeless people.'

There was a pause while she thought about what to say. 'Well, I'm very sorry about that, but it was his decision to sever all ties with us. And it wasn't just me. There's my children as well. He severed all ties with them too. It wasn't enough they had to live with the humiliation of seeing him sent to prison.' She said *my* children, emphasising the fact he was no longer a part of their lives.

'Could we speak to your children?' Denning asked. 'Is it possible they may have been in contact with Ray without your knowing about it.'

'My daughter is at university in Durham, though she'll be home soon for the Christmas holidays. And my son is at work at the moment. He'll be back this evening. But I can assure you neither has had any contact with Ray since his trial.'

She seemed certain of this, but Denning knew children often told their parents what they thought they wanted to hear, which wasn't always the truth. 'We may still need to speak to them,' Denning said. 'It's just possible they might know something.'

She looked sceptical. 'I'll inform them, but I really wouldn't hold out much hope, Inspector.'

'Mrs Bowden, I appreciate my next question might be a difficult one for you, but can you remember much about the fraud itself? Did Ray ever discuss anything with you?'

She shook her head. 'No. I told this to the police at the time. I took little interest in Ray's business affairs, and he had little interest in what went on at the gallery. I mean, he supported my work and always offered me encouragement, but that was as far as it went.'

'Did you believe him when he said he was innocent of the fraud allegations?'

There was a beat before she replied. 'Of course I believed him. At first. But after the evidence was presented, it was difficult to blind myself to the truth. Ray had certainly been involved, even if it was simply to advise his investors to put money into the project.'

'He hadn't been planning to leave the country around the time, as far as you know?' Denning asked.

'Look, I went over this all at the time. I knew nothing about what Ray was up to until the police knocked on the door one morning and arrested my husband for fraud. It came as a massive shock to me, just as news of his murder came as a shock to me today. But then, as now, I was unable to tell them anything.'

Denning had to admit she was putting on a convincing performance, but there was something about what she was saying that just didn't quite ring true. Try as he might, he just couldn't work out what it was. 'Has anyone been in touch with you lately asking about Ray? Or has anyone been seen hanging around? Either here or at the gallery?'

'No. Nothing.' She sighed and gave another shake of the head. 'Until today I hadn't even thought about my ex-husband. I assumed he was either still in prison, or he was dead.'

'Well, he's certainly one of the two, Mrs Bowden. And we're hoping to find out who killed him.'

She looked shocked, as though slightly taken aback by his words. 'I'm very sorry to hear about Ray, Inspector. Despite his failings, he was a good man at heart. But I really can't help you. You mentioned that he'd been living rough with some homeless people. I would suggest you look there for your culprit.'

Back in the car, Neeraj said, 'God, talk about cold. She didn't seem all that bothered that her ex has been murdered. I know they were divorced and all, but you'd think there would be a shred of pity for what happened to him. It was like we were talking about a distant relation rather than the father of her children.'

Denning wasn't so sure. It had felt to him like she was trying her best to act calm, but there had been something about Andrea Bowden that suggested the murder had hit her harder than she would have liked to admit. And then there was the bigger mystery that he couldn't fail to ignore: if Ray Bowden had severed all ties with his family after he'd been found guilty, how had Andrea managed to go on paying the mortgage on a house in affluent Holland Park? It was unlikely her career as a sculptor and co-owner of an art gallery – however posh – could justify the kind of expenditure needed to live somewhere as flash, so where had the money come from?

As they passed her house, he caught a glimpse of Andrea Bowden through standing by the sitting-room window. She was on the phone to someone, and he wondered who she was talking to.

# Chapter Seventeen

Molly and Trudi were asked by a well-mannered receptionist to wait in the tastefully appointed outer office of
Carver Investments Limited. The carpet was deep and the
sofas comfortable. The abstract works of art adorning the
office walls looked like they would cost more than Molly
earned in a month.

The offices were located just off Oxford Street, roughly
halfway between Oxford Circus and Bond Street Tube
stations. The company had previously been known by
its original name: Carver Bowden. That was until Ray
Bowden had been arrested for fraud and subsequently
been airbrushed out of the company's history. This much
Molly had gleaned from the internet. She was hoping
Malcolm Carver could help fill in some of the missing
pieces.

Malcolm Carver was a busy man, at least according to
the receptionist, and was in the middle of an important
Zoom call. The call was due to finish in a couple of
minutes, so Molly and Trudi were asked if they would
mind waiting.

Molly wanted to point out this was part of a murder
investigation and they didn't have time to waste, but she
realised it was probably more important to get Malcolm
Carver in a good mood if they were to have any real
chance of getting him to cooperate.

After a few minutes, Molly and Trudi were shown into Carver's office. Minimalist furniture, with a couple of hard-backed chairs facing a wide desk. The muted sounds of Central London could just about be made out from beyond the windows.

Carver was in his mid-to-late-fifties and had a thin, slightly angular face. His hair looked to be way too dark for someone of his age, and Molly suspected the colour was aided by some hair dye. He wore a well-cut grey suit with an electric blue shirt open at the neck, and a tuft of greying chest hair poked out from the top of the shirt. Carver greeted them with a broad smile, that managed to appear both cheesy and slightly lecherous at the same time. 'How can I help two very charming ladies?' His accent was educated Home Counties, but slightly affected, making Molly think of a character from a PG Wodehouse novel.

Molly briefly caught Trudi's eye and tried not to laugh. She'd already decided Malcolm Carver was probably a bit of a prat.

'It's about your former business partner,' Molly said. 'Ray Bowden. I'm afraid he's been found dead. Murdered.'

A brief look of surprise passed over Carver's face. He opened his mouth as though he was going to say something then shut it again. 'Murdered? That's awful.' A shake of the head. 'Poor Ray. Life really did kick him around.'

'I'm very sorry,' Molly added.

'What happened?'

Molly explained about Bowden's body being found stabbed to death in an abandoned Tube station.

'Homeless?' Carver asked, sounding incredulous. 'Poor bloke. OK, he almost destroyed our business, but I wouldn't wish that on him.'

'I take it you're referring to the fraud case,' Molly said. 'Ray Bowden served time for that. I imagine it must have been difficult for you.' She was curious to know why Bowden had ended up in jail for fraud while his erstwhile business partner had emerged from the whole scandal unscathed.

'As I explained to the police at the time,' Carver said, 'I had absolutely no idea what Ray was up to. I had been ill when it all kicked off – appendicitis – and had taken quite a bit of time off work to recover. Ray had been responsible for the day-to-day decision-making in my absence. Any major decisions he would run by me, but clearly not everything was discussed. I had no idea about this fraud case until the police arrested Ray.'

'Ray Bowden always maintained his innocence,' Molly said. 'He initially claimed he'd been set up and had believed the investment to be genuine.'

Carver nodded. 'That was his defence in court. He claimed he'd been hoodwinked by clever fraudsters and had recommended the investment in good faith.'

'But that wasn't the case?'

Carver sat back in his chair and observed Molly, before briefly glancing at Trudi, then clearly decided his charms, such as they were, would be better spent on Molly. 'It's the first rule of investment – always check out the fine print. If something seems too good to be true, then it probably is. If Ray had taken more care, he would have seen that the returns being quoted were completely unrealistic, planning permission for the project had only been agreed in principle – there was nothing in writing – and most of all, the company behind it was registered to a shelf company based in the Cayman Islands.'

'Easy to say in hindsight,' Trudi offered.

Carver ignored her and looked at Molly when he replied. 'It's our job as financial advisors to ensure we cover ourselves. It took me a long time to undo the damage Ray did to this company. I had to rebuild our reputation from scratch. I had to reassure my regular investors that their money was safe and I had to ensure our staff still had jobs at the end of it. At the same time distancing myself and the company from the effects of Ray's actions. None of that was easy.'

'Ray Bowden paid a heavy price for his mistake,' Molly said. 'First with his liberty and then with his life.'

'If it was a mistake.' He sat forward in his chair and leaned on the polished wooden desk. 'It was never proven at the trial, and Ray always denied it, but the police reckon Ray had been in on the scam from the start. OK, perhaps not in the planning stage, but he was more than likely receiving a healthy cut of the profits. Ray had been planning to leave Andrea, probably to go abroad with his share, as most of the men behind the scam did. His only problem was that he left it too late.'

'Too late?' Molly raised an eyebrow.

'Someone contacted the police. We never did find out who, but very probably one of the investors got twitchy and started asking questions. Questions for which Ray didn't have any answers.'

Molly thought about what she knew about the case so far, coupled with what she was now hearing. There was something bugging her. 'Could Ray have been set up? If the people behind the fraud needed a fall guy, he would have been an obvious choice.'

Carver smiled. 'Ray was shrewd. There's no way he would have allowed himself to have been taken in. Unfortunately, all the evidence pointed to Ray having been involved. He may have tried to portray himself as an innocent victim at the trial, but nobody bought that argument. Not the police and not the jury. In many ways, he got off lightly.'

'Lightly?' Molly was aware her voice had risen a pitch. 'He was sentenced to seven years in prison for a crime he always claimed he was innocent of.'

'Yes, but he wasn't the one who was left to face a group of angry investors. I was the one who had to put up with death threats and accusations that I was involved in the scam. What he did nearly destroyed this business. This business which is my livelihood and which I spent years building up. Only in this past year has the company been anywhere close to where it was before the fraud came to light. And it's been down to solid hard graft on my part. Ray Bowden nearly destroyed me.'

'You sound very bitter, Mr Carver.'

Another cheesy smile. 'And do you blame me? Yes, I am angry, but with good reason.'

'Angry enough to kill him?'

The words had an immediate effect. Carver stopped talking and looked at Molly. 'I didn't kill him. I wouldn't have known where to find him. Until today I thought he was still in prison. Besides, if I was going to kill him, I would have done it five years ago when I found out he'd conned our investors out of several million pounds. There's no point going after him now. The damage has been done.'

Molly thanked him and she and Trudi left. Once they were in the lift heading towards the ground floor, Trudi said, 'What a creep.'

Molly agreed with her: Malcolm Carver was certainly a creep, but did that make him a killer? But there was something else that concerned her.

'Did you notice,' she said to Trudi, 'that when we told him about Bowden's death, he didn't seemed especially shocked. It was almost as though he knew before we told him.'

'How? Bowden's name hasn't been released to the media yet. We only discovered his identity ourselves a few hours ago.'

She was right. There was a press release due to go out that afternoon, but Bowden's identity wasn't yet public knowledge. 'Perhaps I got it wrong,' Molly said. 'Maybe it's just that stiff-upper-lip British public schoolboy thing of never betraying your emotions.'

But as they left the building, she was certain she hadn't got it wrong. She was convinced Malcolm Carver already knew Ray Bowden had been murdered.

## Chapter Eighteen

'Thanks for returning my call.'

'No problem. How can I help you?'

Denning had left a couple of messages with HMP Lewes, the prison where Bowden had served the final year of his sentence. He now found himself talking to the governor: she gave her name as Janice Conway, and had apologised for the delay in getting back to him.

'It's about a prisoner who was released just over a year ago. His name was Raymond Bowden.'

'Just give me a minute.' Denning heard computer keys being tapped in the background as Janice Conway was presumably accessing the prison records.

'Yes. Sentenced to seven years for fraud. Released after four. I can't say I remember him all that well, which is probably a good thing.' There was a moment's silence while she read over the notes on his file. 'As I thought. There were never any problems: a model prisoner. Never in any trouble, kept his nose clean. Seemed to be well educated so he worked in the prison library for a while. Used to help some of the prisoners write letters to their families. Nothing remarkable, except...'

'Yes?'

'Well, I do vaguely remember him now. Very polite, very well spoken, but no one ever came to see him. He never had any visitors. Except once. About a year after he was sentenced. He received a visit on the fifteenth of March from a Malcolm Carver. Carver had put in several requests by the looks of it, but every time the request was declined at Bowden's insistence. Except for this one time, Bowden relented and agreed to see him.'

'I don't suppose you have any idea what the visit was for?'

'Sorry, I'm afraid we're not privy to that information.'

'And there were no other visits during his incarceration?'

'None.'

'What about his relationship with other prisoners? Was he ever involved in any incidents?'

'Like I said, a model prisoner. Never put a foot out of line, seemed to be respected by the other inmates, or at least he managed to keep his head down and avoid trouble. That's not always easy in a place like this.'

She confirmed that arrangements had been made for Bowden to stay at a bail hostel in Lambeth on his release, despite having given an address in West London. As far as she was aware, Bowden had checked into the bail hostel as planned, though he hadn't stayed there very long. She had no idea why he'd left, but she gave Denning the name and contact details of Bowden's probation officer, who might have a better idea of what happened to Bowden after his release.

'Is there anything else I can help with?' she asked.

For a brief moment, Denning was tempted to ask if there was anything on file about the attack on Daniel Placzek, or at least if they were any further forward with finding out who was responsible for assaulting him and why, but he had no authority to request that kind of information, and a seemingly casual inquiry could have been misconstrued as being asked for the wrong reasons.

He thanked her and ended the call.

Next, he rang the probation office. It turned out the probation officer who had been allocated to Bowden had left the service about four months ago, having been on sick leave for some time before that. The person Denning spoke to said it appeared that Bowden dropped off the radar about three months after he was released. He should have reported in to a new probation officer, but it never happened. Due to staff shortages and an ever-increasing workload, his disappearance was never followed up.

Denning made sympathetic noises and ended the call.

He wondered how people managed to completely drop off the radar never to resurface until it was already too late. Quite easily, it had seemed in Bowden's case. His family had clearly washed their hands of him, and as far as the prison and probation services were concerned, he was just another statistic to be processed and passed on and on until he became somebody else's problem.

At least they could rule out one line of inquiry: some kind of prison feud with a fellow inmate. The more Denning thought about it, the more he convinced himself this had something to do with the property scam, though right now there were no obvious answers jumping out at him. Even the questions seemed pretty vague…

McKenna had made her views on the matter clear. He got the impression she wasn't convinced of its relevance, but he wasn't so sure that was the case.

There would be details about the case itself on the Police National Computer database. He logged on to the PNC and brought up the appropriate file. There was the list of victims, though it was reckoned there were probably others, either too embarrassed to come forward, or who had simply decided to write the money off as some kind of tax loss. There were details about Bowden, his company, evidence of his involvement. And the interesting bit: a list of the men suspected of being behind the scam; the planners who pulled the strings. Most of the names meant nothing to him, except for one, near the bottom of the list, a name he recognised and shouldn't have been surprised to see there at all: Alfie Kane.

Kane had spent most of his life on the wrong side of the law: a former gangster who had now reinvented himself as a respectable businessman. Except there was very little that was respectable about Alfie Kane. Naturally enough, there was nothing to link him to the crime, at least not directly. His name had come up during the initial investigation only for it to be dismissed. Terry Benson, the accountant who had helped orchestrate the plan, was also accountant to Kane. Benson had disappeared around the time of Ray Bowden's arrest, rumoured to have fled abroad, and had never been traced. Kane, although apparently questioned, had denied any involvement and, apart from his association with Benson, there was little to connect him to the case.

Denning re-read the information on screen. It couldn't be a coincidence, Kane's name appearing. And now one of the major players in the fraud case was dead – a man who could have potentially put the finger on Alfie Kane, damaging his newly invented reputation as a generous and benevolent philanthropist. It wouldn't have been difficult for Kane to have tracked Bowden down. He had contacts and resources.

Denning's last clash with Kane had been earlier that year, when he had to investigate his links to a corrupt local councillor. Nothing had stuck of course – Kane was too clever for that – but his card was marked as far in Denning's eyes. But try as he liked, Denning could find nothing on the PNC to suggest that Kane was any more involved than any of the other names listed, and even if he was, proving it would be almost impossible. It was certainly possible the other scammers were also criminals of Kane's calibre, but this was one Denning knew. The PNC was useful in as much as it provided relevant background to the case, but he really needed to know the bits that were never made official: the areas the detectives investigating the crime suspected but could never prove. Something that could potentially link this whole thing directly back to Alfie Kane.

He needed to know more about what had really gone on, and just how involved Kane had been. It was time to give Steve Marsh a call…

## Chapter Nineteen

'Good to see you, mate.' Marsh clinked glasses with Denning. Marsh and Denning had been detective constables together some years back. Marsh now worked for the National Crime Agency. The NCA was directly answerable to the Home Office and not part of the police service, though it was well populated by a lot of former police officer.

It had been a few months since they'd last met and it was always good to catch up with an old friend, even if their catch ups inevitably seemed to involve Denning asking Marsh for a favour. The last time Denning saw Marsh was when he'd been seconded to the NCA to help with the arrest of a drug dealer who was also wanted in connection with a couple of murders. Marsh's boss hadn't taken to Denning and had resented his presence on the team. He hadn't been shy in making his resentment known. It had been an experience Denning wasn't keen to repeat.

They had arranged to meet at a wood-panelled pub in Wapping that Denning liked to frequent. It overlooked the river, and in summer was alive with tourists as well as devotees of Jack the Ripper, who – according to local folklore – had drunk in the pub prior to committing his murders.

In winter, the place wasn't so busy. A log fire roared in the main bar, but they chose a quiet corner in the snug, where their conversation was less likely to be overheard.

Denning had got there first and bought the drinks: a pint of craft beer for himself and a pint of Strongbow for Marsh.

'Why is it I only hear from you when you want something, you bastard?'

'You know me too well, Steve. I wish I could say this is the exception...'

Marsh smiled, sipped his pint and laughed. He was dressed in a thick pullover, the collar of a blue-and-black checked shirt poking out from the neckline. His heavy Barbour jacket was lying on the bench beside him. 'OK. What is it this time?'

Denning told him about the murder of Ray Bowden and his suspicions about it somehow being linked to the fraud case. 'I'm almost certain this has got something to do with what happened. Especially when you consider Alfie Kane's name has come up.'

Marsh laughed again, though it sounded forced this time, as if he was trying to make a joke out of something he knew wasn't funny. 'Kane. Seriously, I would let that one go, Matt. You haven't got a hope in hell of pinning anything on him these days. He's so straight, he's practically been canonised.'

'My gut says it's no coincidence that his name came up.'

'Maybe. Maybe not. But there's no way anyone could pin any of this on Kane. He's way too clever to make anything stick.'

Denning sipped his pint. 'You know people who worked on the case. There must have been something that didn't smell right.'

Marsh gave the matter some thought. 'It was years ago. I'm not even sure it's relevant.'

'But you must remember the case? I seem to recall it was all over the press at the time.'

'Yeah, of course I remember it. I didn't work it, but I know a couple of guys who did. They talked about little else for weeks.'

'Well…?'

Marsh stared at his cider for a few seconds, then lifted the glass to his lips and took a long drink. He placed the pint glass back on the table. 'I remember someone saying they thought there was a chance Bowden had been set up, but the evidence suggested otherwise.'

'What kind of evidence are we talking about?'

'The kind that a defence lawyer would struggle to shoot down. Bowden claimed from the off that he didn't know the development was a scam. He insisted he'd been acting in good faith by recommending investors put their money into it. However, Bowden's business partner, Carver, or something, disputed this. He claimed Bowden had known all along the whole thing was a con and was in on it from the start. Carver was the one who told the investigating officers where to look for the evidence that ultimately led to Bowden's conviction. There were computer files he'd made a half-arsed attempt to wipe. Bank statements that proved he must have been aware of what was going on, despite his claims of innocence. According to this Carver bloke, Bowden had been intending to flee abroad with his cut, leaving a wife and two children behind. If we hadn't been alerted when we were, there's a good chance Bowden would have scarpered along with some of the others who were behind it.'

'Who reported it?'

'One of the investors was a retired accountant. He'd become suspicious when emails were going unanswered and Bowden kept refusing to return his calls. He did some digging and discovered there were no plans to start building the marina, and only a token deposit had been paid to secure the land, with a sizeable balance outstanding. He contacted his solicitor, who passed the whole thing over to us.'

'Did you ever have any suspicions about Carver?'

'He was checked out, naturally. But he always insisted he knew nothing about it. He'd been ill and out of the office while most of it had been going on, leaving Bowden to run things. And like I said, he was keen to help with investigation. He said he wanted to try and salvage his name and the company's reputation. He ended up being the prosecution's main witness.'

'Malcolm Carver?' Denning was surprised. 'I can understand him giving evidence against Bowden, but I didn't realise he was the main prosecution witness.'

'And a pretty convincing witness he was too. I guess he felt a sense of betrayal after his business partner did the dirty on him like that.'

It certainly sounded credible, but Denning's grumbling gut told him he had yet to hear the full story. 'Bowden was only the facilitator though,' he said. 'There were others involved. What happened to them?'

'They were either very clever or very lucky. Some went abroad and some just disappeared with their share of the loot. Others were suspected of having been involved, but a lack of credible evidence meant there was no realistic hope of getting a conviction.'

Alfie Kane being one of them, Denning thought.

Marsh put his glass to his lips but rather than take another sip, he paused then put the glass back on the table. He had nearly finished his pint while Denning was barely a third of the way through his. He'd forgotten how much Marsh liked his booze. 'It was strange, though,' Marsh continued. 'There were some funny rumours doing the rounds at the time…'

'What kind of rumours?'

Marsh stared at what was left in his pint glass, refusing to make eye contact with Denning, almost as though he felt like he'd said something he shouldn't have. 'They were only rumours, Matt, and nobody took them seriously.'

'Humour me?'

'At least three of the people alleged to have been involved with the fraud died shortly afterwards.'

'Died? As in suspicious?'

Marsh gave a dry laugh. 'That depends on how much of a conspiracy theorist you are. There was nothing suspicious about the deaths themselves, but the fact three people died in comparatively short succession so soon after a major crime did raise a few eyebrows.'

'Go on.'

'There was Adam Tanner, a banker who was alleged to have helped move the money into various off-shore accounts. The official verdict was suicide, but there were always questions about what really happened. Then there was Keith Prideaux, who was supposed to have been one of the main players. He died in a car accident about six months after it all happened. Skidded off the road and crashed into a tree somewhere in the wilds of Essex.

Again, there were suspicions it wasn't an accident but no evidence to prove otherwise. And then Terry Benson, a minor player, but was some talk down the nick that he was on the verge of fessing up. One day he just disappeared. It was generally believed he'd gone abroad, but he left his wife and kids behind, despite being a family man. He was never traced. Then a few years ago some lag started mouthing off about how Benson was killed shortly after Bowden was sent down and his body is buried in a field outside Colchester. The field was checked – sonar equipment, the lot, but there was nothing.'

'And now Bowden has turned up dead, not long after he got out of prison.'

Marsh laughed. 'I wouldn't take any of it *too* seriously if I were you, Matt. Apart from Benson, there was nothing to suggest the other two were murdered. And even if Terry Benson had been killed, he was a known criminal. He moved in the kind of circles that mean sooner or later he was going to come a cropper. That's assuming he *is* dead. Chances are he's living it up in the Costa del Crime and not giving any of this a second thought.'

'Even if it meant turning his back on his wife and family?'

'It happens. Maybe he met someone younger and fitter without any kids to spoil her figure. Maybe he just he fancied a change of scene.'

But Denning was churning things over in his head. So many people involved meeting untimely ends. It could be nothing, but on the other hand… 'Were any of these deaths fully investigated?'

Marsh laughed. 'You are joking! Like there's the available resources to investigate deaths that probably aren't even suspicious.'

'Do you think those deaths are suspicious?'

'A suicide, a road accident and something that may not have even been a death after all?' He pulled a face. 'OK, I can see how it might seem on the surface, but in all honesty, I think you're looking for stuff that isn't there.'

'Perhaps.' Despite Marsh's words, Denning thought this was worth looking into.

'Anyway,' Marsh said, 'changing the subject. Have you heard anything from Anna Klein recently?'

Anna Klein had been a CID officer based at Islington. She and Denning had been friendly, with the relationship very nearly going beyond friendship until he'd come to his senses. Anna had survived a disciplinary inquiry after it had come to light she hadn't been entirely honest about her relationship with a suspect. It had been Molly Fisher who brought the sorry tale to light, placing Denning in a potentially awkward spot.

'Last I heard she'd transferred down to Devon,' he said. 'Seems she's got family down there and fancied a fresh start.'

'Probably wise.' Marsh finished his drink. 'Time for another? I thought this might have been an excuse for a celebration...'

'Sorry?'

'You. I assume you're going to put in for Betty Taggart's job when she retires? Not long now.'

With everything that was going on, Denning had honestly not given the matter too much thought recently.

'You've heard the rumours then?'

'The NCA isn't as cut off from the real world as you might think.'

Denning glanced out of the window at the silvery grey Thames flowing past. 'I don't know. I'm not sure I want the hassle to be honest with you.'

'In that case, have you considered your options if you don't go after the job? If your particular MIT is disbanded?'

'I tend to take things one step at a time,' he said. Though he knew he was going to have to make a decision soon.

'You could always consider a career with the NCA,' Marsh said. 'I know things didn't exactly go too well last time, but there's been a big shake up in the past couple of months – new management have taken over. They're looking to recruit from police forces.' He sipped his pint. 'The money's not bad.'

Denning wasn't sure money was ever enough of a motivation for him, and the NCA wasn't something he'd seriously considered. But he was also aware he was unlikely to be in a position where he could afford to turn down offers.

'Let me think about,' he said. He had to admit, he was tempted. Even so, he still had a serious crime on his hands. He had to digest what Steve had just told him. The news that three people involved in the fraud investigation had all died. The fact that none of them were around just added to an already complex mystery and made him all the more determined to pursue every possible line of inquiry.

# Chapter Twenty

As soon as Molly was home she locked the door to her flat, pulling the chain across. The landlord had promised to get the front door repainted, but he hadn't said when it would happen.

She hung her jacket on the coatrack in the narrow hallway, then hurried over to the living room window and checked the street outside. She was certain she hadn't been followed on the Tube the other night – it was just a random bloke in a baseball cap – but she couldn't entirely shake off the disturbing feeling that someone had been following her.

She sat on the sofa and checked her phone again. A message from Trudi suggesting drinks some time and a couple of Likes for a recent picture she'd posted on Instagram, but otherwise nothing strange or out of place.

As much as she wanted to dismiss this as paranoia, there had been too many bizarre incidents happening recently that she couldn't easily dismiss. On their own they were nothing serious, but taken together they had unnerved her. The unknown number on her mobile. The feeling someone was watching her. Then the incident tonight on the train…

She'd tried to put it out of her mind during the journey home. Tried to come up with rational explanations for everything, but the fact was she could feel that something wasn't right. She was a police officer, which meant she'd made enemies over the years. It was possible that someone was targeting her.

And then there was her personal life too.

She considered a potential shortlist. Someone she'd helped put away, or a member of their family. Then there was Anna Klein. She'd held a grudge against Molly for some time, after Molly had filed an official complaint about Klein during an investigation they had briefly worked on together. Klein had survived the disciplinary process but had been demoted as a result. She could have paid someone to harass Molly, or even got a criminal contact to do it as a favour. Anna had never struck Molly as being a particularly vindictive person but she couldn't say for sure she wasn't out for revenge.

Then there was Jon, her ex-partner. He'd been behaving very oddly lately. Jon wasn't someone who gave up easily and he liked to get what he wanted. He wanted Molly back. Yes, he had been subtle about it. Offering to help her move into her new flat but at the same time offering to give her space and let her settle in. Jon liked playing mind games. He could easily have asked someone to watch her flat, or even be responsible for the silent phone calls.

She heard a noise outside and glanced through the window again, but there was just an empty street. A motorbike suddenly shot past, then disappeared round the tight bend at the top of the street, and then there was silence.

There was no one there. She was jumping at shadows. Why would someone come after her? The incident on the Tube was nothing more sinister than some random man catching the same train as her. It was late in the evening;

people were heading home. There were literally dozens of men in the station, why should she single him out? Just some random man in the crowd. But that man the other night, the one watching her flat… She hated herself for feeling like a victim.

Try as she might, that was how it felt. She'd known about incidents of stalking, where victims had tried to rationalise events and even tried to normalise them. She'd dealt with them when she'd worked in CID and had silently chided women who'd not said or done anything until it was too late.

She turned on the telly and selected something from Netflix to distract her. She should really be thinking about dinner, but she wasn't hungry. She'd more than likely make do with a sandwich again. Or defrost something from the freezer.

She wanted to focus on the murder investigation, but her mind kept returning to the man who'd been watching her flat. As crazy as it was, she felt there had been something familiar about him. Not the way he looked, rather something she'd sensed about him. Something that reminded her of someone from long ago; a half-hazy memory of someone she once knew… she was trying to make a connection with this man and something in her past – something about him.

Why did she get the feeling she knew this man?

# Chapter Twenty-One

Denning drove into the once familiar street. A long row of almost identical 1980s mellow brick houses, with neat little squares of garden in front of them. The gardens were stark and frost hardened now, but in summer they were usually alive with colour or awash with children's toys.

He parked outside number eleven, turned off the engine and got out of the car.

After their divorce, it made sense for Claire to remain in the family home along with their son. Jake needed security and stability, and Denning wanted to make sure his son and ex-wife would be able to live somewhere familiar.

He rang the doorbell and waited for Claire to answer. Relations were good between them these days. They'd come a long way since the divorce six years ago; the recriminations and guilt had been all but forgotten. But he knew it wouldn't take much for things to swing back the other way. He still had to tread carefully when it came to his ex-wife and son.

Claire offered a weak smile when she opened the door. She was wearing a baggy pullover and her hair was tied back in a loose ponytail.

'Hi, Claire. I wanted to chat about arrangements for Christmas. Hope this isn't a bad time.'

The smile broadened for a brief moment. 'Come in, Matt.'

He followed her into the compact hallway and through into the neat kitchen at the back of the house. She called upstairs for Jake, letting him know his daddy was here. There was a muffled response that came from the general direction of Jake's bedroom, and seemed to indicate he would be down shortly. He was probably playing one of his computer games. Or looking something up on the internet, which he now held in some kind of fascination. There was a time when a visit from his daddy would have seen him stop whatever he was doing and rush downstairs to greet him with a warm hug. But Jake was growing up and Denning could sense his role in his son's life was becoming less significant with each passing year.

Claire switched on the kettle. 'Coffee?'

'Thanks. That would be nice.' Denning looked round the spotless kitchen-diner that formed the rear half of the comfy house. They'd bought the property when he'd been promoted to detective sergeant, not too long after they'd married. They were only the house's second owners, having bought it off the original occupiers who had moved in shortly after the house had been built in the late eighties, not long after the whole area had been transformed from derelict dockyard into a fashionable enclave. They'd been happy there, until their marriage had begun to crumble through a combination of his work and Claire's lack of it. When Jake was born, he'd tried so hard to be a good dad, but somehow work had managed to get in the way. He'd been ambitious, and that meant having to make sacrifices.

'How's Sarah?' she asked, as much out of politeness as general curiosity.

'She's fine. A bit restless, but she's happy she knows she made the right decision.'

Claire dropped a couple of heaped spoons of filter coffee into a cafetiere and added boiling water. She placed it along with two mugs on the kitchen table. After a minute she poured out the coffee, which they drank in silence. Eventually, Denning felt compelled to address the elephant in the room. 'How's...?' He had genuinely forgotten the name of Claire's new partner.

'George,' she said coldly, presumably thinking he was forgetting the name on purpose. 'He's OK. We should all go out for dinner one night. Me and George, you and Sarah.'

He'd only met George once. A PE teacher at a North London comprehensive. George had once played rugby at county level, so he and Denning – who had been in his school's first XV – had found something to bond over. Otherwise, he felt they had little in common. George was divorced with two children slightly older than Jake. They all got on together, and Denning supposed that was what mattered. However, he couldn't help thinking George and Sarah would find little common ground, which would make Claire's suggested dinner-foursome more of a trial than it otherwise would have been.

'I can come round on Christmas morning,' he said. 'If that's OK. I won't be in the way, will I?'

Claire sat at the kitchen table, rubbing at a splash of coffee that had been spilled on the surface. 'George will spend Christmas morning with his own kids, so it won't be a problem.'

'Great.' Denning sipped his coffee, the same slightly bitter but not too strong brand that Claire had always used. 'I still don't know what to get him. Jake, I mean. For Christmas. Has he mentioned anything?'

'Well, he's been on about a dog again, but he knows the score.'

Small footsteps thudded down the stairs. A moment later Jake burst into the kitchen and ran up to hug his daddy. Denning's fear of losing his son – never greater than when Claire and Jake had been held hostage by Daniel Placzek – felt so real now.

He hugged Jake. His son was probably getting too old for hugs, so he should make the most of it. 'Can I get a dog for Christmas?' he asked.

This had been Jake's obsession for some time. Their neighbour had a Jack Russell that Jake would regularly play with; Claire had even looked after it when the neighbour was in hospital. But Claire was too houseproud to allow a dog into her home on a permanent basis.

'What does Mummy say?' Denning looked at Claire, knowing what her answer was.

'She says we can't have one.' Jake pulled a face, though Denning reckoned it was deliberately exaggerated for effect. 'But Uncle George might let me have one.'

Denning looked over at Claire, who shook her head.

So it was *Uncle* George… Denning thought. Things were moving quickly. Perhaps a little too quickly.

# Chapter Twenty-Two

Next morning, Denning was in early. As was McKenna. She was sitting behind her desk checking emails when Denning knocked on the door and entered.

'We've spoken to Ray Bowden's family and to his former business partner,' he said, taking a seat on the other side of her desk.

'And?'

'They seem keen to distance themselves from both him and the fraud case.'

'Understandable. Anything else?'

He repeated what Steve Marsh had told him and concluded, 'I think this changes everything.'

McKenna sat back in her chair, tapping her chin with a biro. 'But what is the truth here, Matt? Realistically, I mean? The chances are our initial instinct is right and Bowden was killed by a fellow rough sleeper. Possibly over drink, drugs, money... who knows?' There was an edge to her voice. 'Listen to me. Despite there being some potentially good leads, I still reckon the chances of us solving this one are slim. The fraud case is too complicated to be worth our time, and may yet turn out to have nothing to do with it.'

He could feel his argument being diminished in front of him. The whole thing slipping between his fingers like grains of sand. If McKenna pulled the plug at this stage, then that would be the end of it: so many questions left unanswered, a murdered man left without justice. *Why was she so keen to direct the investigation away from the fraud case? Where was this coming from? Was she under pressure from someone? If so, who? And why...?* 'You said we had a week. That week isn't up yet.'

She shook her head, still tapping the pen against her chin. 'OK. You can have your week. But I'm telling you, Matt, these kinds of cases won't do your career any favours in the long run.'

'I can live with that.'

'Can you? Look, off the record, if this MIT is allowed to continue in its current form, you'll be a shoo-in for the DCI's post. But only if you don't rock the boat. The murder of homeless people – especially ones with criminal convictions – are not exactly looked upon as a priority by the Great British public. I'm not saying that's right, I'm just telling you how it is.' She breathed through her nose, probably guessing by the look on his face that he wasn't going to let it drop, even in the face of threats and promises. 'OK,' she relented, 'you've still got your week.'

As he headed back to his desk in the main office, Denning found himself wondering what she'd meant about not rocking the boat. Whose boat was he in danger of rocking and why did it concern McKenna so much? He wondered if she was deliberately trying to block the investigation for some reason. But why would she? What did it matter to DCI McKenna who had murdered a homeless man and why?

However, the more he thought about it, the more he thought it was the *why* that was most relevant.

# Chapter Twenty-Three

Molly was grateful for the mug of strong black coffee that was steaming on her desk. She'd slept badly the night before and it had been an effort to drag herself out of bed that morning. As she'd lain awake at two a.m., her brain had been churning over so many thoughts she'd struggled to process them all. When sleep had come, she found herself prey to strange, angular dreams: she'd been running through a forest, chased by some unseen presence. In another she was in an underground chamber, rooted to the spot unable to move, or scream.

She'd woken up in a sweat, and listened to the filtered sounds of London beyond her bedroom window, wondering if she could hear someone inside her flat. She waited until her breathing returned to normal, realising there was no one else there, then she'd chided herself on her stupidity. Despite having slept badly, she knew she needed to focus on the murder investigation. But her mind kept returning to recent events in her personal life, but with the exception of her recent split from Jon, her personal life had been depressingly uneventful for some time. Work tended to occupy most of her time these days.

If someone *was* stalking her, then why? If this wasn't something to do with her personal life, then could it be linked to an investigation she'd worked on? And if so, then why was *she* being singled out? She looked around the

MIT suite: there were detectives like Kinsella who had been around the Met forever and was continually boasting about the number of villains he'd nicked over the years. Or Denning? A fast-tracked DI who had stepped on God-knows-how-many feet on his way up the ladder. Or even Betty Taggart herself? What was so special about Molly that someone wanted to go after her?

She tried to focus on the matter before her. Now that they had a name for their victim it would bring some momentum to the case. She still felt Corey knew more than he was admitting to, and she couldn't be certain what he had already told her was even passingly related to the truth, but he remained their best chance of explaining Ray Bowden's murder. Persuading him to make anything official was going to be an uphill struggle.

She was roused from her thoughts by the sight of Denning standing at the front of the room next to the whiteboard, about to start the morning briefing. The press release had gone out, so Bowden had now been officially named as the murder victim whose body had been found in the Tube station. The press were already running stories about Bowden's involvement in the fraud case, though they were being careful not to imply any connection between that and his murder. At least not yet.

'OK everyone, we now know a bit more about our victim.' The name RAYMOND JOHN BOWDEN was still written next to the post-mortem photo of their victim. It had now been joined by another photo showing Bowden at the time of his arrest. The contrast between the two pictures was remarkable: the earlier picture showed someone in his mid-forties; tanned and fit with slicked back greying hair and a confident expression. The other picture showed an old man, gnarled and withered, in poor health, even taking into account the fact he was dead.

'I'm sure by now you're all familiar with the details of Bowden's crime,' Denning said. Molly looked at the file that had been waiting for her on her desk when she'd arrived that morning. She'd skimmed over it, still half asleep as she read about the property scam that had netted millions for the perpetrators and left Ray Bowden to carry the can. Despite his involvement in the crime, it was difficult not to feel sorry for him.

'What about the others?' Kinsella asked.

'Others?' Trudi looked at him.

'There were at least half-a-dozen men allegedly involved in this fraud. How come no one else was arrested?'

'There was never any proof,' Denning said. 'Bowden refused to name names.'

'It might have helped his case if he had,' Kinsella added. 'Possibly even earned him a lighter sentence.'

'Bowden was believed to be the facilitator,' Denning said. 'As the head of an investments company, he was the one who recommended people invest their pensions and hard-earned savings. He always claimed he didn't know the property investment was a con, and instead he was acting in good faith.'

'But the jury believed otherwise,' Neeraj said.

'Not to mention the poor sods who lost their money.' Kinsella had a smug look on his face, as though his sympathy for the victims was diminished by the fact most of them were already wealthy. 'Now I imagine quite a few of them won't be crying into their beer at the news of Bowden's death.' He gave a slight guffaw.

'Are we going to talk to any of the investors?' Trudi asked. 'They would certainly have a good motive for wanting him dead.'

'That is a possibility, Trudi,' Denning said. 'But if it was one of the victims of Bowden's fraud, how did they find him? It's not like anyone knew he was living there.'

Trudi nodded. 'Good point.'

'That brings us back to square one,' Kinsella said, looking bored. 'Odds on, this is a homeless-on-homeless crime. And one we haven't got a cat-in-hell's chance of getting a conviction for.'

Molly watched Denning sigh. She'd known him long enough by now to be able to read what he was thinking by his facial expression and gestures alone. Denning liked to think he played things cool, but when you spent enough time with someone, you became familiar with how they ticked. She knew he found Kinsella to be aggravating, and she sympathised with him. To people like Dave Kinsella, the world was black and white, and the easiest answers were often the most convenient. Detectives like Matt Denning worked best when faced with a challenge: when the answers had to be searched for and the truth was rarely obvious.

'We have to try, Dave,' Denning said, though from the tone of his voice he didn't entirely disagree with Kinsella.

'Molly, Trudi – you spoke to Bowden's former business partner, Malcolm Carver. What did he have to say?'

'Nothing much,' Molly said. 'Just like Bowden's family, he claims he's had no contact with Ray Bowden since before the court case. A few sympathetic nods at the mention of Bowden's death, but it's clear he blames Bowden for what happened and has erased his former business partner from his life.' She wanted to mention how she was sure Carver was already aware of Bowden's murder before they spoke to him, but this was still little more than a hunch.

Denning wrote Carver's name on the board. 'Let's look into him a bit more anyway. I don't accept he knew nothing about the fraud. It's just possible he knew and was covering for Bowden.'

'This fraud case, boss,' Neeraj said. 'Are you sure it's relevant?'

'We can't rule it out, Deep. It may not turn out to be significant, but it does give us something to work with.'

Molly re-read the details about the fraud case. It was almost six years ago now, but that wouldn't have diminished the suffering felt by the people who had lost money. 'What about the men who Bowden refused to implicate, where are they now?'

'Good question,' Denning said. 'Three of them are now dead. As for the others...? Disappeared. Abroad with the money probably, but none of them could be traced.'

'So why didn't Bowden leg it with the others?' Kinsella asked.

'Another good question.' Denning shrugged. 'The prosecution argued that he was planning to do exactly that when he was arrested.'

'Maybe he had a change of heart,' Trudi suggested. 'Felt guilty and decided he couldn't go through with it after all.'

'It was too late by then,' Denning said. 'Most of the money had been transferred into numerous different bank accounts, none of which could be traced. Even if he had been struck by a pang of conscience, the damage had been done.'

'What about the others players who were involved,' Kinsella said. 'It might be worth checking if any of them have returned to the UK in the intervening years. One of them could have come after Bowden. Frightened he was going to talk.'

'If he was going to name names,' Trudi said, 'then surely he would have done it when he was arrested. Especially if he could have used it to broker a lighter sentence.'

'I suspect only Bowden could have answered that question,' Denning said. 'But, yes, we certainly can't rule out one of the other fraudsters being involved, including Alfie Kane. Tracking the others down may be tricky, but we should at least look into it.' He looked around the team. 'Deep and I spoke to Bowden's widow. It's clear that there's been little or no contact between Ray Bowden and his family for some time.'

'Might explain why they didn't report him missing,' Trudi said.

'I'm guessing there wasn't a great deal of love lost between him and his family,' Molly added, 'but I suppose we shouldn't judge them until we know all the facts.'

'The rest of you, look into the other people who were involved in the fraud. It is just possible someone did manage to find out where Bowden was living and wanted him out of the way permanently.' He looked at Molly. 'This mystery man that Corey spotted with the envelope full of money. This could be significant. We need to find out who he is and why he was offering our victim a wad of cash.'

'Can we believe this Corey geezer though?' Kinsella said. He looked at Molly. 'You said yourself, he's flaky.'

'Right now, Dave,' Denning said, 'he's all we've got. If it turns out he lied about the money, then we can drop this line of inquiry, but until then we need to look into it further.'

'It just seems too far-fetched to me, boss,' Neeraj offered. 'I mean why would someone give a homeless bloke money?'

'And more to the point,' said Trudi, 'why would he turn down the offer of ready cash? Food, even the chance of a warm bed for the night... It doesn't make sense.'

'I don't know,' Molly said. 'But I do think Corey was telling the truth. About that at least.'

'So you trust him?' Trudi asked.

She shrugged. 'I don't know. I think there's more that he's not telling me.' She paused before continuing. 'But I don't think he's our killer.' Even as she said it, she knew she couldn't be certain. Corey didn't *seem* like a murderer, but what did that even mean?

'We need to find out more about this man with the money. Molly, can you and Trudi speak to Corey again? Get an approximate date for the meeting, and then we can start trawling any CCTV from the surrounding area to see if we can identify this man.'

Molly thought about this. There was a good chance Corey had given her a fake address, or even if he hadn't, there was nothing to say he hadn't moved on from there by now. London was a big city; the homeless were mostly anonymous, and often by choice. There were lots of places to stay hidden if he wanted to.

'I can try,' she said. 'I'm not sure how much use he'll be though.'

'That's assuming he's not our killer,' Kinsella added drolly.

'OK,' Denning said, ignoring Kinsella. 'Let's look into every aspect of Ray Bowden's life. The money angle – if true – gives this case some added complexity.' Denning was looking around the room when he spoke, but Molly sensed he was directly addressing Kinsella. 'Because I don't think this murder is anything to do with the unhoused community.'

## Chapter Twenty-Four

Denning wanted to speak to Ray Bowden's children. His daughter wouldn't be back from university until the weekend, but his son was around. The chances were that he had nothing further to add beyond what Andrea Bowden had told him earlier, but until he had spoken to the lad he couldn't say for certain.

When Andrea Bowden opened the door to Denning, she made an initial attempt to hide her displeasure at seeing him there, but quickly dropped the act when she realised he wasn't going to be easily fobbed off.

'Has your son left for work yet, Mrs Bowden?'

'Not yet. But he's just about to leave, as am I. And as I told you yesterday, he won't be able to tell you anything. He's had no contact with his father since the trial.'

Denning offered her a reassuring smile. 'I understand that. But if I could have a word with him anyway.'

She sighed, and then showed him into the plush sitting room. 'Finlay, there's someone here to see you,' she shouted up the stairs.

She breezed into the sitting room, throwing Denning another disdainful look. 'I hope this will be an end to the matter, Inspector. I really am very sorry about what happened to Ray, but he's part of our past and I really don't want my children upset by having it all dragged out again.'

She was interrupted by the arrival of her son. Finlay Bowden was in his mid-twenties. He was a good-looking lad, slim, with soft features and a fringe of dark hair that partly covered his face. Andrea explained why Denning was there. He proffered a hand in Denning's direction. He had a firm handshake. 'Finlay?' Denning asked, confirming that he'd heard the name correctly.

'It's Finn, actually. Only Mum calls me Finlay.' He sat on one of the armchairs by the fireplace and looked like he might burst into tears at any moment.

'OK, Finn. Firstly, I'm very sorry about your dad,' Denning said. 'I appreciate you may not have had much contact with him over the past few years, but it must still have come as a shock to hear he'd been killed.'

Finn Bowden nodded. 'Yeah, I'm sorry. But I don't know what I can tell you. Like Mum said, we hadn't spoken since he went to prison. He told us he didn't want us to visit, so we never saw him.'

'How did you feel about that?' Denning asked.

He shrugged. 'If that's how he wanted it then there wasn't much we could do.'

It almost felt like he had been primed by his mother to repeat verbatim what she'd told Denning earlier that day. Andrea Bowden was sitting on the other armchair watching the conversation unfold. Keeping her eye on her son the whole time, perhaps ensuring he didn't go off script for any reason.

'And your sister…?'

'You would have to ask her, but I imagine she felt the same. She never mentioned him.'

Denning sensed that he felt uncomfortable talking about his father. Presumably his mother had informed him of his father's death, perhaps assuming that he should feel the same distant feelings towards him that she did. But Ray Bowden had been the lad's father. Even allowing for their estrangement, there was still a connection there. However, it was clear that Finn Bowden hadn't seen or spoken to his father for some time. There was probably very little he could add.

'OK, well thank you. Both of you. We'll let you know when Ray's body can be released so you can make arrangements for the funeral.'

'The funeral?' Andrea Bowden seemed genuinely surprised.

'Despite the circumstances,' Denning said, 'you are still his next of kin.'

Andrea Bowden looked like she was about to say something, when a sound came from the hallway. Someone else had just come down from upstairs. Denning briefly wondered if it was Bowden's daughter home early from university, but when the sitting room door opened, a middle-aged man entered. 'I'm off now, darling,' he said, bending down to kiss Andrea Bowden on the cheek. 'I'll give Finn a lift into work if he's ready.' He suddenly spotted Denning sitting on the sofa and gave him a puzzled look. There was something familiar about the man; Denning was certain he'd seen him before somewhere, and it had something to do with the investigation.

'My husband,' Andrea Bowden said, indicating the stranger. She introduced Denning as the inspector investigating Ray's death. 'And if you have no further questions, I'd really appreciate it if you would leave.'

The stranger extended a hand, and greeted Denning. 'Oh, yes. I believe I spoke to a couple of your colleagues the other day.' He smiled, and suddenly everything fitted into place as Denning realised the man he was talking to was Malcolm Carver.

# Chapter Twenty-Five

Molly had had no luck trying to get hold of Corey. In the meantime, she turned her focus to Malcolm Carver. There was something about Carver that Molly hadn't liked. It wasn't just the feeling of sleaziness; he was no sleazier than many men she'd had to deal with over the years. Actually, it was more a question of there being something about him she didn't trust. The ease with which he'd passed the blame firmly onto the shoulders of Ray Bowden and failed to accept any part in the fraud. His concern being about his reputation and not the fact that his former business partner was dead. And dead in tragic circumstances. There was not a shred of compassion for someone who had once been a business partner and possibly even a friend.

An internet search hadn't thrown up anything useful. His professional history and education were laid out for all to see on his LinkedIn profile, and there were a couple of interviews with him in financial magazines and a feature in the *Sunday Times*. He was always very careful to omit any reference to the fraud case, and it was clear he was trying hard to put it behind him.

She had to scroll onto the second page before she found anything that might even be construed as interesting. About ten years ago, shortly after Bowden and Carver had set up the financial services company, a former employee had taken them to court for constructive dismissal. The employee had eventually lost the case on grounds of her having been found to have been in breach of her employment contract. The short piece from the *Financial Times* website was light on detail, but it did give the complainant's name: Karen Higgins. Molly did a quick Google search. There were several Karen Higgins with active social media accounts, meaning it would take a while to trawl through them all to find a connection. She typed 'Karen Higgins financial services' into the search box and was directed to the homepage of the Unicorn Pensions Trust, a company based in the City of London. Though this felt like a long shot, Molly noted Karen Higgins's contact details and decided to give her a call.

'Good afternoon, Karen Higgins,' a polite voice sounded down the phone.

Molly explained who she was, that she was phoning in connection with a murder investigation, and asked if it was possible for them to meet for a chat.

'I'm sorry to hear about Ray Bowden,' Karen said, 'but I don't think I can help you, I'm afraid. I left the company ten years ago, and I've had no contact with Ray since. I certainly don't know anything about his death.'

Molly felt she had to come clean here. 'To be honest, it's really Malcolm Carver I'd like to ask you about. Ray's business partner. I was just looking for a bit of background on him.'

'Malcolm?' Molly could tell from the tone in her voice that the name didn't merit the same level of sympathy as Ray Bowden's had, something which immediately intrigued her.

'I have to point out that Mr Carver isn't a suspect in this investigation. However, we think it is just possible Ray

Bowden's death is somehow connected to the property fraud he was involved with. Any information would be helpful.'

There was a lengthy pause from the other end of the line, then Karen Higgins suggested they should meet.

—

Half an hour later, Molly was sitting opposite Karen Higgins in her office in London's Square Mile. The office was on the fifteenth floor of a modern building a couple of streets from the Gherkin. Karen was in her early forties, smartly dressed with neat hair. Unlike Malcolm Carver, her charm seemed genuine and not put on.

'Ray was a charming man,' she said, greeting Molly with polite professionalism. 'A real gentleman. Malcolm was the one you had to watch.'

'In what way?'

She smiled disarmingly at Molly. 'I'm not sure I should be discussing any of this. For a start it was ages ago and secondly, I don't see how any of this is relevant to a murder investigation.'

'Anything you tell me will be in the strictest confidence,' Molly said. 'And at this stage of the investigation, any piece of information might be relevant, even if it doesn't appear so.'

Karen sat behind her desk with an impressive view of London stretching out beyond the window. Molly glimpsed the Thames in the distance. 'Ray started the business. I know they ran it together, but it was his idea. Ray had the drive and the determination, but Malcolm had the contacts.'

She could see that Molly looked puzzled. 'Ray was a self-made man. He came from a relatively humble background, joined a bank straight after school. Studied accountancy at night school, worked his way up. Malcolm had led something of a charmed life. Public school educated, joined a top City firm after Cambridge. He never had to reach for anything. Everything he wanted was handed to him, or was always easily within his grasp. He made a name for himself when he was quite young, still in his twenties. He was a natural risk taker, and most of his risks paid off. Some big time. He knew how to make money and people trusted him to make money for them. Ray, on the other hand, was more what one might call an honest plodder. He liked to pursue safer, long-term investments: property portfolios, pharmaceuticals, energy companies. Industries that, while not very exciting, did at least offer steady, long-term growth.'

'A case of opposites attract?'

'Yes, but in so many ways they worked well together. A mix of secure and steady growth, or the chance of making a quick buck if you wanted a faster profit.'

'I get the impression all wasn't as good as it seems?'

Karen smiled again. 'Quite. I say they worked well together, that wasn't to say there weren't areas where they disagreed. Malcolm was ambitious – he wanted to expand the company, but Ray was more cautious.'

'I understand you had a disagreement with them?'

She laughed awkwardly. 'Ah, yes, the constructive dismissal. I had been with the firm for about three years and things had been going well. Unfortunately, Malcolm began picking fault with my work, deliberately under-mining my contribution in front of clients, that kind of thing. If I was even five minutes late for work, and it didn't matter what the reason was, he would be on my back threatening me with a written warning. It was almost as though he wanted me out the company. I spoke to Ray about it, but he said it was just Malcolm's style and I shouldn't take it personally. In the end, I couldn't take it anymore and I quit. I was lucky I was able to find another job quite quickly. But I resented the way I'd been treated. They settled out of court and I dropped the case. I suspect that was down to Ray and not Malcolm.' She gave Molly a curious look. 'That was the strange thing. I was always so surprised when it was Ray that was arrested for fraud.'

'Why was that?'

She blushed and lowered her voice, as though she'd been caught telling tales out of school. 'There was something about Malcolm that I never fully trusted. He was forever wining and dining flashy businessmen then claiming it back on expenses, even though it didn't necessarily have anything to do with the business. And we were never entirely sure where Malcolm's wealth came from. Somebody said he'd inherited money from his grandparents when he was young, but he never mentioned his family.' She gave a twitchy smile. 'I would have thought that if either of them were to have gone down for fraud, it would have been Malcolm and not Ray.'

# Chapter Twenty-Six

Kane's house was large and, from the outside at least, superficially impressive. At first glance, it resembled a mock-Georgian mansion, complete with a stucco-pillared entrance and wide sash windows. It stood on the site of a 1930s bungalow that had mysteriously burned down some years earlier, when planning consent had been refused to demolish it. The bungalow had been surrounded by almost two acres of land, which had been added to over the years, and subsequently converted into manicured lawns and a wide terrace that ran along the rear of the property.

Rather than looking classy, as had been the original intention, Denning thought it just looked ostentatious. Whatever the case, Alfie Kane had loudly announced his presence: he had money and success and he wanted the world to know it.

Denning had announced his own presence via the intercom at the gate. After some muffled grumbling the electronic gates had swung open and he'd pulled up in front of the red-bricked mansion with the view of Epping Forest, slipping his Ford Focus into a space beside an S-Class Mercedes and a slick, black Range Rover.

Alfie Kane had started his career as a petty criminal, hanging around Soho in his youth, running errands for bigger, badder men who thought nothing of slitting someone's throat if they looked at them the wrong way. He'd worked his way up the greasy ladder, taking advantage of every opportunity that came his way, successfully avoiding police scrutiny along the way. It had always been rumoured – though naturally never proven – that he'd had at least a handful of senior police officers either on his payroll or in his favour. A few years ago, he'd turned his back on crime and was now a self-proclaimed respectable businessman. Or at least, that was the official version.

The heavy polished front door was opened by a man Denning knew as Stuart Braxton, a muscle-bound thug with a scar on his chin who served as Kane's security-man-cum-butler. He and Denning had met before: his dealings with Kane over the years had made him a familiar face amongst Kane's team.

He gave Denning a curt nod, led him through an impressive marble-floored hallway and into a vast conservatory at the back of the house.

If Kane wasn't happy at the sight of Denning standing in the doorway, he made a good show of hiding his displeasure.

'Inspector Denning, how are you? I hope this isn't a professional visit.'

The slight smirk on the edge of his lips implied he knew this was exactly that. The vast conservatory was lit by discreet lighting concealed within the ornate, white-painted ironwork that formed the skeleton of the room, which consisted of lush plants and heavy cane furniture. As the growing gloom of dusk descended outside, the glass walls threw back eerie reflections.

Kane poured himself a brandy from a decanter and offered one for Denning, which he declined.

'Not while on duty?' He gave a light, throaty laugh. 'So this *is* a professional visit after all.'

He indicated for Denning to take a seat. Denning was familiar with Kane's routine: pretend to be your new best friend, but always subtly reminding you he was a man who liked to come out on top. He had to be handled with care. If McKenna knew he was there...

'It's about a man named Ray Bowden,' Denning said, keeping his voice light. 'Do you recognise the name?'

Kane shook his head. 'I can't say I do. Should I?'

'He was murdered a couple of days ago.' Denning paused, waiting for a reaction, but Kane didn't even offer a flicker of emotion. 'He was stabbed to death in an abandoned Tube station.'

Kane's forehead wrinkled in puzzlement. 'What was he doing in an abandoned Tube station?'

'He was living rough,' Denning said matter-of-factly. 'He had been since his release from prison a year ago.'

Kane looked blankly at him. It was as though everything he'd just said had either failed to register or he just wasn't interested in listening to what Denning had to say. Denning suspected it was the latter.

Kane took another drink of his brandy. 'I'm sorry to hear about that, Inspector Denning. I admit, the name does ring a bell. Something about a property fraud if I remember rightly. A load of unfortunate investors conned out of their savings. It's very unpleasant and I feel for them, I really do. But I never knew Ray Bowden and I can offer no light on who's responsible for killing him.'

Kane's accent was clipped yet smooth, like he'd worked hard to rid himself of the East London inflections. But it was still there if you listened carefully enough. A glimpse of the real Alfie Kane poking through the polished veneer.

'I thought you might know something about the investment scam. Your name came up in connection with it.'

Kane looked at Denning but said nothing. After a moment, he got up and poured himself another brandy. 'Are you sure you won't have one? It's good stuff. Louis XIII de Remy Martin Rare Cask Grande Champagne Cognac. None of your shop's own crap.' He smiled as he said it, swilled the dark liquid around the crystal glass and took another swig. He sat back down opposite Denning. 'You see, I like the nice things in life, but unlike you, I've never had anything handed to me on a plate. All this' – he waved a hand around the luxuriously furnished, glass-walled room – 'I've got through sheer, hard graft. I don't need to con gullible pensioners out of their savings, Inspector Denning. Contrary to whatever it is you think of me, I'm not a criminal.'

Not now, maybe, Denning thought, but so much of what Kane valued had been bought either directly or indirectly through the proceeds of crime, including, Denning surmised, the house they were currently sitting in. 'I just wondered if you knew anything about the fraud,' Denning said calmly. 'I believe Ray Bowden's murder might have something to do with it. The more facts I have at my disposal, the more likely I am to find his killer.'

'I wish you well – one can't help feeling sorry for someone who ends his days sleeping rough in a derelict railway station – but you seem to be wasting your time here. And mine.'

He watched Denning as he swilled the expensive brandy round the glass and then drained it in one gulp.

Denning gazed at his own reflection in the darkened glass of the conservatory. He thought he spotted something moving in the gloom outside, scuttling across the garden. A fox, perhaps, or a badger...

'Someone offered Bowden money before he was killed,' Denning said. 'He refused it. And then he was murdered. It was almost like someone was trying to buy his silence, then when that didn't work they took more drastic action. Whoever did that must have had a lot to lose. And it would need to be someone who was very ruthless. Someone prepared to go to any lengths to ensure they didn't risk anything – or anyone – who might pose a risk to their very nice life.'

There was a silence, which Kane eventually filled. 'You remember Justin Morrow? Councillor with the GLA?'

Of course Denning remembered. Morrow and his wife were responsible for the deaths of two people: a former senior detective and an investigative journalist who had got too close to finding out the truth. Before Denning had had a chance to arrest Morrow, he had stepped in front of an express train. Denning had been chasing him at the time. An investigation by the Professional Standards Department had cleared Denning of any wrongdoing, but the guilt had lingered.

'I remember Justin Morrow,' Denning said coldly.

'You wouldn't back off then, and now he's dead. And you can never, I mean never fully, be certain of his guilt, can you? Whatever your lot say about you not being responsible, you've still got his blood on your hands. You still see his face in your dreams. You know that – at the end of the day – his death is on your conscience.'

Denning knew when he was being baited. But he was damned if he was going to let Alfie Kane rattle him.

'I don't see how any of this is relevant to the murder of Ray Bowden.'

'It's about you, Denning. It's about you poking and prodding into things you should just stay away from. Nothing good ever comes from harassing people, and another slip up on your part might not see you get off quite so lightly next time.'

'A threat…?'

Kane stood up. 'This conversation is now at an end. Don't come round here again unless you have some kind of proof that I've done something. And as that will never happen, this is where we say goodbye. Take care, Mr Denning. Lots of it.' With those parting words, he walked out the conservatory, leaving Denning sitting there, feeling for all the world like he'd just been threatened, but knowing there was bugger all he could do about it.

# Chapter Twenty-Seven

By the time Molly arrived at work the next day, Denning was at the front of the office waiting to start the latest briefing. She'd slept badly again, sensitive to any strange noise that sounded out of place. She'd been woken at one point by what sounded like two foxes fighting, and had struggled to get back to sleep.

Denning waited until Molly was seated and then began the briefing.

'Andrea Bowden has remarried,' he said to a sea of bemused faces. Molly couldn't think how this was relevant to the case. 'Her second husband is Malcolm Carver, Ray Bowden's former business partner,' he continued. 'Presumably they knew each other before Ray Bowden's arrest, and obviously, as consenting adults, they're both free to marry whoever they like.'

'But it does raise some awkward questions,' Kinsella said. 'Like why she would want to marry him?'

'Love is answerable to no one,' Trudi said, a twinkle in her eye. 'I don't have to tell an old romantic like yourself that, Dave.'

Kinsella pulled a face.

'Yes, but her jailed husband's business partner,' Molly said. 'It may have just been convenient.'

'Convenient?' Kinsella was shaking his head. 'What is with you two? One of you puts it down to love, the other one thinks it's a marriage of convenience.'

'Maybe she just fancied the bloke,' Neeraj offered, though his comment seemed to fall on mostly deaf ears.

Molly thought back to her meeting with Malcolm Carver. *Fanciable* wasn't a word she'd have used. 'What I meant was that she would have been in a vulnerable state. This was someone she knew who could offer her stability and support. Maybe that's why she turned to him.'

'That's a good point, Molly,' Denning said. 'Have a word with Andrea Bowden, or Carver, whatever she's calling herself, and see if you can find out anything more about when and why they got together. It is just possible there could have been something going on between them before Ray Bowden was sent down.'

'I don't imagine Bowden would have been too happy about the situation,' Trudi said. 'If it were me, the first thing I'd do when I got out is to have a word with them both.'

'More than just have a word,' Kinsella said. 'If it was me, I'd knock Carver's bloody head off.'

Denning wrote Andrea Bowden and Malcolm Carver's names on the whiteboard. 'So if Bowden had paid them a visit after he was released, then we need to know about it. But tread carefully – neither Andrea Bowden nor Malcolm Carver has actually done anything wrong by getting married. I mean this could all be nothing.'

'Or it could give one or both of them a motive,' Kinsella said.

'Really?' Neeraj wasn't looking convinced.

'Think about it,' Kinsella said, leaning back on his chair. 'All the time Bowden's banged up, they're safe.

Then he gets out. I can't imagine he'd be too chuffed to discover his wife and his former business partner have got it together in his absence.'

'Especially if Carver had already screwed him over the fraud case,' Molly said.

'Interesting,' Denning said. 'Care to elaborate on that point, Molly?'

'I spoke to someone who worked for Bowden and Carver, Karen Higgins,' she said. 'She seemed to be of the persuasion that, of the two of them, Carver was more likely to have been involved with the fraud. I got the distinct impression she thought Bowden was the honest one, while Carver was the one who liked taking risks. What if it was Carver who was responsible for the fraud and let Bowden take the blame for it?'

Denning nodded. 'I had been wondering that myself. But there's no evidence that Malcolm Carver was involved in the fraud or even knew anything about it.'

'Besides,' Trudi said, 'why would Bowden deliberately take the rap for Carver? I mean covering up for a minor mistake or the odd dodgy investment as a favour or to help a friend out is one thing, but to actually serve time for a crime you didn't commit? Bowden would have to be insane to agree to that.'

'Bowden did insist he was innocent,' Neeraj argued. 'Maybe he was, and he was just protecting Carver.'

'I refer you back to previous point,' Trudi said. 'Protecting him by going to prison for four years? It's crazy.'

'Maybe there was some kind of pay-off?' Neeraj suggested. 'Carver couldn't handle the thought of prison, so he paid Bowden to take the rap?'

'Carver came from a pretty privileged background,' Molly said. 'Deep might have a point. If he thought he couldn't handle prison, then Bowden agrees to go down for it in return for... what? Money?'

'So where's the pay-off?' Kinsella said, pointing out the obvious. 'He's sleeping in a derelict railway station?'

'The money,' Molly remembered. The cash that Corey said someone had handed to Bowden in an envelope. *A smartly dressed man...* he'd said. That would have fitted Carver's description.

'He'd been out of prison for a year by the time the money was offered to him,' Denning said. 'And besides, according to your witness, Bowden turned the money down. But I accept, this does potentially give Andrea and Malcolm Carver a motive. I seriously believe the fraud is the key to all this. I'm not sure how all the pieces fit together but there has to be a reason why Ray Bowden chose to lie low. His prison record is excellent, so this has nothing to do with anyone he might have pissed off while he was inside. The police have as good as admitted the drugs were more than likely planted to get rid of the rough sleepers. So I think this has all got something to do with Bowden's work. And the property developer, Steven Hodge, have we found out anything more about him?'

There was a general shaking of heads. 'Seems legit,' Trudi said. 'Spent fifteen years working for Harvey Thompson Estate Agents in Chelsea, then branched out into property development about a decade ago. Mostly residential properties but has recently moved into the commercial sector.'

'OK,' Denning said, 'but let's keep an eye on him too. Molly, have another word with Karen Higgins – find out what was really going on at Carver Bowden Investments. And where are we up to with Corey?'

'I'm working on it…'

## Chapter Twenty-Eight

Molly phoned Karen Higgins. She felt like they'd got on well together the previous day and that a body of trust had been built up between them. At least enough for her to get in touch again without feeling like she was harassing the poor woman.

'It's really just a quick follow-up call,' Molly said. 'I was looking for a bit more background on Ray Bowden's relationship with Malcolm Carver. I know you said they were different people, but what was their working relationship like?'

There was a pause from the other end of the line. 'Good, I suppose. There was certainly no animosity between them. I imagine that situation would have changed after the fraud came to light.'

Molly tried to arrange her next question in such a way that it wouldn't seem in any way impertinent. 'What about Mrs Bowden? Did she ever come into the office, or phone up?'

'She would phone the office sometimes. I did meet her a couple of times – office party, that kind of event.'

'What about Andrea Bowden and Malcolm Carver? Would you say they got on together?'

'Ah, I think I can sense where you're going with this. There were rumours that Andrea and Malcolm were… close. I never believed them, but one of the secretaries, someone who had been there since they set the company up, claimed they'd been having an affair behind Ray's back.'

'Did Ray suspect anything?'

'To be honest with you, I'm not convinced there was anything to suspect. You know what it's like in these small companies. People like to gossip, especially about their bosses. But if it was true, then no, I don't think he did.'

'But just assuming there was any truth in the rumour, how long would the affair have been going on?'

'Well, I suppose all the time I worked there. So at least five years.'

'Just one last question, Karen, then I won't take up any more of your time. Malcolm Carver claims he was unaware of the fraud because he'd been off work recovering from an operation. Can you confirm if that was the case?'

There was a momentary silence from the other end of the line. 'Well, yes and no. Malcolm was off work for a while, but he still came into the office from time to time. Ray took some time off – he claimed it was for personal reasons – and Malcolm had to come in then.'

'How much time did Ray take off?'

'A week. Maybe ten days.'

'And he didn't say why?'

'No. Like I said, it was for personal reasons. But it was very unlike Ray to take time off. He was a bit of a workaholic. And it was strange…'

'Strange? In what way?'

'Ray seemed different when he returned to work. I can't say what it was, but something had obviously happened. He was usually very cheerful – laughing and making silly jokes. He seemed, well, more subdued.'

'And he never said why?'

There was another silence from the other end of the line. 'I could just have imagined it. I mean, it could have been nothing. It was shortly after that that the shit hit the fan and Ray was arrested.'

Molly thanked her and ended the call.

Clearly something had happened to Ray Bowden that had necessitated taking time off work. Had he discovered his wife and his business partner were having an affair behind his back? But then why return to work? Especially if it meant working alongside the man his wife was cheating on him with. But if there was any truth in the rumour that Andrea Bowden and Malcolm Carver were having an affair then it could potentially have given one or both of them a motive for wanting Ray Bowden dead. If he came out of prison and discovered they were now married, he could potentially have caused a lot of trouble for them.

Then there was the Google search Molly had done on Malcolm Carver's business interests. Although there was nothing to directly connect him to the fraud case, there had been a couple of allegations of financial misconduct that had been made against Carver, though nothing had ever been proven. The more she looked into his life, the more Malcolm Carver seemed to come across as a slippery customer.

She checked the address Denning had given her. It was time she paid Mr and Mrs Carver a visit.

-

Denning had been right about the house. Admittedly it was in a posh part of London, so it was going to be nice, but Molly hadn't been prepared for the sheer opulence of the place. The large gilt-framed mirror over the mantelpiece looked like something that belonged in Downton Abbey.

Andrea Bowden, or Carver as they now knew her to be, was eyeing Molly suspiciously from the comfy-looking sofa. Finn Bowden sat next to his mother, clearly wishing he was somewhere else. He was already late for work, Andrea had explained, so they would appreciate it if Molly could ask her questions quickly.

'I'm not sure what else I can tell you,' Andrea said. 'We've already spoken to an Inspector Denning. Twice. There's really nothing more to add.'

'I understand that, Mrs Carver, and I won't take up too much of your time.'

'It's Bowden, actually,' she said coldly. 'I prefer to use the name Bowden, as I have already explained to Inspector Denning.'

Molly made a mental note. 'That's actually one of the reasons I wanted to speak to you. I didn't realise you had married Ray's business partner.'

'Ray's former business partner. Ray no longer had anything to do with the company. He made that choice the day he chose to steal from their clients, leaving Malcolm to pick up the pieces, which let me tell you wasn't easy. Trying to sort out the mess Ray had left behind. And not just the business, us as well.' She looked at Molly like a teacher patiently explaining something to a slow child.

It felt like she was trying to get things off her chest: a cathartic release, perhaps partially motivated by grief. 'I can understand that,' Molly said. 'I realise it must have been difficult.'

'It isn't helped by having the police asking me loads of questions. I know nothing about Ray's murder. I hadn't seen him for over five years.'

'This is more about us trying to fill in the blanks about his life,' Molly said. She wanted to add it was also about trying to find out what she could about her current husband, and his possible involvement in her first husband's death. 'We believe his death may have something to do with the fraud case. It's possible one of the investors may have tracked him down and killed him.' She paused before continuing. 'There's also the possibility one of the other men involved in the fraud may have killed Ray in order to keep him from talking.'

'That's absurd. Considering where he was living when he was murdered, I would have thought you should be going after one of those homeless people he was dossing down with. Maybe one of them found out who he was. Perhaps they thought he had money.'

'Is it possible Ray could have had access to funds? I presume Malcolm bought him out of the business when he went to prison?'

'I don't know about that. I don't think there was any money to spare after what Ray did. He left us with the mortgage on this place. Can you imagine how much that cost every month? Then there were our children's school fees. I couldn't manage on what I earned from the gallery. Our savings had been depleted paying for Ray's legal team. If Malcolm hadn't stepped in and helped us, then we would more than likely be the ones living rough.'

Molly glanced around the lavish room: the house must be worth a small fortune. Why didn't they just sell it and buy somewhere smaller?

'I know what you're thinking,' Andrea said. 'But this is our home, why should we have to sell it? *We* hadn't done anything wrong. If anything, we're as much the victims here as the people Ray conned the money out of.' She sighed and smiled. 'I'd known Malcolm for many years. I knew he was a good man. He stepped in to help save both our family and the business. I... we owe him a great deal.' She looked at her son when she said this. But the look on Finn Bowden's face suggested he didn't share his mother's enthusiasm for his stepfather.

'Finn...?' Molly looked directly at him. 'How did you feel when Malcolm came into your home?'

He stared at her for a couple of seconds before he answered. 'Yeah. It's like Mum says.'

'You didn't feel he was trying to replace your dad?'

'What sort of question is that?' Andrea Bowden was glaring at Molly, her eyes reduced to narrow slits. 'I thought you wanted to find out who killed him. I can't see how you're going to manage that by asking questions about our personal life.'

'Like I said, Mrs Bowden, until we can build up a full picture of Ray's life, we haven't got much to work on. Anything that can give us an insight into his life will help.'

Andrea Bowden didn't look convinced. She opened her mouth to say something but before she had a chance, Finn spoke: 'Yeah, Malcolm's great. He got what he always wanted – a ready-made family and the business all to himself. It's worked out well for him, hasn't it. Not worked out so well for Dad. Living rough with a bunch of dropouts. He didn't deserve that, even if he was a rubbish dad.'

Molly was shocked by his tone and the level of aggression. So much of that could be put down to grief, but there was something more here; it was like something had been unleashed that had been boiling away under the surface for years. She looked at Andrea to gauge her reaction to her son's sudden outburst. He seemed to be singing from a different hymn sheet to his mother.

But Andrea Bowden kept calm.

'I wouldn't want you to get the wrong impression, Sergeant,' Andrea said, 'Ray Bowden wasn't some kind of hero. Yes, it's terrible what happened to him. But he was dead to us long before this week. Long before he went to prison if you really want to know. He made his choices and he had to live with them.'

Molly wanted to know what she meant by that, but it was clear the interview was over. Andrea Bowden had got to her feet and was indicating Molly should do the same.

'As I told your colleague yesterday, Detective Sergeant, if we can think of anything that might be useful to your investigation, we'll be in touch. Until then, I would appreciate it if you left us alone.'

# Chapter Twenty-Nine

Denning was at his desk. He kept throwing glances in the direction of McKenna's office. He should really be running his theory by her, but he knew exactly what her reaction would be. Even if they could prove Ray Bowden's murder was somehow linked to the old fraud case, any information relating to it would have to be passed on to the NCA.

He thought again about Steve Marsh and the chance to switch horses and work for the NCA. The work was varied enough to be interesting yet tended to avoid the goriness of murder investigations. There might even be something approaching sensible working hours. It might mean working away from home a lot, but that wouldn't necessarily be a problem. Sarah often worked away from home and they were used to living something approaching separate lives whenever work demanded it.

He would need to discuss it with Sarah before he came to any decision. With Claire too…

Denning tried to put it out of his head for now. He had other thoughts to occupy his brain. Specifically, the details surrounding the deaths of the other men involved in the fraud case. And a man serving time in prison for it while others were still free.

Most had either moved abroad, somewhere beyond the reaches of UK extradition deals, or had simply slipped through the net due to lack of evidence. People like Alfie Kane, Denning surmised.

He thought about Kane.

Shortly after he'd returned from visiting Kane in his mock-Georgian mansion, he'd received an anonymous text message. Well, not so much a message: it was just a photograph. A church. But it wasn't just a church. It was the same church in East London where Daniel Placzek had held Claire and Jake hostage.

The meaning was clear.

Denning had little hope in proving who had been responsible for sending the photo. There had been no number, and even if he did manage to trace the sender, chances were it would have come from a burner phone which had long-since disappeared.

Kane was clever enough to make sure there was no way it could be traced back to him. Even if Denning were to go to McKenna with this, or if he were to go over her head, he would have to explain why he had spoken to Alfie Kane in the first place. Any justification he could put forward for visiting Kane would be tenuous at best. There was very little to directly link Kane with the fraud case, and even less to connect him with Ray Bowden's murder.

But he couldn't ignore his instincts.

Steve Marsh had emailed over the files on the fraud case: what they knew and had been able to prove, and what they'd speculated on, but had little or no chance of finding enough evidence to put before a jury.

There were believed to have been almost a dozen men involved with the fraud either directly or indirectly. Of the six main players, three were now dead, four if you included Terry Benson. From the remaining two, one was in prison for an unrelated matter, and the other – who was also wanted in connection with a number of similar crimes – was believed to be living in Algeria. The others involved were people like Kane: rumoured to have had a hand in the operation but who had kept their distance.

While the deaths were undeniably suspicious, there was nothing on the system that hinted at foul play. This would be a hard sell to get past McKenna at the best of times. With her constantly reminding him his job was potentially on the line if he put a foot wrong, then now was clearly not the best of times.

If only he could find something that proved all the deaths were linked. At least then he could go to McKenna and insist this was about something else: this was more than just a brutal murder of a homeless man. They could make it official and call for more resources, maybe even share intel with the NCA. But there was nothing, at least nothing obvious that tied the crimes together. Then, if it wasn't obvious, he would have to look for it. He would have to dig around in the dirt and find the missing pieces. And all the time keep the plates of a murder investigation spinning.

# Chapter Thirty

Molly checked Google Maps on her phone: Kempton Way wasn't far from Whitechapel Tube station. Ironically, Whitechapel had been the Tube stop before Shoreditch when the old East London Line was still running.

Molly and Trudi were in one of the pool cars: a Toyota Yaris that already had a couple of bumps on the passenger door and a lengthy scratch along the bonnet.

They found Kempton Way easily enough: a short stub of a street running from Whitechapel Road to what looked like a sports centre at the other end. One side of the road was a row of shops, take-aways and an off licence. On the other side were 1950s-style council flats set slightly back from the road. She went into some of the shops and asked if anyone had seen someone who fitted Corey's description hanging around, but she was met with confused looks followed by denials. She decided to try the flats opposite. A woman pushing a pram just shook her head when she asked.

The flats were typical red-bricked council houses of the era: five storeys high with a couple of concrete walkways running along the first and third floors. Covered stairwells at either end. They looked out onto a children's play area at the front, which was separated from the road by a low metal fence.

'This looks like the place,' Trudi said, slipping the Yaris into a parking space behind a battered Transit van. 'Do we have an exact address?'

About a third of the way along the ground floor one of the flats had been boarded up; the brickwork around the front door and windows was slightly blackened, as though there had been a recent fire. The boards were presumably a temporary measure until the council could get around to repairing the property. Boards that could easily be removed...?

'I'm guessing it's the one whose occupants are the least houseproud,' Molly said, pointing at the boarded-up flat.

They approached the building cautiously. Molly still wasn't convinced this was a good idea. Even if Corey was there, they couldn't assume he'd want to talk to them. But as he was all they had in the way of an even halfway credible witness, he was going to have to talk.

And God knew what else they might find on the premises...

She pressed her ear against one of the boards that had replaced a burnt-out window. There were voices coming from inside: male, but after a moment she heard a woman's voice. Unmistakably Zella.

There was a metal padlock on the board covering the front door; it had been snapped off. A pair of decent bolt cutters would have done the trick easily enough. Molly reached out and touched the padlock. Behind the plywood board the door to the flat was still intact, twisted and scorched by the fire, the glass panels smashed.

'Maybe we should call for back-up,' Trudi suggested. 'At least get some uniforms to come in with us and make the whole thing look official.'

'This *is* official,' Molly said. 'We're not calling round to wish them well in their new home.'

'You know what I mean.'

Molly ignored her. She pushed open the remains of the front door and went inside.

The flat smelt of smoke, as well as a musty stench that suggested the place hadn't been occupied until now. The fire looked like it had started in the hallway: the walls were blackened and there was ash on the floor.

The voices were coming from a room off to the right. They obviously hadn't heard Molly and Trudi entering the flat as no one had appeared to ask why they were there.

They entered what was presumably the living room: not as badly fire-damaged as the hallway, but with walls that bore evidence of smoke damage. There was still furniture in the room: an old sofa and a couple of rickety armchairs, and a battered old sideboard that looked like it would fall apart as soon as anyone opened one of the doors.

There were three people in the room: Corey, Zella and another man of around the same age, with a scraggly beard that partly hid a thin face. Corey and Zella were sitting on the sofa, while the bearded man lay on the floor, smoking a joint. Three opened cans of lager sat on the floor next to an empty crisp packet and some chocolate wrappers.

The man smoking the spliff looked up when he saw Molly and Trudi standing here, gave them a quizzical look, then snorted a laugh. Corey and Zella looked round.

'What the fuck are you doing here?' Zella asked.

'I need to speak to Corey,' Molly said.

'How the fuck did you find us?' Zella's narrowed eyes were fixed on Molly.

Molly ignored her, focussing instead on Corey. 'Can we talk outside, Corey?'

'You're not chucking us out of here,' Zella said. 'We've got nowhere else to go.'

Molly surveyed the room: dust and ash, fire-blackened walls and furniture that belonged in a skip. This really was all they had. What right had she to take that away from them? It was a council-owned property and they were homeless. In Molly's eyes they had as much right to be there as anyone.

'I just need to speak to Corey. Then I'll be out of your hair.'

'He doesn't want to talk to you. And you can't make him. We know our rights. So why don't you fuck off?'

'Corey,' Molly said calmly. 'We only want to ask you some more questions.' She smiled at him, trying to reassure him. 'We can get something to eat if you like...'

Zella shot her another filthy look, but out of the corner of her eye, Molly caught Corey trying to hide a smile. Any reluctance he might have felt at talking to the police, and the subsequent cold shoulder from Zella, was clearly overruled by his stomach and the need to fill it. The offer was clearly too good to refuse. Despite a warning nudge from Zella, he got to his feet and smiled at her. 'Look after my stuff, babe,' he said and then followed Molly and Trudi out the squat.

They found a café on Whitechapel Road. Molly had been here once before when she'd been investigating a family murdered in their own home. Their son had run a company called Party Animals, which had an office in a building across the road from the café. The café was still there though Party Animals was long gone.

She and Trudi ordered sandwiches and a couple of lattes for themselves, while Molly told Corey to order whatever he wanted; he opted for scrambled eggs on toast and a mug of tea. The table by the window was taken so they sat nearer the counter. Luckily the young woman behind the counter seemed more interested in her phone than in their conversation, so it was unlikely they would be overheard. The woman had given them a wary look when they had pitched up, but after Molly had ordered and paid for the food with her debit card, tossing a couple of quid's worth of loose change into the tip jar, her concern had quickly waned.

Corey seemed edgier than last time they'd met. She supposed he hadn't earned himself any favours by associating with the police. In their eyes, Zella had a good point: the police couldn't be trusted.

Once their food arrived, Corey ate his with gusto. Molly and Trudi picked at their sandwiches. The café was unpretentious but the food was tasty.

'I don't think Zella likes me,' Molly said, offering a smile. She wanted to put the lad at ease.

'She's alright when you get to know her. We kind of look out for each other.'

'But she doesn't like you talking to me?'

'She doesn't trust you.' He smiled at her through a mouthful of food. 'It's nothing personal. She doesn't trust police. Or anyone come to think of it.'

'But she trusts you?'

He gave her a look that said he wasn't entirely sure. 'Suppose...'

Molly smiled. There was something endearing about Corey. If life was fair, he would be at college now, or university, or working in a job. It wasn't too late... There were so many questions she wanted to ask him about his life. She wanted to tell him there was still time to turn it all around. She'd managed to turn hers around, with a lot of help…

'We've identified the man who was murdered at the old station,' Trudi said, reminding Molly why they were there. 'His name was Ray Bowden.'

Corey looked blank, the name clearly meant nothing to him.

'He had a family,' Trudi continued, 'a son and daughter about the same age as you and Zella.'

The lad munched his food. 'Sorry,' he said, taking a sip of tea.

It wasn't clear what exactly he was sorry about: the news that Bowden had a family, or that he was unable to provide any further information beyond what they already knew.

'We need to ask you about the man with the envelope of money, Corey. It's important you try to remember as much as you can about what happened.'

He took another mouthful of food. 'I told you all I could remember last time. He was just some bloke. I couldn't really see that well. It was dark.'

'Did Ray say anything to you about this man? Or the money?'

He carried on eating, ignoring the question. Probably hoping they'd go away and leave him alone. But that wasn't going to happen. Not until he'd given them something useful.

'Corey,' Molly prompted. 'This is important. Ray Bowden had a family and they deserve to know who killed him. And right now, you're the only person who can help us find that person.'

'He was just some bloke. Average. Smart gear.'

'Would you recognise him if you saw him again?'

'Maybe.'

Molly looked at Trudi, who was silently shaking her head. They were getting nowhere. It was time to try something else.

She'd downloaded a photo of Malcolm Carver from his website, and another one from his Facebook page. One showed him smiling at the camera, the other featured him very slightly in profile. She showed the photos to Corey.

'Could this be the man you saw offering money to Ray before he was murdered?'

Corey glanced at the pictures and shook his head. 'I don't recognise him.'

'Take another look, Corey. Closely this time.' She could sense that he was reluctant to talk to her. Had someone got to him? Was it Zella warning him off talking to the police again? She just knew that it was going to be impossible to get him to make any kind of formal statement.

He took the photographs from her and looked at them. 'I don't know.' He screwed up his face. 'It was dark and I didn't get a good look at his face.' He stared hard at the man in the pictures. 'But it could be him. I mean it looks like it could be him – same build and the like. But I don't know...'

'Try and remember, Corey. Think back to when you saw him.'

It had only been a few days ago, less than a week probably. But so much had happened to Corey in between, it was understandable that he might be confused. Or had simply tried to block the whole thing out of his mind. But right now, he was all she had. 'Corey... This is serious.

Very serious. There's a killer out there and we need to find him. There's a chance he might kill again.'

The last bit was deliberate exaggeration aimed at scaring the lad into cooperating. She felt bad that she was manipulating him, but it was the only thing she could think of to shake him out of his stupor. 'Take a good long look.'

'Yeah,' Corey said eventually. 'Yeah, that was him. That was the man.' He handed her back the photos.

She slipped the photographs back into her bag.

He'd said it too quickly. She couldn't be sure whether he was being truthful, or just saying what he thought she wanted to hear to get her off his back.

'Corey, I'm going to have to ask you to make a statement to confirm that you saw this man speaking to the man who was murdered.'

'Will I have to go to court?'

She wanted to lie and say he wouldn't. But she owed him the truth at the very least. 'If it turns out that he's the man responsible for the murder, then there's a very good chance you might have to go to court. All you would have to do is confirm what you saw. You wouldn't get into any trouble.'

'He won't do it.' A voice behind them.

Molly turned round. Zella was standing by the doorway. She came over and sat down next to Corey, putting her arm protectively round his shoulder. 'I was worried about you. I tried a couple of places, then some geezer I know said he saw you come in here with these two.' She shot Molly and Trudi a disdainful look, then turned back to Corey. 'They can't make you do anything you don't want to do, mate.'

Molly knew she was in danger of losing Corey if she didn't act quickly. Zella was becoming a thorn in her side. She was either going to have to get her to back off or get her on side: the carrot or the stick approach, which was likely to work better?

'Zella, a man has been murdered. He had a family. A son and a daughter, probably the same age as yourselves. Don't they have the right to find out who killed their father and why?'

'That's not our problem.'

Molly wanted to say that she could easily make it their problem — arrest them for obstructing a murder invest-igation — but where would that get them? They would just clam up and deny everything. 'I only need Corey to confirm that this was the man who offered Ray Bowden the money in the envelope. Once he's agreed to that, you won't see me again.'

Zella glowered at her. 'That's the thing though, isn't it? We won't see you because we're of no further use to you. You've got what you want from us and then we go back to being nothing to you. Just some more dirt that you and your mates can move on whenever we're in the way. He doesn't want to get involved, and neither do I, so do yourself a favour, lady, and hop it.'

'This isn't going to go away, Zella. I can come back with a court order. I don't want to, but I will if that's the route you choose to go down.'

'Do what you like. We don't care. But just get the message and leave us alone.'

'He had kids,' Corey said. 'I remember now he told me something about his family. It didn't make much sense at the time.'

'Shut up, Corey. Don't tell her anything else.'

Molly raised a hand to silence Zella. 'What was it, Corey?'

'He said something about trying to keep the truth from them.'

'The truth about what?'

'I don't know. He never made much sense at the best of times.'

Molly wondered what he'd meant by this. Did it refer to the fraud case? Or something else? Something relating to his family?

'Try and think, Corey. Did he say anything else?'

Corey shook his head. Zella stood up, moving in front of him, blocking him from Molly. For a second, Molly thought she might be about to hit her. She could arrest her, or call for back-up, but she wasn't sure there was much point. They weren't going to tell her anything else. She needed to get Corey on his own, away from the influence of Zella. She might have thought she was protecting him, but she was simply making an already difficult job even harder.

As they left, Molly began to think that Ray Bowden was a man with many secrets.

# Chapter Thirty-One

Fiona Tanner was in her late forties. She was, she explained, just back from the gym, but could spare Denning five minutes.

She lived in Kilburn, in a pleasant semi-detached house on a street not far from Kensal Green Cemetery. She showed him into the living room. There was a framed photograph of her and her late husband on a table by the window. Denning had googled Adam Tanner but apart from the information about his alleged involvement in the fraud case, there was little of note.

'You said you wanted to talk about Adam,' Fiona said, sitting opposite him. 'I don't really know what I can tell you. It was nearly three years ago now.'

She'd come home from work one day to find her husband in the bath having taken an overdose of sleeping pills and drunk half a bottle of whisky. The coroner had said it was suicide, and there was nothing to suggest he hadn't taken his own life. But Denning wanted to make sure everything had been looked into.

'He suffered from depression,' he said. It was as much a statement as a question.

'Off and on,' Fiona said. 'The pressure of the fraud investigation didn't help. The police had initially thought he was one of the major players. In reality he'd become involved unwittingly. He always insisted he didn't know it was a fraud. He'd dealt with Ray Bowden and Malcolm Carver for years – we knew Malcolm socially – and he trusted them. The whole thing came as a massive surprise.'

'The allegations were that Adam had helped to dispose of the money after it had been transferred into various dodgy bank accounts. It was believed that he knew what he was doing, and was aware that it was illegal.' Denning offered her a propitiatory smile. 'I'm not passing judgement, only telling you what I know. Which, I have to say, isn't very much.'

'The police investigation cleared Adam of any wrong-doing, although his employers weren't so understanding. He was, let's just say, *encouraged* to leave his job. He took voluntary redundancy, we sold our house in Surrey and moved in here. We lived off my money for a while – I run my own accountancy firm – then he eventually found a job managing a market garden in Wembley. It was a difficult time in our lives, but we got over it. I thought Adam had managed to put it behind him, but perhaps he hadn't. There were always rumours and gossip. We lost a couple of friends over it. They obviously believed he was guilty. Some of the neighbours wouldn't speak to us. Until we moved round here and nobody knew.' She looked at him quizzically. 'And this is to do with a murder, is it? Ray Bowden? I can't see how Adam's suicide fits into that?'

He explained about the other deaths; how he was certain there was a connection there.

'I think the men behind the scam, I mean the ones who organised it all, got away scot-free and somehow wanted to make sure the men left behind kept quiet.'

She opened her mouth, then shook her head. 'You think Adam might have been murdered…?' She said it like it was the most fantastical thing that could ever have happened to them.

'At this stage, it's nothing more than a possibility, and something that I have to consider.'

'Why would anyone kill Adam?'

'It's possible he was going to tell the police what he knew. Maybe he had a change of heart about the whole thing. The men behind this scam are dangerous and powerful. They're the kind of people that will go to any lengths to protect themselves. Including, I'm afraid, murder.'

He was referring specifically to Alfie Kane, but it was very likely the others involved were cut from a similar cloth. Fiona Tanner looked shocked. It was as though this was all something alien for her.

'And you think the same people are responsible for Ray Bowden's murder?'

'It's one avenue of inquiry. We also have a number of other angles to investigate.'

She sat back on her chair. 'I'm not sure I can take this in. If Adam was murdered, why wasn't it investigated as a murder at the time?'

'The evidence would have suggested it was suicide. Unless there was anything concrete to contradict that, then the investigating officers would have had nothing to work with. Did Adam leave a note?'

'No, but apparently that's not uncommon in suicides. Or so someone told me at the time.'

That much Denning was aware of. 'What was his behaviour like just before his death? Was he acting out of character? Did he seem scared, or worried about anything?'

Fiona rubbed the back of her neck as she tried to think back to what must have been a difficult time in her life. 'No. No, he was a bit quiet, but that wasn't unusual for Adam. Sometimes he'd withdraw into himself. He seemed OK though. It wasn't like other times he'd struggled with depression. But I suppose he never really came to terms with having to leave the bank, and the gossip and everything.'

'He never mentioned the fraud case?'

'We didn't discuss it. It had happened and it was over and done with.' She sighed. 'But, of course, that doesn't mean that he had come to terms with it. There's a good chance it was festering away inside him.' She looked at Denning. 'I wish I could help you more, but I just can't believe Adam was murdered. It's taken me the best part of three years to come to terms with his suicide, and now I feel I'm finally getting some closure, you come along and stir things up again. I just want to forget about it and move on.'

Denning understood and sympathised. 'I'm sorry, Mrs Tanner. I realise these questions must be uncomfortable for you, and I can only apologise. Just a couple more things. What did you think of Ray Bowden and Malcolm Carver? Or Andrea Bowden?'

'I knew Andrea socially. We weren't especially close, but we had a couple of friends in common, and I admired her as an artist. I can't say I really knew her husband that well. I mean, I knew he was supposed to be this great financier, and I think he and Adam may have met up socially from time to time. They both played golf, but I wouldn't say they were all that friendly.'

'What about Malcolm Carver?'

'Like I said, we were friendly with Malcolm, but we didn't live in each other's pockets. Adam used to play golf with him, but like with Ray Bowden, I wouldn't say they were very close friends.'

'Did you know Andrea Bowden was now married to Malcolm Carver?'

Fiona looked shocked for a moment, then smiled. 'Well, that wouldn't surprise me. Andrea always liked the nice things in life. I suspect she knew a good thing when she married one.'

Denning noted the cynicism and wondered if it was motivated by a personal dislike of Andrea Bowden, or simply that she seemed to be one of the few people who had come out of the whole situation relatively unscathed. 'Do you think it was possible Andrea Bowden was aware of what Ray was up to?'

'Oh, I wouldn't say that. If you want to think that, then that's up to you. I'm just saying Andrea Bowden never struck me as being anybody's fool. She would never have got herself into something messy without seeing an obvious escape route.'

Denning saw himself out. There was someone else he wanted to speak to. He typed their address into the satnav and started up the engine.

—

Brian Deacon was in his thirties, balding with a nose ring. He had been the partner of Keith Prideaux, another of the men believed to have been behind the planning of the fraud. Denning had agreed to meet Deacon at the pub in Blackheath where he worked.

'I want to make one thing clear,' Deacon said, 'Keith and I had split up long before he was arrested for that fraud.'

'But you were still friends?' Denning said. The pub served Guinness and he was tempted to ask for a pint, although he was officially working.

'Oh yes. We stayed friends right up until he had his accident. Good mates. We'd always been mates, even before we got together. Didn't see any reason to stop being mates just because it didn't work out between us.'

'You mentioned the accident. Car crash, wasn't it?'

Deacon turned to serve a customer who had ordered a pint of lager, but he continued talking to Denning as he served them. 'Coming home from the pub one night. Probably over the limit, though the police never said. Anyway, he swerved to avoid an oncoming car. Drove straight off the road and into a tree. They never found the other driver.'

'Was it caught on CCTV?'

Deacon finished serving the customer and returned to Denning's end of the bar. 'There weren't any cameras on that stretch of road, so there wasn't much to go on. They tried to trace the other driver but no luck. The police did find a stolen Toyota burnt out in some nearby woods a few days later. They reckoned it was probably the other car. Nicked by joyriders then set on fire.'

'But no arrests?'

He shot Denning a withering look. 'You're the police. Aren't you lot always going on about limited resources?' He sighed. 'No, Inspector, there were no arrests. There was nothing to prove the car was involved in Keith's accident, and no clue as to who was driving it.'

Denning paused before asking his next question. 'But you're convinced it was an accident?'

'What does that mean?'

'The police didn't say anything to you that might have suggested it was deliberate?'

'Look, mister, Keith and I weren't even together at the time. The police didn't tell me Jack Shit. I found all this out second hand. But no, nobody seemed to think it was deliberate. OK, so Keith wasn't exactly an angel, but he had no enemies. Not real ones anyway.' He sniffed and started polishing a small patch of the bar in front of them. 'Well, maybe he had pissed off one or two people over the years but no one would have wanted to kill him over it. He was a laugh – people liked him.'

'What about Alfie Kane? Did Keith know him?'

'You're not going to trip me up, mister. OK, I know Alfie's insisting he's a good boy these days, but he's a man with a reputation, and I like my life now. So, whether or not Keith knew Alfie is neither here nor there.'

'About the fraud case,' Denning said. 'I don't want to know whether or not you believe he was guilty, but did he ever talk about it? Especially in the days leading up to his accident?'

Deacon thought about this for a moment. 'No. He never mentioned it.'

'Did Keith know Malcolm Carver or Ray Bowden?'

'He knew them. He worked with Ray Bowden yonks ago. Knew him and trusted him. Didn't know he was going to do the dirty on everyone and drop them in the shit.'

'So you believe Ray Bowden knew what he was doing?'

'I reckon he was the brains behind it all. Keith was a nice bloke but he was easily swayed. I suspect he let Bowden talk him into it. You know how these things go – the promise of easy money.'

'Can you think of anyone who would want to kill Ray Bowden?'

He looked at Denning for a moment. 'If you mean did I hold a grudge against him because of what happened to Keith, then yeah – I suppose for a while I did. But enough to kill him…?' He pulled a face. 'No way. Not my style. And besides, until you came calling today, I thought Bowden was still banged up.'

'OK, but if you can think of anything else, give me a call.'

He took Denning's card and nodded. Denning thanked him and left the pub.

It was cold outside, a bitter chill reminding him winter was here. Christmas wasn't far off and Denning hadn't even thought about what he was going to do. Right now, he had other things on his mind, like whether he had called this wrong and was barking up the wrong tree altogether. The link between Bowden's murder and his involvement in the fraud case now looked to be on shaky ground.

## Chapter Thirty-Two

When Molly returned to the office, there was no sign of Denning. Neeraj was poring over his computer, trawling through a list of emails, humming to himself while crunching an extra-strong mint. He always kept a packet on his desk but only ever offered them to someone if he thought they looked like they were about to ask him for one. Molly had learned it was probably fairer just to let him keep them to himself rather than force him to share.

'Do you know where Denning is?' she asked.

He didn't look up from his emails. 'We're not joined at the hip you know.'

'I didn't ask if you were. I just wondered if you knew where he was.'

'No. If I did, I would have told you.'

Either Neeraj was in a mood or he was enjoying being difficult. She decided to play him at his own game. 'I'd love a mint, Deep.' She took the packet from his desk and helped herself to one of the sweets. 'You don't mind, do you? Cheers.' She made a loud slurping sound and replaced the mints on his desk. She heard him grumble something under his breath, which she couldn't quite make out. Smiling to herself, she headed back to her desk.

She was intrigued by what Corey had told her about Bowden. There was something they were missing and she had a nagging feeling it was something obvious.

Somehow, Malcolm Carver seemed to be the key to this. Corey had identified him as the man with the envelope full of money; a lot of money, Corey had said. But what had motivated it? Guilt? At stealing Bowden's family? Or had he felt guilty about something else…?

She remembered what Karen Higgins had said about being surprised to discover it had been Ray Bowden, when her money would have been on Carver having been behind the fraud. What if he had been? What if their initial thoughts had been right and Carver had somehow persuaded Bowden to take the rap for the scam? Not with bribery, but blackmail? What if Carver had something on Bowden that he'd used to persuade him to agree to take the blame? It would have had to have been something big to convince him to spend four years of his life in prison. Then there had been Finn Bowden's discomfort at the mention of his father, followed by his mum's comment about Ray not being as innocent as people thought. The whole family dynamic there had felt strange, like they were performers acting out the role of a happy family when all the time it was just a pretence. There was a secret there, a secret which the family either knew about or strongly suspected.

Denning was right when he'd said the murder wasn't down to a random homeless assault. It was personal. Someone had deliberately sought out Ray Bowden and murdered him.

She googled the name Ray Bowden in the hope of finding something that they'd missed. They knew about the conviction for fraud, what if he'd served time for another crime that hadn't been flagged on the system?

The first lot of pages that came up concerned his murder and the ongoing investigation. Most of the news stories mentioned his conviction and some even went into detail about the trial. She jumped to later pages, but there was nothing that seemed especially relevant.

She typed in 'Ray Bowden and Carver Bowden Investments'. There were a couple of pages about the company itself. She scanned them, but there was nothing she didn't already know.

She couldn't see it, but she knew it had to be there somewhere. She looked up as she heard Denning enter the office. He was looking exasperated, clearly frustrated by the lack of progress.

'Any luck tracing the mystery man with the money?' he asked.

'Corey positively ID'd Carver from a couple of photos.'

'That's good, isn't it? It should be enough to bring him in for questioning.'

She sighed. 'To be honest, I don't even know if there was a man with any money.' She shook her head. 'I can't help thinking Corey is stringing me along – telling me what he thinks I want to hear.'

'Why? What's he got to gain from that?'

She didn't want to tell Denning about the cash she'd considered giving Corey, or the meals she'd bought him. Reason enough to keep her dangling on the end of a proverbial piece of string and make her look like a fool for admitting it. 'I don't know,' she said. 'It's just a feeling…'

'Let's be honest, it's not like we've got much to go on here. Any kind of break would be good.'

'You still think this is all connected to the fraud case?' She couldn't really see it herself. The fraud was years ago, and surely Bowden had already paid the price with a lengthy prison sentence and the loss of his marriage, home and reputation. But Denning was like a dog with a bone sometimes: if he got an idea in his head, it would take a JCB to shift it.

'There's something there. Bowden's death comes after several others died. I think he was killed to keep him quiet. I believe he knew something, maybe he knew who the real players were in the fraud case, and they're trying to save their own backsides.'

Then Denning was distracted by his phone ringing.

He lifted the phone and swiped to answer it. 'DI Denning?'

Molly could just about make out a young woman's voice on the other end of the line. Denning's face gave no indication as to who the other person might be.

When the voice on the other end of the line stopped speaking, he said: 'OK. When and where?'

A muffled response followed. Denning said: 'Sure. See you then,' then ended the call.

He slipped his phone back into his jacket pocket. 'That was Sophie Bowden. She wants to meet. Apparently there's something she wants to tell me.'

# Chapter Thirty-Three

Sophie Bowden wasn't at all what Denning had expected. Not moody and sulky like her brother, or spoilt like her mother. They'd agreed to meet on what she'd called 'neutral territory': a smart coffee shop not far from the Victoria and Albert Museum.

'Mum doesn't know I'm meeting you,' she said, sipping a caramel latte. 'Neither do Malcolm or Finn. And I'd rather they didn't find out. I wasn't due to come down until the weekend, but as soon as I found out about Dad, I had to come home.'

Denning had stuck with an Americano, which he sipped as she spoke. 'Anything you tell me is in the strictest confidence,' he said. 'But if you do have any information regarding your father's murder, or the incident with your mum, then you do need to let me know.'

She stuck a spoon into the tall latte glass and stirred. Denning was struck by how together she seemed. He knew she was in her final year at uni, and there was a noticeable confidence about her.

'Unfortunately, I can't tell you anything about my father's murder. I hadn't spoken to him for years. To be perfectly frank about it, we were never all that close. My dad seemed to prefer his sons. Well, to be more accurate, one of them.'

'Finn?' Denning guessed.

She shook her head. 'The other one. The one we were not supposed to know about.'

Denning paused, he thought about what Corey had said about Ray.

'Theo, or Leo?' he asked, trying to remember the name Corey had used.

'Leon,' Sophie corrected, with a smile. 'That's his name. I never met him, but I know Finn was in contact with him.'

'When was this?'

She shrugged. 'I don't know the exact date, but it was before Dad was sent to prison. I don't know what they talked about, apart from our shared father presumably. You would have to talk to Finn about that, though don't be surprised if he denies it. Finn likes to keep his secrets.'

She stopped stirring her latte, placed the spoon on the table and looked directly at Denning. 'But I don't want to talk about Finn. The reason I asked to meet you is because I think we all need to start being honest with each other.'

'That would be helpful.'

She threw him another half-smile. 'You're probably aware of the unusual background to our family. Dad trying to keep two different families happy. Well, it was never really a problem for us. Finn and I were both aware that something wasn't quite right when we were growing up. Mum had her work and then the gallery. She didn't seem too bothered about Dad being away a lot. As long as he paid the bills and we had a roof over our heads, she was happy to play along with the charade of happy families. But it meant that lies were normalised in our house. Dodging the truth in return for convenience almost became a way of life. And that never changed, even after Dad went to prison and Mum married Malcolm.

Even now, they present this façade to the world to pretend everything is fine.'

'Sophie, I don't doubt any of this has had an effect on you, but I'm investigating a murder.'

'I think someone has threatened Mum and Malcolm. They've been acting very cagey. I can't stop myself from worrying that whoever killed my dad could come after my mum next.'

'What makes you think they've been threatened?'

'I overheard her and Malcolm arguing the day I came back from uni. I don't think they realised I was there. Malcolm had received a phone call from someone, he wouldn't say who it was, but it freaked him out. He was arguing with the person on the phone, threatening to go to the police.'

'And you have no idea who he was talking to?'

'No. I assumed it was either a business contact or a client. Sometimes Malcolm…' She paused, shaping the words carefully in her brain before continuing. 'Sometimes Malcolm wasn't always as scrupulous with other people's money as he should have been.' She looked appealingly at Denning. 'What I just said is strictly off the record, by the way.'

Denning nodded. 'Go on. What happened after the phone call?'

'He told Mum she wasn't to go out, to stay away from the gallery and don't answer the door. When she asked him why, he refused to say at first, until he eventually admitted that she might be in danger.'

'In danger? Those were the exact words he used?'

'Yes. He wouldn't go into detail and Mum refused to take it seriously. She thought it was probably some crank trying to cause trouble after what happened to Dad.'

'A threat? You're certain?'

'No. But I can only tell you what I heard and what little they told me. Now I don't know if any of this will help you find my dad's killer. This may have nothing to do with anything. However, I do know Malcolm has made a few enemies over the years. He cuts corners and he's obsessed with money. And he's never been overly concerned about how he comes by it.'

Denning took another sip of his Americano then placed the cup back on the table. 'You're saying he's a criminal?'

'Criminal is rather a pejorative word. And it means different things to different people. To a serving police officer, anything that is in breach of the laws of the land makes one a criminal. But in a broader sense, crimes are often committed on a daily basis by perfectly ordinary people for the most banal of reasons. Parking in a disabled bay, for example, or fiddling the figures on your tax form.' She looked at Denning. 'Sorry, I've just finished a module in criminal psychology, specifically exploring society's perception of what's considered "acceptable" and "unacceptable" crimes.' She paused. 'Actually, I'm thinking about joining the police when I graduate.'

It was Denning's turn to smile. 'Based on one module?'

'I've also completed modules in forensic psychology and penology, as well as an optional module in comparative criminal justice. Trust me, it's more than a passing whim.'

He was impressed. His initial impression of Sophie Bowden being mature beyond her years was turning out to be pretty accurate. 'There are worse career options,' he said. He just managed to stop himself from adding that there were probably better ones too. She was young and keen. And bright. In theory, he should be doing everything he could to encourage her in her choice of career. 'Your degree would certainly give you an advantage.' Along with her unassailable self-confidence, he thought.

'Your degree must have helped you?' she said.

He looked puzzled. 'I'm sorry...?'

'I googled you before we met. I was intrigued. Someone with a social conscience catching criminals. It must make you something of a rarity in the Metropolitan Police?'

Denning thought about detectives like Dave Kinsella or McKenna. Or the rest of his team for that matter; detectives who had worked their way up through the ranks. Solid, reliable officers who were first and foremost team players who covered each other's backsides. But the Met was evolving. Fast-tracked graduates were the detectives of the future. The Dave Kinsellas and Liz McKennas of the world were dying out. 'The Met's changing,' he said. 'The idea of the jaded detective spending his lunch hours in the nearest pub exists only in nostalgic TV crime shows.'

Sophie smiled at him again and took another sip of her caramel latte. 'I apologise if I sounded flippant just then. I actually admire the way you took my dad's murder seriously. To a lot of people, he would have been nothing more than another homeless person whose death would have attracted little interest and even less sympathy.' She dropped her voice, and for a moment Denning could glimpse the vulnerable young woman behind the confident exterior. 'Despite our estrangement, he was still my dad. He was still a part of me, and I really hope you do manage to find his killer.'

'One last thing – this threat to your mother, do you have any idea what it could have been in connection with?'

'If I had to guess, I would have said it was some kind of warning.'

'A warning?'

'I think my stepfather may have become involved with something questionable and this was someone's way of making sure he kept the details to himself. But that's only my guess. It's unlikely he'll admit to any of this, especially if it's been spelled out to him that his family's life could be in danger.'

Denning thought about this. There was one person who would think nothing about threatening someone in such a way and who had a vested interest in keeping someone quiet. And he felt it was time he paid this person another visit.

He thanked Sophie, paid for their drinks and left, promising to keep her up to speed with the investigation.

# Chapter Thirty-Four

'Christmas. Have we decided what we're doing?' Denning asked Sarah.

She was sitting at the dining table, writing Christmas cards. A large glass of Cabernet Sauvignon beside her, half drunk. 'I haven't given it much thought,' she said. 'We said something about seeing my parents on Boxing Day, but I haven't really given Christmas Day any thought.' She took a sip of her wine. 'Besides, how do I know you won't be working?'

It was clearly half said in jest, but it was always a possibility. If a murder or other serious crime was recorded on their patch, they would at least have to put in an appearance.

But besides, Denning was still thinking about Sophie Bowden. He had been impressed by her honesty and her directness. That was assuming she was telling the truth. There was always the possibility she'd been playing him, driven by some intense dislike of her stepfather, and had seen this as an opportunity to drop him in the shit by making up a false story.

'I'll spend the morning with Jake and Claire,' Denning said, 'but the rest of the day will be ours.' It was the same every year since he and Sarah had got together: he always hoped she would organise things, while she was happy to leave everything to him. As a result, Christmas was usually something of a last-minute mad dash round the shops, or frantically ordering things online and then desperately hoping they'd arrive in time. Every year he promised he'd be better organised, and yet, somehow, it never seemed to happen. This year was no exception.

'We've got our office party next week,' Sarah said. 'I expect I'll be going on my own as usual.'

Denning sighed inwardly. They had this discussion every year, too. 'I don't want to make a promise I might not be able to keep,' he said. 'You know how things are at the moment.'

She made a sound he didn't quite catch but he could sense the sentiment behind it. Her concern at his absence was more down to embarrassment than anything else. People at work knew she was married, but they so rarely met her husband he suspected there might be some people at Bishop & Willetts who thought she'd invented him. Christmas was inevitably a flash point for them. It was a juggling act, trying to keep everyone happy. He would at some point have to arrange to see his own parents in the run-up to Christmas and organise some kind of drinks get-together for his team, but that all depended on how the investigation progressed.

Then, his mind kept returning to what Fiona Tanner and Brian Deacon had said, too. Neither seemed to think the deaths of their respective loved ones had been suspicious, at least not until he'd mentioned it. Perhaps McKenna was right and he was looking for things that weren't there…

He thought about Ray Bowden; life hadn't been fair to him. Betrayed by his family and his business partner, and reduced to living rough. What kind of Christmas would he have had? Or the others who had been living rough alongside him? Then there were people like Kane, Carver and the others who had done alright on the back of other people's misery. And they got away with it.

Perhaps the best way to deal with people like that was to hit them where it hurt. Go after their finances, find out where the metaphorical bodies were buried if the real ones couldn't be found. And perhaps the NCA would be his best opportunity to find those bodies.

Kane's threat was buzzing round inside his brain. The photo of the church. Kane would have known about it: it was all over the news at the time.

Denning looked over at Sarah, sipping her wine and putting any cards he was expected to countersign in a separate bundle to those that were for posting. For someone like Sarah, the thought of ending up homeless was something she could never be able to countenance, not seriously. She believed people were responsible for their own destinies and if life threw anything unpleasant at you, then it was down to you to find a way round it.

'What are you thinking?' she asked. 'You looked like you were miles away.'

'Have you heard of Carver Investments?' he asked. 'They're small time compared with the kind of funds you deal with, but I just wondered if they'd ever come up on your radar.'

She shrugged. 'Can't say I've heard of them. Why?'

'There was a big fraud a few years ago. Investors were conned into putting their money into a dodgy property scheme that never materialised. Carver Investments, or Carver Bowden as they were known at the time, were involved.'

'I could ask around if you like. Someone at work might have heard of them.'

He tried a different approach. 'How easy would it be for someone to organise something like that without their business partner knowing?'

She put her pen down and looked at him. 'The company would have to be registered with the financial regulation authorities, who would conduct routine audits, so whoever was planning something like that would need to be very careful. Or very clever.'

That was what had been bugging Denning. Ray Bowden was clearly an intelligent man, but according to Molly, Karen Higgins had described him as being an 'honest plodder'. Someone who liked to play it safe. Trying to outwit his investors, the financial regulators and his business partner would take a lot of mental juggling. Bowden just didn't strike him as the sort of person whose brain worked that way. 'But the business partner? He would have to have known something was amiss. Or at least had his suspicions?'

'Unless he was an idiot.' Sarah took another sip of her wine. 'It does happen though. If someone's clever enough at covering their tracks then it would be possible to pull the wool over the eyes of the people they worked with. But you'd be taking a huge risk.'

*A huge risk…* And what was it Molly Fisher had said about Bowden not being a natural risk taker?

## Chapter Thirty-Five

Molly hadn't seen Jon since the summer, when they'd agreed to keep their distance from each other. There was once the chance they could build a friendship on the back of their failed relationship, over time.

But things had changed. She was now certain she was being followed by someone. She hated using the word 'stalked'. She had worked on a stalking case a few years ago: a young woman who was being harassed by a former colleague she'd been friendly with. The ex-colleague had misinterpreted the friendship, seeing something that wasn't there, and had made her life a living hell for several months. It had been a difficult and emotionally challenging case. The ex-colleague wasn't nasty and had never explicitly threatened her; rather he'd turned out to be shy and socially awkward and had little experience with women. He'd been sentenced to eight months in prison. The victim had subsequently moved out of London fearing what would happen when he got out. Molly was determined she wasn't going to go down the same road.

The doorbell rang.

She took a deep breath and answered the door. She could feel her heart pounding in her chest. She hadn't even planned what she was going to say. Accuse him outright, or humour him and hear what he had to say.

'Hi Molly.' He had put on weight, though only a few pounds and being slightly over six foot and of a big build, he mostly seemed to carry it off. He'd grown a beard since she'd last seen him too, perhaps just because he couldn't be bothered shaving.

'I'm good, Jon. Thanks for coming.'

She showed him into the small living room. She'd only been living there for a few months and had yet to make the place feel like hers. The furniture came with the flat, and the dull daubs on the wall presumably belonged to the landlord.

'Nice place.' It was the first time he'd seen her new flat. It was almost clinically tidy, unlike his house in Crouch End, which had always had a 'lived-in' feel about it, and was permanently cluttered with his things. He thrived in mess, while she had learned to tolerate it. She had learned to tolerate a lot of things.

'Do you want something to drink?' she asked, quickly adding, 'I've got tea or coffee.' She didn't want to offer anything alcoholic. Not only might it throw out the wrong signals, but one beer or glass of wine could so easily lead to another, and Jon was so often unpredictable when he'd had a few.

'I'd love a cup of tea.'

She went into the kitchen to make some tea, returning a few minutes later with a pot and two mugs. She put the tray on the table. 'Do you still take sugar?' There was milk and sugar on the tray. Sometimes Jon would try and cut down on his sugar intake, but such resolutions rarely lasted.

He helped himself to milk and plopped two sugar cubes into his mug. Molly poured the tea.

So far, so civilised, she thought. How long could they keep it up for?

'How have you been?' he asked. 'How's work?'

She told him she was OK, and work was full on, as always. He told her he was doing alright, and had been given the offer of full-time work at the university where he was teaching. She knew it wasn't really what he wanted to do, but it was work, and it was in his chosen field of journalism, so at least the work interested him. 'Rowan was asking after you,' he said. 'I know she'd love to see you again.'

Rowan was Jon's daughter from his second marriage, or had it been his third? There were times when they'd been together that Molly had struggled to keep up with his complicated history of broken marriages and forgotten children. Admittedly, he'd matured in his later years, but she had never been able to shake off the fact that Jon had a track record for treating relationships a little too casually.

'Give her my best when you next see her.'

She drank some tea; despite the milk, it was still hot enough to slightly burn her lip. She knew they couldn't keep going with banal small talk all evening. If she was going to confront him then she might as well get it over and done with.

'Jon, there have been some odd things happening to me lately.' She paused and looked into her mug, contemplating another sip before deciding against it. 'Well, not odd, just... unsettling.'

'Unsettling? In what way?'

She struggled to find the right words. 'There was some graffiti on the front door the other night. It said "You're next".' The landlord had sent someone round to paint over it earlier that morning, all evidence now removed. In hindsight, perhaps she should have left it there. Now Jon and anyone else only had her word that it had ever been there. 'There have been a couple of silent phone calls,' she added. 'And someone's been following me. The other night, on the Tube. And then someone was watching the flat.'

'You think it was the same person?'

She couldn't be sure. She was now convinced the man at Bethnal Green Station the other night was nothing to do with any of this, but her brain was so fried with it all she couldn't be certain of anything anymore.

'I don't know. But taken together with what was written on the door…?'

'After what happened here, something like that is always going to attract ghouls…'

She cut him off. Naturally he knew about the murder and how it had made the news, but equally he knew something like that would never have bothered her. 'No, it's not the flat. It's…' She struggled to say it, to admit that she felt like a victim; the one thing she vowed she'd never be. 'I think someone's stalking me. And I think it's someone who knows me.'

She let the silence hang in the air until the penny slowly dropped.

'Me?' He made a great show of looking incredulous. 'Why the hell would I do something like that? Why would you even think that?'

She waited until his indignant outrage had passed, then continued. 'Like I said, I'm pretty certain it's someone who knows me. They know where I live, or at least it hasn't been too difficult for them to find it out. They know my phone number too.' She told him about the silent phone calls. 'And it feels like I'm being watched. In fact, I think they might even know where I work.'

'So, you think it has to be me? Not some nutter you've put away? Or someone from work who's got a grievance against you? You'd rather think I would stalk you? I mean, why, Molly? Why would I want to do something like that? I still care about you.'

'Perhaps that's why, Jon. Perhaps it's exactly because you still care about me.' She sighed. 'I've made it clear how I feel, but you've made it clear you want me back. In these kinds of situations, in a significant number of cases, it's down to someone the...' She just stopped herself from saying 'victim'. 'It's down to an ex-partner.' She'd researched it on the internet. She was familiar with the startling statistics: over 700,000 stalking and harassment offences in England and Wales in the past year; only five per cent of stalking cases resulted in a charge. Of the cases that did end up in court, the conviction rate for stalking offences was around sixty per cent. More than half of reported cases ended with the victims not supporting further action. A number of victims were subsequently killed by their stalker...

She accepted the man she'd seen watching her wasn't Jon, but could he have persuaded a friend to watch her for him? It sounded crazy, but not impossible to believe.

He was staring at her open-mouthed, the mug of tea in his raised hand, as though he'd been frozen in time. Had she done the wrong thing by confronting him? If it was him, then she was trapped here with him. There were people in the flat upstairs, but apart from the occasional 'hello' whenever they bumped into one another in the narrow communal hallway, she didn't know them. But she was being silly. Even if Jon was her stalker, did she really believe he would actually harm her?

'Molly, I can't believe you'd think...' He placed the mug of tea back on the table with a slight thud. 'Look, it's not me.' He reached out and touched her gently on the arm, just like he always used to do when they were together and he could tell she was upset. 'It isn't me. Which means it's someone else. Have you mentioned it to anyone at work?'

'I don't want to involve work.'

'But you're with the police. Surely they must have specialist teams who investigate this kind of thing.'

*This kind of thing*, she thought. Stalking. 'They do, but they're under-resourced and overburdened. I don't want to add to that.' She didn't want to say that it was mostly because part of her still refused to believe this was actually happening. Deep down, she was still willing to believe this was nothing more than her imagination picking up on something that wasn't there. But as the days went on, it was getting harder and harder to convince herself that was the case.

'You should at least mention this to Denning. OK, I know he can be a bit of a knob sometimes, but at least he could help. Or Betty Taggart. She might be more receptive to taking things further.'

Molly couldn't be sure Jon wasn't just putting on a convincing act. If he was stalking her then he was hardly likely to admit it without further prompting, but if he was trying his best to persuade her to make this official...

'I don't want to go to either Denning or McKenna with this. At least not yet.'

'What happens if things get worse? What if this nutter actually tries to harm you?'

She didn't have an answer to that. She was hoping she could successfully nip it in the bud before things got any worse. In a way, she'd been welcoming the distraction of a murder investigation to stop her from having to think too hard about the other things that were happening in her life.

'I don't know,' she said eventually.

Jon finished his tea and poured out another two mugs, adding milk to Molly's and milk and sugar to his. 'I think you should move back in.' She opened her mouth to argue: this was the absolute last thing she wanted. 'Just for a few weeks until this is sorted,' Jon said, cutting her off. 'Look, it's almost Christmas. Unless you have plans, we might as well spend it together – as friends, nothing more.'

She hadn't even given Christmas a thought. She could spend it with her mother and stepfather, though they often went abroad for Christmas and New Year, or splashed out on a cruise if they were feeling flush. 'I'm not sure, Jon...'

'What are the alternatives? Staying here on your own, jumping at every shadow? Spending it with Trudi and her bird in their pokey flat? Three of you squeezed in there like herring in a barrel?'

'Jon, I...'

He reached over and held her arm again, reassuringly. 'Don't say anything now. Just have a think about it. There's no agenda. You'd be helping me out. Rowan and Eli want to spend the day by themselves, so I'd be on my own otherwise. You know what I'm like – I don't want to spend the day brooding and overthinking stuff.'

Jon was no stranger to depression and sometimes there was a danger his gloomy moods might threaten to engulf him. And while Molly could see the appeal of taking him up on his offer, there was the risk of throwing him the wrong signs. She had made it clear she wanted space between them; moving back in, even if it was only temporary, was a backwards step. And then if Jon was the one who was stalking her, and if he was doing it to get her back, this was potentially playing into his hands.

She looked at him, smiling at her while holding her arm, tenderly like he used to do at the beginning, when things were still good between them.

'Can I think about it?' she said. Even though she had already made her mind up and was now just trying to find a way of letting him down gently. Already she was regretting asking him round tonight. She couldn't help feeling she had fallen into a carefully prepared trap.

# Chapter Thirty-Six

Sheila Gorton nodded at Denning as he passed under the inner police cordon and made his way towards her.

A member of the public had phoned it in around twenty minutes ago. They'd actually phoned for an ambulance but considering what was said during the 999 call, the police had attended the scene as a matter of course.

By the time Denning and Neeraj arrived, the alleyway had already been sealed off and a team of forensic officers was checking for evidence.

Corey was slumped roughly halfway along the narrow street. It was only a few metres from the squat, and it hadn't been established whether he'd been killed there, or elsewhere and had his body dragged there.

'Pierced his heart by the looks of it,' Gorton said gravely. 'He would have died quickly, if that's any consolation.'

Denning didn't reply.

'Do we know his name?' Gorton asked.

'According to DS Fisher, his name was Corey.'

Molly, having found Zella at the squat, had informed her what had happened to Corey.

Zella was talking to a uniformed officer. Denning asked Molly to speak to her and get some details, ideally a next of kin. He glanced over at Zella, who was now having an animated conversation with Molly. 'His friend might be able to help, though I doubt it.'

'I'll confirm the cause and approximate time of death as soon as I've completed the post-mortem.'

Denning was working through likely events in his head. Why would someone kill Corey? The obvious answer was that he knew more than he had admitted to about Ray Bowden's murder. But the only person he had spoken to at length about that was Molly, and even then he hadn't really told her much.

He could hear Zella and Molly arguing: voices carrying across the street. 'What's the problem?' he asked when he was close enough to try and calm the conversation down.

'She's to blame for this. It's all her fault,' Zella shouted, her face streaked with tears.

'I understand you're upset, but—'

'Her.' She jabbed a finger at Molly and then wiped a hand over her eyes. 'If she had left him alone like I told her to Corey wouldn't be dead.'

'You can't blame DS Fisher for what happened to Corey,' Denning said calmly. 'She was doing her job.'

'If she hadn't kept hassling him, he would still be alive. It's her fault. And it's your fault.' She spat at Denning and turned on her heel. Molly made to follow her.

He grabbed Molly's arm. 'Leave her for now, Molly. Let her calm down. She won't be going far. We can speak when she's had a chance to process what's happened.'

'I need to explain...' Molly began, but it was clear she didn't know what to say.

'It might be easier if I speak to her,' Denning said. 'You talk to Sheila Gorton. Try and find out what exactly happened.'

He approached Zella. She was standing by a wall smoking a roll-up. She glanced over when she saw him approaching and flicked ash onto the hard ground. 'What now?'

She looked at him defiantly.

'I need to find out who killed Corey. I think he was killed because he knew something about Ray Bowden's murder. Anything you can tell me will help us find his killer. And it will be in total confidence. You have my word.'

She smoked the rollie for a few seconds, thin plumes of smoke hanging in the icy air. 'Why should I trust you? You don't get it, do you? We were all fine until you lot came charging in, chucking us out of where we were living. That's when everything started going wrong for us.' She started to cry again. Despite the aggressive stance, he could sense that she was just a vulnerable teenager who was trying to make the best of what life had thrown at her. And she had just lost her friend, possibly her boyfriend. He imagined when you were struggling just to survive, you grabbed hold of those closest to you in order to try and stay afloat against the sweeping tide of despair that threatened to engulf you on a daily basis.

'Zella, I'm sorry about what happened to Corey. And I'm sorry you were moved on from the old station. I can't do anything about the latter, but I can do something about Corey. I can find the person responsible and bring them to justice. But only if you help me.'

She finished her cigarette and wiped another tear from her cheek. 'I think he was scared.'

'What about?'

'I don't know. I think someone was after him. He kept saying that he'd said too much to her. Fisher! He kept saying he should have kept his mouth shut.'

'Had someone threatened him?'

Zella nodded. 'I asked him what it was. He wouldn't tell me. He said it was nothing to worry about and it would sort itself out. But it didn't, did it?'

Denning was thinking. If someone had been threatening Corey, how would they have found him? Perhaps someone with good connections to the streets?

Someone like Alfie Kane.

# Chapter Thirty-Seven

Later that afternoon, Denning held another briefing. A greater sense of urgency was now taking over the investigation. Another murder meant things had shifted up a gear. A new feeling of momentum underpinned everything.

Molly looked at the whiteboard. Corey's photo was pinned next to Ray Bowden's. Two desperate people who had been thrown together and forced to survive against the odds. A chance connection made through mutual hardship that should have endured, but had ultimately ended up with both of them dead. Stabbed through the heart in the most callous of ways.

'Our victim is Corey Gates. As yet, we know very little about him, except for his name and the fact he was a member of the unhoused community. We don't have details for any next of kin. Obviously we need to identify them as a matter of urgency.'

'What could Zella tell us about him?' Molly asked. She was struggling with feelings of guilt. If she hadn't pressurised Corey into talking to them, when he clearly didn't want to, then there was a good chance that he might still be alive. She knew she had to put those feelings to one side. What mattered now was finding Corey's killer and, presumably, whoever had killed Bowden.

'She didn't tell me a whole lot… It might be useful for you to talk to Zella again.' Denning gave Molly a sympathetic smile.

'Really, boss?' Neeraj interjected. 'After what she said earlier?'

Denning shot Neeraj a filthy look, which silenced him immediately. Molly wondered what Zella had said about her, but could guess the gist of it: blaming her for Corey's death, just as she already blamed herself.

'I might not be the best person to speak to her,' Molly said. 'Maybe someone else might be better?' She looked over at Trudi, but Trudi was staring at a pile of notes on her desk.

'She knows you, Molly. OK, she's angry at the moment, lashing out at authority figures that she blames for what's happened. But she'll stop being angry and when she does, she's going to want to find out who killed Corey. Maybe even tell us who he is.'

'Assuming she knows,' Molly added. 'I get the impression they only use first names. Perhaps not even their real names.'

'It's all we've got to go on at the moment,' Denning said.

'We must have some serious suspects by now,' Kinsella said. 'I reckon the ex-business partner is worth another look.' He turned to Molly. 'Didn't you say this Corey bloke ID'd Carver from a couple of photos?'

'He couldn't be certain, but he seemed to think it was Carver who paid Bowden a visit just before he was killed,' Molly said.

'You didn't get him to sign a statement to that effect?' Denning asked.

She only wished she had. 'I think, given time, I could have persuaded him. As it was, he just wasn't up for it.'

'Zella seemed to think he was frightened by someone. We need to find out who that person was. There's a good chance it was Carver. Let's check him out further. Find out where he was when both men were killed. See if we can get anything that connects him to these murders.'

'There's something else,' Molly said. 'About that family. There's something they're not telling us.'

There was a heavy silence in the room and Molly realised they were waiting for her to elaborate on what she'd just said. The only problem was, she didn't know where she was going with it. It was really nothing more than a hunch.

'Go on,' Denning said after the silence had gone on for too long.

'I don't know,' she said. 'I mean, not exactly. There's just *something*. Something Bowden wanted to keep secret. I think he was being blackmailed.'

'Blackmailed? Who by?' Denning was staring at her now, encouraging her to finish what she'd started.

'Carver. Well, I assume Carver. It was just something Andrea Bowden said about Ray Bowden not being the person people thought he was. I think he was hiding something.'

'Maybe he'd committed other crimes,' Neeraj said. 'Ones we don't know about.'

'Like what?' Kinsella asked.

'How would I know,' Neeraj replied. 'I just said we don't know about them.'

Kinsella folded his arms across his chest and harrumphed. 'How would that be relevant to him being murdered?'

'If he refused to go on being blackmailed,' Molly said, 'perhaps he'd reached the point where he just didn't care anymore. If it had something to do with Carver, then maybe he felt he had nothing to lose by going public with the truth about what really happened over the property scam.'

'It all feels a bit tenuous,' Denning said. 'But taken along with what Sophie Bowden said about liars and there having been something suspicious surrounding Andrea's accident, it certainly won't do any harm to take a deeper look into the Bowden family. If they are hiding something, let's find out what it is. Carver, specifically. He claimed he knew nothing about the fraud because he'd been away from work recovering from an operation. Let's get this confirmed and find out exactly how long he was absent from the office for.'

'You think he's lying?' Molly asked.

'I don't think he's been entirely honest with us during this investigation. I reckon he knew more about what Bowden was up to than he claims. Let's find out what it is he's hiding. And, while we're at it, let's check out both his and Andrea Bowden's alibis for the night Ray Bowden was killed.'

'What about the property developer?' Trudi asked, checking her notes. 'Steven Hodge? He's certainly got a motive.'

'He wanted the homeless people out of his property,' Kinsella said, 'which is kind of understandable. But do we really think he resorted to murder to achieve that? It seems a bit extreme.'

'It's still a motive,' Trudi said. 'What if Corey got it wrong, and it was actually Hodge who was offering

Bowden the money? They're both of a similar age. If it was dark, it might have been difficult to recognise them.'

'Why target Bowden?' Neeraj asked.

'As one of the older people in the homeless community, maybe he thought he offered the best opportunity to persuade them to move out. When that didn't work, and Bowden threatened to expose him, he killed him. Corey was a witness.'

'Hodge's name is definitely in the mix,' Denning said. 'But right now, I think Carver has the greater motive. This isn't just about work, it's personal too – all the time Bowden was alive, he was a risk to Carver's life with Bowden's ex-wife. If it turns out Carver has a solid alibi for both nights in question, then we can rule him out. Until then, I'd say he remains our strongest suspect.' Denning turned to face the whiteboard. He underlined the words 'property investment fraud' in marker pen. 'I still think we need to look into the company a bit more. Find out any discrepancies in the accounts. According to Mrs Bowden, Carver managed to bail the company out after Bowden was sent down. Where did he get the money from?' He looked around the team. 'And let's look over any CCTV and possible witnesses to Corey's murder. At least then we might have something solid to work with.'

Molly looked down at her notepad. She realised she'd spent the past two or three minutes doodling, and her mind had started to wander. She was thinking about the fact she had let Corey down. Zella was right, if it hadn't been for her then there was a good chance Corey might still be alive.

She was suddenly aware of someone beside her and looked up to see Denning standing at her desk.

'I know what you're thinking. But there's no point in going down that route. You were following a lead in talking to Corey – doing your job. The only one responsible for his death is the killer.'

She nodded, touched by his reassurance. However, there was no denying the feelings that were running through her right now. 'I could have handled the situation better from the start. Instead of pursuing Corey, I could have explored other options. Corey felt like the low-hanging fruit. In reality, I'm not sure how much he actually knew about Bowden's murder and how much he made up for attention.'

'Hindsight is a wonderful thing, Molly. And it would make our job so much easier if we had it beforehand.'

It meant a lot to her to have Denning on her side, but even his words felt hollow. 'I've spoken to Karen Higgins again,' she said, changing the subject, beginning to feel uncomfortable at the direction the conversation was taking. 'It turns out Carver was back in the office for a couple of weeks, even though he said he was away for some time. So there's an inconsistency that needs to be followed up.'

'Right. Good. Carver's hiding something – let's find out what it is.'

## Chapter Thirty-Eight

Molly had agreed to meet Zella in the café on White-chapel Road where she and Trudi had taken Corey for lunch. Molly felt a pang of sympathy for Zella. Whatever the nature of her relationship with Corey, Zella had lost someone she cared about. She was facing up to this grief on her own, and that was a lot to ask of anyone, let alone someone as young as Zella. In fact, it was her youth that seemed to affect Molly the most. Someone that age should have parents, or at least some family members, looking out for them. All Zella had for emotional support had been Corey, and now he was dead.

The girl behind the counter gave Molly a wary look when she walked in, as though she sensed trouble would be following in her wake. Molly ordered a tea and a black coffee, paying the girl and telling her to keep the change. The girl sighed and told Molly to take a seat.

Zella looked like she'd been there for a while. A mug of stewed tea sat on the Formica-topped table in front of her while she stared out the window at the busy street.

'I just want to say I'm sorry, Zella. About Corey. He didn't deserve that. Neither of you deserved it.'

She could see from the redness around her eyes that Zella had been crying. She wondered how girls like Zella survived on the streets. Homelessness was brutal enough for anyone, but especially worse for women, who never escape the feeling of being vulnerable. Molly thought about her own situation: at least she had somewhere she could feel comparatively safe; a door she could close behind her at night.

'Thanks,' Zella said dryly. 'Your sympathy is noted.'

The girl from behind the counter placed their mugs on the table, taking away Zella's mug of stewed tea. 'Have you thought about what happens next?' Molly asked.

Zella wrinkled her face. 'What do you mean? With Corey? A funeral hopefully. If you can find his family. And good luck with that.'

'No. I don't mean that.' Molly sipped her coffee, trying not to grimace at the acrid taste. 'I meant you. Christmas isn't far away. Where will you go?'

'I'll jet off to my villa in the south of France.' Zella gave Molly a hard look. 'What the fuck do you think I'll do? I'll stay on at the squat until I get chucked out, and then find somewhere else to doss down and hope it's watertight. Do I look like I have a choice.'

Molly wanted to ask about her family, but what would be the point? Families weren't necessarily always what they were cracked up to be. And she should know that: her own family was about as dysfunctional as possible. She imagined Zella's family, if she even had one, wasn't somewhere she wanted to be. Not if sleeping in derelict buildings was a better alternative. 'There are charities that help out over Christmas,' she found herself saying. 'They offer shelter. At least you'd be somewhere warm and get something to eat.'

Zella just looked at her like she was talking fluent gibberish. 'They ask you a million questions and get social services involved. We did that once, me and Corey. We said we'd never do it again. They ask you questions about your family. Why you're homeless.'

Molly suspected most of the questions were asked out of concern rather than prying. 'It's your life, Zella. No one can make you do anything if you don't want to do it.'

Zella sipped her tea, clasping her hands around the mug to keep them warm. 'We had plans, me and Corey. Nothing special, just find a place together, get a job. He wanted to be a chef. He said we should open our own restaurant one day. He had dreams.' She placed the mug back on the table with a thud. 'But that's all they ever were. Dreams. Corey was a dreamer. He couldn't cope in the big bad world. He always seemed to be one of life's victims. If there was a dog turd on the pavement, then Corey was the one who would step in it.' She smiled when she spoke, their sparse shared happy memories rekindled.

'We will need to inform his family,' Molly said.

'They won't give a toss about him,' she replied. 'He hadn't had any contact with them for years. He said his mum was dead and his dad and his step-mum couldn't care less about him.'

'Even if they couldn't give a toss,' Molly said, 'they've still got a right to know.'

'He told me he came from Sheffield, or just outside it. His parents ran a pub. Until his mum died, then his dad sold it and moved in with his new wife. They'd been seeing each other before his mum died, or so he said. You could never be sure when Corey was telling you the truth or when he was spinning you a line. He liked talking shite, just to make himself seem more interesting.'

'Did he say what the pub was called?'

She shrugged. 'Something like "The Birds and the Bees". He said it had a stupid name. It was near a river.

He and his mates used to go fishing there after school. Until they got told off and his dad belted him.' She stared into her mug of tea, thinking. 'He said his gran used to be a local councillor.' Her eyes flashed at Molly. 'But like I said, Corey talked a lot of shite.'

Molly made a mental note to chase it up. If any of it was even halfway true it might give them a lead. A way of identifying the young lad now lying cold and dead in a mortuary.

'He must have had his watch on him,' Zella said suddenly. 'He said his dad gave it to him. Or his uncle. Anyway, he always wore it. He claimed it was worth a few quid. I used to tell him if it was worth anything, he should flog it, but he said he couldn't ever part with it. Silly sod.' Her mouth twitched into a smile at the memory.

'We can check,' Molly said. The post-mortem was due the next day. All his belongings would have been bagged and tagged. 'Would you like the watch? I imagine he'd like it to go to someone he cared about.'

Zella gave another shrug. 'To be honest with you, I reckon he nicked it. It was just suddenly there one day. He showed it off to me, but told me not to say anything to anyone.'

'Did Corey tell you anything else? Anything about the night Ray Bowden was killed? It's possible he saw or heard something that's in some way relevant.'

'Nah. Corey didn't always make a lot of sense at the best of times.'

Molly wondered at the unaddressed mental health issues that had seen Corey abandoned by his family and then ignored by a system that struggled to cope even when you approached them directly and asked for help. Unhoused and invisible, Corey would have stood little chance of getting the help he needed when he needed it most.

And then there was Zella… The girl was clearly bright. Bright enough to know when to keep her mouth shut perhaps…

'What about you, Zella? Did you see or hear anything?'

She shook her head. 'Even if I did, why would I tell you?'

'Because this isn't just about a random man who was murdered, Zella. This is about Corey. If you do know something, it's not going to help Corey if you keep it to yourself.'

She didn't answer for a moment. Then she said, 'I saw him arguing with someone. A couple of days before he was killed. I didn't get a good look at the bloke he was arguing with. I assumed it was just some random knob-head Corey was trying to blag some money off. Corey had a way of winding people up. None of us likes begging, but sometimes you ain't really got a choice.'

'Where was this?'

'Near the park. The one beside the old station. I was coming back from getting some food and I saw them. I couldn't hear what they were saying, but it looked like there was some serious shit going down between them.'

'The man he was arguing with – could you describe him?'

She shook her head. 'I didn't see his face. He had a hood up. He was tallish, slim, not skinny, just not big. He was wearing a dark jacket – scruffy, but not dirty. He had his hands in his pockets. I didn't really look, to be honest. It was raining. Well, more like sleet… I just wanted to get inside as quickly as I could.'

'Did you ask Corey about this?'

'He said I'd imagined it.'

'Had you seen this man before?'

Zella picked at a loose fingernail for a moment, worrying it until she decided she'd had enough. 'I dunno. There was something familiar about him, but the way he was dressed... You see a lot of guys like that, especially on the streets.'

'You think he was homeless?'

She returned her attention to her fingernail, then said: 'I think I maybe saw him in the station. At least someone dressed like him. I mean, the same jacket. Well, similar. Dark grey with a fur hood. Like a coat but not as long. But like Corey said before, people come and go all the time. You see someone one day, then you never set eyes on them again.'

'Thanks, Zella. That's a help.' Molly gave Zella her card. Corey arguing with another homeless man. It shouldn't be that strange, yet somehow Molly felt this was significant. 'Get in touch with me any time. If you want to know about Corey. Please just call me. And if you can think of anything else, again, please call me.'

When she left the café she was certain she saw Zella crying.

# Chapter Thirty-Nine

Denning pulled up outside the Bowden's smart house in Holland Park. He was certain Molly was right and the answers to Ray Bowden's murder lay somewhere inside those four walls.

'This isn't convenient,' Andrea Bowden said, glowering at Denning when she opened her front door. 'I'm just about to go out.'

'This is important, Mrs Bowden,' Denning said. 'I really do need to speak to you and your husband.'

Andrea Bowden sighed. Realising she probably had little choice in the matter, she let him in, then showed him into the elegant sitting room. At the end of the wide hallway, he could just make out Finn Bowden pottering around in the kitchen. Denning asked if he could join them.

'You really are wasting your time here, Inspector,' Andrea Bowden said, the indignation clear in her voice. 'We've been over this again and again. I have nothing further to add, and Finn hasn't seen his father for years.'

'I'd still like to speak to him,' Denning said. 'And what about Mr Carver? Is he here?'

'He's at work,' she said.

'On a Saturday?'

'When you run your own business, you don't always manage to keep to a nine-to-five schedule.'

Denning nodded. Sarah worked in finance and often worked weekends. 'That's no problem,' he said. 'I can speak to him at the office.'

Finn Bowden suddenly appeared in the doorway, looking sulky. He glanced over at his mother and then came into the room and sat on the arm of the sofa opposite Denning.

'Thanks, Finn,' Denning said. 'I appreciate you joining us.'

'He can't tell you any more than I can,' Andrea Bowden insisted. 'He barely remembers his father.'

'I don't think that's entirely true though, is it, Mrs Bowden? I think Finn's memory of his father isn't quite as distant as you think.' He looked at the lad, who was refusing to give him eye contact. 'The prison got back to me. They confirmed what you told me about Ray refusing all requests to visit him. However, they also informed me that about six months before he was released, he contacted Finn, asking to meet him. Finn refused to meet his father. In fact, Ray contacted you twice, and both times you turned him down.'

Before Finn had a chance to speak, Andrea jumped in. 'That was his choice. If Ray had made it clear he didn't want to see any of us when he first went into prison, then why should he expect us to see him when it suits him?'

'Because I think he wanted to explain to Finn the truth… I expect he wanted to come clean to Finn about something.'

'What exactly do you mean by that?' she asked.

'I think maybe you should tell me.' Denning sat back on the sofa making it clear he wasn't going to go anywhere until one of them finally told him the truth about the

Bowden/Carver family, and the secrets that lay at the heart of this.

'I don't know what you're getting at,' Andrea said. 'But I don't see how these questions are going to help you find Ray's killer.'

'Finn…?'

The lad finally looked up at Denning. 'His other family,' he said, throwing an apologetic look at his mother. 'There's little point in not telling him. He's a detective, he'll find out eventually.' He sighed, ignoring the angry look his mother was throwing at him. 'Dad had another woman. I think the old-fashioned word is mistress. But it wasn't like that. Well, not really. We knew he'd disappear from time to time. Spending time with her, although we didn't know that at the time. We thought he was working away. There were always excuses.'

'And you never suspected something was up?' Denning asked.

Finn looked over at his mother. 'Of course I suspected something was up,' Andrea Bowden said. 'I'm not an idiot. I suspected there was another woman.' Her face fell. 'We didn't know about the boy though.'

Both Finn and his mother fell silent, clearly uncomfortable talking about something private; dirty washing aired so very publicly. 'Boy?' Denning asked after a moment.

'Ray had a child with this other woman,' said Andrea. 'We didn't know about that until Malcolm told me. The whole sorry saga came out after the trial. Malcolm knew everything. He knew about this bloody woman, and about the brat. He said Ray was waiting until the children – our children – were old enough, and he was going to leave us for her and start a new life together.'

'Malcolm told you this?'

'Yes. He'd known about it for years. He never said how he found out – whether by accident or Ray had told him – but he'd agreed to keep it quiet. To protect me and the children, he said.'

But also, Denning thought to himself, to ensure he had a hold over Ray Bowden. 'We will need to speak to them,' Denning said. 'They'll need to be officially informed of his death.' The details were already out there; the news of Bowden's death had appeared on various news websites and were no doubt available on social media. But they would still need to speak to them formally.

'I don't have any contact details for them,' Andrea said.

'But you know her name?' Denning said.

There was a moment's pause before she spoke. 'Alison Harvey,' she said. The contempt for the 'other' woman clear in her voice. 'I believe she lives in Hammersmith, though I have no idea where.'

There was one more thing before he left. 'I realise this may seem like an impertinent question, but were you and Malcolm Carver seeing each other before Ray went to prison?'

'Certainly not! And yes, that is an impertinent question.'

But Denning sensed from her reaction that he might just have hit a raw nerve.

# Chapter Forty

Molly tied her scarf around her neck and pulled up her collar. She checked the address, and found it was off the main road. She wasn't sure what to expect when she walked up the short path to the front door. It was a modest-looking terraced house, approximately halfway down a street of similar looking houses.

'Mrs Harvey?' she asked when the door was opened by a middle-aged woman in a thick pullover and a pair of faded jeans.

'It's Miss Harvey, actually. How can I help you?'

Molly explained why she was there.

'Ray?' she asked. 'You'd better come in.'

The house was cosy; homely might have been the polite way to describe it. It reminded Molly of a slightly tidier version of Jon's house in Crouch End. The living room was cluttered: a stack of magazines neatly piled in one corner; a couple of opened novels on the coffee table, next to a cooling mug of coffee. A contented-looking spaniel wagged its tail in a dog basket next to an electric fire, which seemed to be the only source of heat in the room. Molly sat in a comfy, if slightly worn, armchair.

'Would you like something to drink?' Alison Harvey asked, spotting Molly looking at the mug of coffee. Molly, who was still twitching from the industrial-strength coffee she'd had at the café with Zella, politely declined.

'I have to inform you that Ray Bowden is dead,' she said. 'He was murdered.'

If Molly had been expecting Alison to become suddenly overcome with uncontrollable grief at the news, then she was going to be disappointed. Alison nodded to herself and then sighed. 'Do you know, I wish I could say this has come as a shock to me. I really wish I could.' She sighed again. 'I just knew something had happened to him.' She sighed. 'OK, maybe not murdered. I thought he might end up taking his own life one day.'

'You thought he was suicidal?'

'There was always something about him. Something fragile.' She blushed awkwardly. 'I imagine you know the background to our relationship?'

Denning had filled her in on the details. He'd uncovered the secret at the heart of the Bowden family. But if Molly was being honest, Alison was not what she'd been expecting. She'd assumed Alison would be younger and less… comfortable. 'Yes,' she said. 'I admit I don't know the details, and I don't really need to know. I know the two of you have a son together.'

'Leon.' Alison nodded at a framed photograph on a table near the window. A lad in his late teens – straight hair and Harry Potter-style glasses. At first glance he could have been mistaken for a younger, cleaner version of Corey. 'He died,' she said, a slight catch in her voice. 'About a year before Ray was arrested. A brain tumour.'

She remembered what Corey had said: *Leo… or Theo…* That was who Bowden had been thinking about. Corey had reminded him of his son. His other son. His *secret* son.

'I'm so sorry.'

Alison Harvey nodded. 'Ray was devastated. We both were.'

Molly quickly did the maths in her head. If their son was in his early twenties, then the affair had been going on for almost as long as Ray Bowden had been married to Andrea. It was beginning to look less like an affair and more like a full-on relationship.

'It couldn't have been easy for you,' Molly said. 'For either of you.'

'In a way it was harder for Ray. He had to keep so much of his grief hidden. Even when we were together, it was like he was trying hard to be strong, when all I really wanted was for him to share his grief with me.'

'While Leon was growing up,' Molly said, choosing her words carefully so as not to prise open an old wound, 'it must have been difficult to accept the situation. With Ray, I mean.'

She wasn't suggesting Alison had a strong motive for killing Ray Bowden, but it was a possibility she had to consider.

'Leon and I accepted the situation was what it was. I suspect Leon would have preferred it if we'd all lived together as a family, but he knew the score. His dad had another family and that was that.'

'Did he resent Ray's other family?'

She thought before she answered. 'Perhaps a little bit. It was never easy for him. Having a part-time father. But as I told him many times, some people don't have dads. At least he was there, even if it wasn't all the time.' Molly knew all about that. Her father had long since severed any ties with Molly and her brother, preferring instead to stay in Australia with his new wife and new children. Her stepfather had been more of a father to her, and even that was a far from perfect relationship.

'Ray was never happy with Andrea,' Alison continued. 'She was always criticising him. Nothing was ever good enough. Although they were comfortably off, they were never rich enough as far as she was concerned. She always had to keep up with her rich friends. The art gallery she ran was always draining money, but Ray let her have it as a hobby. And he was certain she was having a relationship with his business partner behind his back. She always denied it, naturally. And Ray could never prove it. He knew he could never leave her while the children were at school – she would have taken him for everything, including that big, posh house in Kensington. He was going to wait until they were at university. Sue her for divorce on the grounds of her affair with Malcolm Carver. But, of course, it never happened.'

Molly wondered if it ever would have happened. How often did men like Ray Bowden promise to leave their wives and families, but never did. It was always jam tomorrow. It struck her that Ray Bowden seemed to be happy to have his cake and eat it.

'Until Ray was arrested,' Molly said. 'And then everything came out?'

'Malcolm blackmailed Ray into taking the blame for the investment scam. Don't get me wrong, Ray knew all about it and was happy to go along with it. He thought it would be a quick and easy way of making money. Malcolm said he was going to disappear abroad with his share, making it look like he was the one behind it all. Ray thought this seemed like the perfect solution – get rid of Malcolm once and for all and a bit of money in his pocket, which would come in handy if the divorce from Andrea got messy.' She rubbed a hand over her face. 'At least, that was the plan. Predictably, it didn't turn out like that.'

No, thought Molly, it hadn't turned out like Ray Bowden had planned it. Perhaps Malcolm Carver had had his own plan, one that didn't involve him having to disappear abroad and spend the rest of his life looking over his shoulder. 'Malcolm Carver framed Ray? And he went along with it?'

Alison threw Molly a sad look. 'I think by then Ray just didn't care. After Leon died, it was like he'd had the stuffing knocked out of him.'

A situation Malcolm Carver took full advantage of. But did that give him a motive for murder?

'I'm sorry to bring this all up again. I appreciate it isn't easy for you.'

The other woman nodded but didn't say anything.

Molly thanked Alison for her help. 'I'll be in touch if there are any further questions, but hopefully that's it for now.'

She was about to leave the house when her phone rang. It was Denning. She swiped the call to answer. 'Boss...?'

'It's Andrea Bowden,' he said, a note of urgency in his voice. 'There's been an accident...'

# Chapter Forty-One

Denning met Neeraj at the entrance to Charing Cross Hospital. Neeraj had already established that Andrea Bowden was in a private room on the third floor. As they made their way up in the lift, he asked Neeraj to fill him in on what had happened.

'We got a call from uniform in West London,' he said, popping another mint into his mouth. 'They recognised her name. Apparently she stepped out into the path of an oncoming car – didn't see it until it was too late. Driver didn't stop.'

This must have happened only minutes after Denning had left her. Maybe if he hadn't delayed her... But there was no room for guilty feelings; the accident had happened, assuming it *was* an accident...

'Has it been picked up on CCTV yet?' Denning asked.

'Not yet. But we're hopeful we'll get a sighting.'

'A description of the driver...?'

Neeraj shook his head.

The lift doors opened with a ping. Denning showed his ID to the woman behind the desk, asking for directions to Andrea Bowden's room.

She was lying in bed flicking through a copy of *Hello*. She tossed the magazine onto the bed when she saw them. 'I really don't think I'm up to talking to the police,' she said. 'I gave a statement to someone when they were putting me into the ambulance. I really don't know what happened.'

'We won't stay for long,' Denning said, pulling up a chair beside the bed and indicating for Neeraj to do the same. 'We just need to ascertain whether or not this was an accident.'

Her face twisted into a vision of panic. 'What makes you think this wasn't an accident?'

'We have to ask,' Denning said, keeping his voice calm. 'Your ex-husband is murdered then a few days later you're the victim of a hit-and-run. Of course it could all be coincidence but we have to make sure it wasn't something more.'

'Why would someone want to kill me?' The panic in her face was now present in her voice. 'It was an accident, wasn't it?'

'The driver didn't stop,' Neeraj said.

'But…' She looked confused, like she couldn't understand what they were saying. 'But that's nonsense. Why would someone want to kill me? I've had nothing to do with Ray for years. Why would his killer come after me?'

It was a good question, and one that Denning couldn't answer just yet. 'Like I said, it may yet turn out to be a coincidence.' He tried to offer her a reassuring smile. 'Did you get a look at the driver?'

'No. Like I told the officer at the time, everything was a bit of a blur. I stepped out onto the road and the car just came out of nowhere. I was certain I'd looked before I stepped into the road, but…' She shook her head. 'I honestly can't remember. It all happened so quickly.' She panicked again. 'Has someone told Malcolm? He'll be worried?'

'I'm sure uniformed officers will have informed him, but I can check. There's nothing else you want to tell us about what happened? Nothing else strange happened recently?'

'You mean apart from my ex-husband being murdered?'

'I mean have you received any strange phone calls? Threats? Anything like that?'

She shook her head. 'No, of course not. I'd have informed you if I had.'

'What about Malcolm?'

'What about him?'

'Has he felt under threat recently? Or has anything happened to him?'

She put her hand to her mouth. 'Oh God, you have made sure he's alright, haven't you?'

'I told you – we'll speak to him. We'll make sure he's OK. Look, please try not to worry. This could all turn out to be nothing. Some kid going too fast, didn't see you until the last minute then panics and doesn't stop. Incidents like these are more common than you think.'

She relaxed slightly, partially reassured by Denning's words, but he wished he could believe what he was telling her. He couldn't help feeling that there were too many strange things happening to people who had been close to Ray Bowden, and that wasn't a coincidence.

He thanked her and promised to be in touch. Once they were back in the lift heading down to the entrance, Neeraj asked him, 'Do you really think it was an accident, boss?'

'I think we should ask for a uniformed officer to keep an eye on Andrea Bowden, for the next few days – just to be on the safe side.'

Molly spoke to the shopkeeper who was closest to where Andrea's alleged accident had happened. He hadn't seen anything, but he'd heard it. A car accelerating suddenly then a screech of brakes, a cry and a sickening thud.

He agreed to let Molly have any CCTV from the shop, though the coverage didn't extend much beyond the front of the shop. He unloaded the disk and handed it to her anyway.

She asked some more shopkeepers as well as a fast-food shop across the road and got a similar response in all of them: everything had happened so quickly that no one had had a chance to fully take it in until after Andrea had been hit by the car. Even the descriptions of the vehicle differed: someone saying they thought it was a BMW, someone else insisting it was an Audi. She cursed to herself. This was more than likely going to turn out to be another wild goose chase. She would put money on the incident being nothing more than an accident: Andrea Bowden momentarily distracted; not looking where she was going and she steps out into the path of an oncoming car; the driver panics and drives on.

There were at least a couple of CCTV cameras in the street: one at the end by the traffic lights, another overlooking a noisy pub by the T-junction. Both would have covered the stretch of road where the incident took place.

A part of her hoped she was right and this was an accident. Because if she was wrong, and whoever had killed Ray Bowden and Corey was now coming after other members of his family, then this whole shitshow was about to get even messier.

# Chapter Forty-Two

Denning was convinced that Andrea Bowden's hit-and-run was somehow connected to the two murders. 'I think we should be treating what happened to Andrea Bowden as attempted murder,' he said. 'Our priority is to find the driver,' Denning said. 'We're checking CCTV and have confirmed that the car was a black BMW. The number-plate matches that of a Vauxhall Astra that was stolen in Chiswick yesterday afternoon. The car hasn't been located yet, but we're looking for it.'

'This doesn't prove that the hit-and-run was deliberate,' Kinsella argued. 'A stolen car, joyriders. They're off their moronic faces on something, mow down some poor sucker in the street, then panic and abandon the car. It's a predictable course of action.' He sighed. 'We'll find the car dumped in the middle of Epping Forest before the week's out.'

Denning shook his head. 'I don't think so, Dave. Check out the CCTV footage. There's only one driver, and he's seen accelerating towards Andrea Bowden the moment she steps off the kerb. She was deliberately targeted.'

'Why?' Trudi asked. 'Assuming this is connected to the murders of Ray Bowden and Corey, what could Andrea Bowden have to do with it? Unless we're saying she was somehow involved with the property scam, which I can't see.'

'At the moment, Trudi, that would appear to be our best connection. Andrea Bowden's daughter believes her mother and stepfather recently received a threatening phone call. If she's right, then that would suggest someone is out to harm Andrea Bowden and Malcolm Carver. It's possible that someone is trying to get to Carver via his family.'

'If they're in danger, then shouldn't we issue an Osman Warning?' Molly suggested. 'That's a bit extreme,' Kinsella said. 'For a hit-and-run.'

'It might be worth suggesting it to Carver,' Denning said. 'Though he's currently sticking to the story this was an accident and that we're overreacting. There's an officer outside Andrea Bowden's hospital room and we've advised Carver and his family to be vigilant. Unfortunately, unless he agrees to comply with an Osman Warning, there's not much else we can do at present.' An Osman Warning was issued if it was felt there was a risk of death or serious harm against an individual. It was a route Denning was reluctant to go down unless it was absolutely necessary.

'If our killer is now targeting the family,' Trudi said, 'then there's a good chance Carver could be next.'

'We don't know for certain that Carver was involved in the fraud case,' Kinsella said. 'Where's the evidence?'

'I spoke to Alison Harvey,' Molly said. 'She seemed certain Carver was behind it, and I believed her. According to her Carver blackmailed Ray Bowden into taking the blame for the fraud.'

'That's a hell of a leap,' Kinsella said. 'Covering up for someone is one thing, but four years inside? It would be easier just to tell the missus and fess up.'

'Aren't you always telling us how marriage feels like a prison sentence for you, Dave?' Trudi chortled to herself while Kinsella rolled his eyes.

'I said there was no evidence linking Carver to the crime,' Denning said. 'That's not the same as saying he wasn't involved. If we work on the assumption that he was one of the men behind it, then what Molly's saying sounds credible.'

'I refer you to my previous point,' Kinsella said. 'Seven years inside. I can't see him agreeing to go along with that, no matter what hold Carver had over him.'

'But he didn't know he'd go down for seven years,' Molly argued. 'He pleaded innocent. Assuming he was actually innocent – at least in terms of having organised the fraud – then there was a very good chance he would have got off.'

'Or perhaps he thought he'd get a lighter sentence,' Neeraj said.

'Either way,' Trudi said, 'why go after Andrea Bowden? How was she involved?'

'I think she knows more than she's admitting to,' Molly said. 'It wouldn't surprise me if Carver and Andrea Bowden didn't deliberately set out to frame Ray Bowden to get him out of the way, then when he was eventually released, they have him killed to keep him quiet permanently.'

'And Corey?' Trudi asked.

'A possible witness?' Molly said. 'I'm not sure. Even if Corey had witnessed who had killed Bowden, there was very little chance of getting him to testify in court. Trying to persuade him to make any kind of formal statement wouldn't be easy.'

'Any luck trying to trace his next of kin?' Denning asked.

'I've not had a chance to chase up the local CID in Sheffield,' she said. 'But I'll get on to it as soon as we've finished the briefing. Though the scant details Zella gave me about his family background are unlikely to be of much help.'

'You know what?' Kinsella said, addressing the room with a wide sweep of his arm. 'I think we're missing something here.' He said 'we' but he was looking at Denning when he spoke, making it clear where he thought the blame really lay. 'The money that was alleged to have changed hands. This has to be significant. Until we find out what happened to it, we're in danger of barking up the wrong tree. Which brings me back to the drugs angle. That's what kicked this off in the first instance. Personally, I think that's the key to all this.'

'So, what about Andrea Bowden?' Trudi asked. 'How does she fit into your theory, Dave?'

'Like I said: wrong place and wrong time. Unless we know for certain it wasn't joyriders, then we can't go assuming anything. I reckon what happened to her has got nothing to do with any of this, and we shouldn't allow ourselves to be distracted by it. Let's look at what we already know...' He counted the facts off on his fingers. 'Our first two victims were stabbed. Drugs are found on the premises. We've got half a tale about money being offered to the first victim. Assuming that's true, how do we know he didn't take the cash? The only person to allegedly witness this transaction is also now dead. What if they split the money? We know they were pally. If you're living in a rat-infested hole, then any cash is going to come in handy.'

'Dave's got a point,' Neeraj said. 'And if he's right, then this girl Zella would be an obvious suspect. Why don't we bring her in?'

'I don't think Zella's responsible,' Molly said. 'I think Corey meant a lot to her. I can't see her doing it. She mentioned a man Corey was seen arguing with near the station a couple of days before he was killed. She could only give a vague description of the man. By the sounds of it, he was wearing a Parka jacket. And there was something about a watch that belonged to Corey. I need to speak to the pathologist as it seems to have gone missing.'

'She's only telling us about this now?' Denning said.

'I think it's something of a miracle she's even talking to us at all,' Molly said. 'I'm still not sure she trusts us.'

'OK,' Denning said. 'I think this man could be relevant. He's certainly worth talking to. Try and get some more details from Zella. Failing that, ask around for other witnesses and have another look over any CCTV from the area.'

'What about this watch?' Trudi asked.

Denning gave the subject some thought. 'I don't know. If he had something of any value, I can't believe he didn't try and sell it.'

'Is this watch even relevant?' Kinsella asked.

'We have to assume everything is relevant, Dave,' Denning said. He heard the phone on his desk ping with a voicemail message.

'Then how do we know this Zella girl didn't take the watch when she killed Corey?'

'You're barking up the wrong tree here, Dave,' Molly said. 'Zella isn't our killer.'

Her comment was met by silence from her colleagues.

'OK, Molly,' Denning said after a moment. 'You've spoken to her. You know her better than most of us. However, we have to put her name on the board. We can't rule her out entirely at this stage.'

He wrote her name on the whiteboard.

'How would she be connected to the Andrea Bowden incident?' Trudi asked.

'If we're working on Dave's assumption, then we would have to discount what happened to Andrea Bowden,' Denning said. 'But until we know otherwise, I'm going with the theory that these incidents are all linked. So let's find the driver and speak to them. If we can conclusively rule them out, then we start to look at the possibility this is about something else.'

Denning would have to run this past McKenna first. The two deaths, and now Andrea's hit-and-run, meant the case was now snowballing. At the very least he would ask her for an extension from the week that she gave him to solve the case. Even then, he wasn't feeling confident about solving it this side of Christmas – not unless they were to get a lucky break.

As soon as the briefing was over, he checked his phone. There was a message from Sophie Bowden. He rang her number and she answered immediately.

'Thanks for getting back to me. I'm not sure if I should be talking to you, but I think it's important. It's about Mum's accident...' There was a pause from the other end of the line, as though she was waiting for him to prompt her.

'Whatever it is, Sophie, it's better if you just tell me.'

'I walked in on them arguing in the hospital room the evening it happened. Malcolm said he had tried to warn Mum. After the threatening phone call that I mentioned

235

to you last time we spoke. Mum was furious. They stopped talking when they saw me standing there. When I asked them what was going on, they just said it was nothing for me to worry about. After Malcolm left, I asked Mum about it. She said Malcolm was being silly and overreacting. She kept on insisting it was an accident and hadn't been looking where she was going.'

'But you didn't believe her?'

'When I got home, I confronted Malcolm. He told me to mind my own business and then said a few choice words about Dad. I asked him about the phone call. He initially denied it, then said there were things it would be better I didn't know about. When I pressed him, insisting that if Mum or any of us were in danger, then we had a right to know, he told me it had been a warning. A warning to keep his mouth shut. He said if I spoke to the police they would go after Mum again. Then he stormed out. To the nearest wine bar, I imagine.'

'You've done the right thing, Sophie. We've got someone outside your mum's hospital ward and we can arrange protection for you and the rest of your family too, but you need to tell me who had threatened Malcolm. Was it a man called Alfie Kane?'

He wanted her to say yes – say yes and they would be able to nail Kane forever.

There was a heavy silence from the other end of the line. Eventually, Sophie spoke. 'I don't know. Malcolm wouldn't say. I just know that whoever it was, Malcolm was more scared of them than he was of the police.'

# Chapter Forty-Three

Denning pressed the intercom by the ornate metal gates and waited until he got an answer. The bored voice that grunted a response belonged to Stuart Braxton, the security-guard-cum-butler, who always went out of his way to make it clear Denning was as welcome as dog mess in a children's playpark.

'I'm afraid Mr Kane doesn't want to speak to you. He spelt it out last time you called round.'

But Denning wasn't going anywhere until he'd spoken to Kane.

'I'm here on police business,' Denning said. 'I can come back with a warrant if that's going to make things easier.'

There was a muttered response, most of which Denning couldn't hear, though he was sure the word 'fuck' was faintly audible. A couple of seconds later the gates swung open with an electronic buzz and he pulled up on the gravel driveway and parked the car beside the flashy Merc.

If it turned out that, as he suspected, Malcolm Carver had been behind the investment scam rather than Ray Bowden, then Carver would have been no more than a bit-part-player in the whole sorry saga. The main man behind it all was the person Denning was here to speak to.

He got out the car, marched up to the front door and rang the bell. From somewhere in the depth of the mansion he heard it chime.

The front door was opened by Braxton. His impassive face gave nothing away, but Denning could sense his very presence on his boss's property pissed him off. He'd run a PNC check on Braxton: he had previous for GBH and ABH. His last term inside had been six years ago, where he'd served half of a four-year sentence in Belmarsh for assaulting a man in a pub in Chelmsford. Since his release, he'd been in Kane's employ and apparently keeping on the right side of the law. For now at least.

'Is he here?'

Braxton stared impassively at Denning for a few moments, barely managing to conceal his animosity. If Alfie Kane was all that stood between Stuart Braxton and another spell inside, then his loyalty to his devious boss was as understandable as it was admirable. Eventually he stood aside to allow Denning into the expensive house.

Denning wondered which of the palatial property's many rooms Kane would be lurking in this time. The man led him to a vast living room where Kane was relaxing on one of the plush sofas. Kane and his butler-cum-security-guard exchanged a look when Denning was shown into the room.

He was led into what looked like a library. There were bookcases around three of the four walls, and a large billiard table in the centre of the room. Denning suspected the books in the bookcases were – as they used to say in smart shops – for display purposes only, but the billiards table looked like it saw regular use.

Kane was half sitting, half lying on a ruby-coloured leather Chesterfield, chatting to someone on his phone.

He looked up when Denning entered the room. 'OK, no problem,' he said into the phone. 'We'll speak later.' He ended the call and tossed the phone onto the sofa. 'Thanks, Stuart. If you want to give me and Mr Denning here a few minutes, then show him out.'

Braxton nodded, threw a glance at Denning then left the room.

Kane poured himself a whisky from a crystal decanter on an antique sideboard, added a splash of soda and sat back on the Chesterfield. There was no offer of a drink for Denning.

'I wish I could say it was nice to see you again, Mr Denning, but we both know I'd be lying.'

The only other chair in the room was a hard-backed seat that looked decidedly uncomfortable. As Denning didn't fancy joining Kane on the Chesterfield, he remained standing, with his back to the window.

'Andrea Bowden,' Denning said, coming straight to the point. 'I know you were responsible for her so-called accident. I know about the threats, and I can hazard a fairly accurate guess as to what lay behind it. You're worried Malcolm Carver is going to talk. Talk about your part in the investment scam that Ray Bowden was sent down for. And more too, perhaps. Which does raise the obvious question, what exactly is it you're trying to hide?'

Kane's brow creased. 'You're going to have to be a little more specific here I'm afraid. I haven't the foggiest what you're on about.'

'The scam you and Malcolm Carver orchestrated between you. You made sure everyone involved kept quiet. Either bought off, or if it looked like they were going to have a wobble and confess, then they were silenced. Adam Tanner, Keith Prideaux, Terry Benson,

Ray Bowden. And those are just the ones we know about. How many of them are dead, Kane?' Denning asked. 'Suicides, road accidents. Mystery disappearances?' Denning wanted to make Kane sweat. He wanted him to know that he was on to him. That no matter how well-polished the legitimate-businessman-act, Denning knew what he really was, and it was only a matter of time before he caught him out.

Kane shrugged and pulled an exaggerated face. 'I still haven't got a Scooby...'

'That's the clever thing about getting away with murder. Either you have no body, so it's harder to prove. Or you make it look like something else – accident or suicide, or whatever.'

'Oh, right. I'm with you now. You're still trying to link me to this fraud case that Ray Bowden was done for. Well, I'm terribly sorry, Mr Denning but, as I've already told you, I had nothing to do with that. And I wouldn't want to have to speak to that nice DCI McKenna about this continued harassment. I can't imagine she'd be too happy about it.'

Denning wondered what he meant by the mention of McKenna again. It was clearly a very pointed comment aimed at unnerving him, but why would a former criminal have the ear of a serving police officer, especially one as high-ranking as a DCI?

'I know you're behind this, Kane. I don't know how I can prove it, but I know you're responsible for those deaths.' Denning moved in closer, so he could smell Kane's expensive aftershave. 'And don't try threatening me again. Sending pictures to my phone. It's not clever and it isn't going to intimidate me.'

Kane pulled a face. 'It's OK, I understand. The strain of a murder investigation, even if the victim's only a homeless ex-con, it must get to you. You wanna try destressing. Christmas will be here before we know it. Try thinking about your family rather than work for a change. Christmas is the time for families after all.'

Denning struggled to fight the overwhelming urge to punch Kane's smug face. It would be the end of his career and he could kiss goodbye to any chance of joining the NCA. Instead, he lowered his voice and said, 'Your luck will run out sometime, Kane. And I'll be the one to make it happen.'

Kane just sat back on the sofa and smiled. 'I don't think DCI McKenna would appreciate one of her senior detectives harassing someone without any real evidence to back up the claims they were making.' He almost hissed the word 'evidence' to give it emphasis. 'I don't want to have to make this official, Denning, but I'm beginning to tire of these constant interruptions.'

Denning said, 'If you're responsible for what happened to Andrea Bowden, then who's to say you weren't behind the murder of Ray Bowden and Corey Gates too?'

'Unless you can prove any of this nonsense, I suggest you go away and stop bothering me. I really don't want to take this any further, but I'm beginning to feel that you're leaving me with no choice.'

'I don't scare easily, Kane. You can try and threaten me, but I'm not going to go away. I could arrest you here and now for the attack on Andrea Bowden and the murder of Ray Bowden.'

'Except you've got no evidence to back any of this up. And even if you could prove it, you wouldn't have a hope in hell of getting this nonsense anywhere near a court. And we both know that.'

Kane got up from the sofa. Denning was aware of Stuart standing in the doorway behind him. He was effectively trapped. If Kane or his goon wanted to turn nasty there was little he could realistically do to stop them.

Kane was now standing directly in front of him. 'You've led something of a charmed life, DI Denning. Facing down that nutter that took your wife and kid hostage. Being responsible for the death of Justin Morrow, and then your brush with psycho drug lord, Jason Hart. Until now, it seems like you've always had luck on your side. But, like most things in life, luck runs out eventually.'

Denning tried to appear calm. Nobody knew he was here. Yes, his mobile phone was switched on and was transmitting a signal, so eventually he could be traced to Kane's house. But by that time it might all be too late.

'I didn't kill Ray Bowden,' Kane said calmly. 'If I were you, I'd look more closely at his rotten family. That's where you'll find the answers to this. Now get the hell out of my life.' With that, he turned his back to Denning, and sat back on the sofa, indicating their impromptu meeting was over.

Denning felt a hand on his elbow as he was gently but firmly led back into the hallway and guided towards the front door.

## Chapter Forty-Four

Denning wasn't happy about being fobbed off. Within minutes of him pulling out of Kane's driveway, McKenna had texted insisting she wanted to speak to him. He could predict McKenna's reaction to his recent visit to Kane and he knew she would make her opinion clear. McKenna was in one of her formidable moods. Denning could sense it. She sat behind her desk looking at him like he was deliberately wasting her valuable time just for the sake of it. Despite this, he needed to get something off his chest.

'You were warned,' McKenna said as soon as he entered her office, not even giving him a chance to sit down. 'You were warned to stay away from Alfie Kane, but yet again you ignore what I tell you. You really are pushing your luck, Matt. If this goes further I can't promise I can cover your backside.'

'I've done some more digging, and from what I can find, the only two men who have done OK on the back of the fraud case are Kane and Carver. Everyone else who was believed to have been involved is dead or has disappeared. I think Kane is behind this whole thing. The incident with Andrea Bowden was a warning to make sure Carver keeps his mouth shut.'

He waited for her response. She sat there, fixing him with her infamous gimlet stare for a moment. 'You're going to have to drop this, Matt. I thought I made it clear to you – keep your nose clean and think about your future. Your petty obsession with Alfie Kane isn't doing you any favours. Kane has been rumoured to have been involved in just about everything from the assassination of JFK to the kidnapping of Shergar. If you're seriously suggesting we're going to find enough evidence to link him to the murder of a homeless ex-con, then you really don't understand how this job works. And I think that's going to do you a lot of harm if you want to progress in the Met.' She drummed her fingers on the desk. 'Politics, Matt. That's what matters in an organisation like the Met. One that is under constant scrutiny – from the government, from the media. From the public. And let's be honest here, from other forces. Did you know there are police forces in the country that hold the Metropolitan Police up as an example of what not to do? That's the game we're playing here. That's what you're up against if you're serious about sitting in this chair. And going after people like Kane, who is regarded very much as a pillar of the community, not to mention the fact he more than likely has got friends in high places, is going to unleash an entire barrelful of problems neither of us needs. Have you got that?'

'Kane's lying,' Denning said. 'He practically admitted he was behind what happened to Andrea Bowden.' He didn't mention how Kane had denied any involvement in the murders of Ray Bowden and Corey Gates. It was probably better just to let McKenna believe there was an obvious connection between the incidents.

She sat back on her chair watching him. '*Practically admitted* is not evidence we could put before the CPS, is it?' She exhaled heavily through her nose. 'And even if we could, this isn't our case. Andrea Bowden's accident, or non-accident, whatever we're going with, is now being handed by West London CID. Or at least I thought it was.'

'We can't ignore the obvious connection between Andrea Bowden being deliberately knocked down by a car and her husband's murder. The two things can't be coincidental.'

'Firstly, they can. And secondly, none of this proves Alfie Kane had involvement in either incident. There's, what, a tenuous suggestion he might have been behind the hit-and-run? OK, even if we accept that, it doesn't tie him in with Ray Bowden's murder. Andrea Bowden was hit by a car – Ray Bowden was stabbed through the heart. It's a totally different MO. For the final time, Matt – let this drop. Your obsession with Kane isn't doing your career any favours in the long term.'

He knew this was going to be a tough fight, but he had to go for it.

'Maybe the reason Kane's got away with it for so long is because no one has had the guts to really go after him. We could find the evidence if we looked hard enough for it.'

McKenna sighed. 'Look, Matt. I'm telling you now to forget about Kane. Leave Andrea Bowden to the regular CID. You can liaise with them if they think there's anything that looks like it might be relevant, but otherwise I need you to concentrate on finding the killer of Ray Bowden and Corey Gates. Have we made any progress since we last spoke?'

He filled her in on what they'd found out about Malcolm Carver and Bowden's secret family. The Bowden/Carver family secrets being laid bare.

'You think this could be relevant?'

The truth was, he didn't know. This murder invest-igation should have been so straight forward, yet it was turning out to be more slippery than he'd expected. 'It's one avenue we're exploring. It can't be a coincidence that Bowden's son died shortly before all this kicked off. I think he was, I don't know... out of his mind with grief... whatever. I think Malcolm Carver took advantage of the situation and used to it to frame him for the fraud.'

'What about Corey Gates? Are you certain the same person killed him?'

'The PM results have been emailed through. It's confirmed that they were both murdered by a single blow to the heart with a bladed instrument. It's looking like it's the same killer.'

McKenna gave this matter some thought. 'And you don't think we're missing the obvious here? Both our victims were homeless. This could very easily be someone deliberately targeting homeless people. In which case, there's a very real danger we've got a serial killer out there. Have you ruled that out?'

This was something Denning had considered, even before Corey's murder. Kinsella had brought it up at the first briefing. Only it didn't feel like that was the case. 'This feels like something personal,' he said. 'I think Ray Bowden was the intended victim and Corey was in the wrong place at the wrong time. Either that, or he knew something, or possibly witnessed something.'

McKenna looked like she wasn't entirely convinced. 'OK, if that's your gut feeling here, but I do think we should keep our options open. Even if this really does have something to do with the fraud case, NCA might be better suited to find the connections. Hand it over to the NCA. They've got the time and resources to look into this.'

'Even though there could very well be a connection between the fraud case and Bowden murder?'

'Until such time as we can get proof of that, we let it drop. We have to.'

He accepted that she had a point, but he was certain there was a link there somewhere. He just had to find it.

He thought very carefully about his next comment. There was always a danger of pushing McKenna too far, and he was perilously close to that point now. But he had to get something off his chest; something that had been bothering him for some time. 'What is it with you and Alfie Kane? You seem very keen to let him off the hook any time his name comes up in connection with anything.'

He waited for her reaction.

She gave an awkward laugh, a little too exaggerated to be fully convincing. 'That is nonsense. I know that if we do ever decide to go after someone like Alfie Kane we need to be one hundred per cent sure of our facts. We'll need strong evidence to nail him for anything, especially as he's made damn sure he's squeaky clean these days. The man is almost Teflon. He knows it and he knows we know it. It'll take bigger bastards than us to bring Alfie Kane down.'

'But it's more than that, though, isn't it.'

'What does that mean?'

He paused before he spoke, allowing the silence to sink in. 'Kane knew about our conversation. He knew what we'd discussed. Now, either he's bugged this office, or you and he have been chatting. About police matters.'

'Is that what he told you? He's bluffing.'

'Is he?'

For a brief second, she looked rattled, her composure slightly askew. He'd caught her on the back foot. 'Are you actually suggesting I discuss operational matters with a former gangster?'

'You tell me.'

She tried fixing him with the gimlet stare, but its intended power to diminish had worn thin over time. 'That's absurd. Any dealings I've had with Kane have been purely professional. You know that. I don't even know why we're having this conversation, Matt. It's not appropriate and it ends now.'

He thought about her. Thought about how she'd worked her way up the ladder through sheer grit and graft, earning herself the not entirely flattering nickname Betty Taggart along the way. The kind of journey someone like himself or Sophie Bowden couldn't possibly imagine. McKenna was tough because that was all she'd known. It was a different world, but it didn't excuse her possible association with a former criminal, who may potentially be linked to a murder. Before, there had been her connection to an undercover officer who had been discovered to have had links to a known drug dealer, which she'd kept quiet about. It had turned out to be entirely innocent, but it showed that there were a lot of things in her private life McKenna was happy to keep secret.

Kane's words had stuck in his head. He'd done his own research, pointed in the right direction by Steve Marsh. Denning said, 'Your ex-husband – he knew Kane. There were rumours he was involved in the Security Direct robbery. Even a possibility he was going to be investigated for alleged corruption for his involvement. The rumours were never substantiated because he retired from the force before anything could be taken further. But I've spoken to a couple of people who were around at the time. They reckon that if there had been an official inquiry, your ex wouldn't have been allowed to retire on a full pension. In fact, there was a good chance he could have ended up serving time for police corruption.'

He waited a moment for his words to take effect.

McKenna refused to give him eye contact, her gimlet stare now directed at the paperwork sitting on her desk.

She looked defeated.

After a moment, she spoke. 'What I'm about to tell you doesn't ever go beyond these four walls. There had always been suspicions that Kane was involved in the infamous Security Direct robbery. Nothing was ever proven, but a lot of people made a lot of money over that. My ex-husband was one of the officers who investigated that particular incident. The sums involved were colossal – millions. At least double what was reported in the press at the time. One of the reasons so many people got away with it is that many police officers were bought off. You have to understand, Matt, this was a different era. Corruption was more common than you might think. Police officers were underpaid and undervalued. A lot of them came from the same background as the criminals they were arresting. People like Alfie Kane knew that as long as they had a few tame coppers on the payroll, then blind eyes would be turned to certain crimes. Obviously nothing serious like murder – they weren't stupid. But money being taken from a warehouse. A lot of that money coming from dubious sources in the first place. A hefty insurance payout.'

'You're saying your ex was bought off by Kane.'

She didn't answer, but the look on her face told him all he needed to hear. He'd heard about McKenna's ex-husband: a big bear of a man who didn't suffer fools gladly. A bruiser. He'd retired to Spain some years back, long after he and McKenna had split up. Denning knew he'd had a reputation for cutting corners, but to have an accusation of corruption as good as confirmed by a senior officer was disconcerting to say the least.

'I'm saying Kane made him an offer that he foolishly accepted. He'd become so disillusioned with the job by this stage. Then our divorce. He wanted to get out and start afresh. Kane's money enabled him to do just that.' She looked apologetically at Denning. He'd never seen McKenna looking contrite before. Angry, impatient and often sarcastic, but never like she felt she had to apologise for anything. 'It was a different time, Matt. That doesn't excuse what he did, and he certainly wouldn't get away with that now. But it happened. He's left the Met and he's left me.'

'I still don't see why you're protecting him. This was years ago and the two of you are no longer together.'

'You don't understand. He's been unwell… He doesn't need the stress. His partner left him six months ago, and well, whatever else happened, we're still close. I still care about him. I hate myself for it, but it's how I feel. If any of this were to come out it would destroy him.'

Denning couldn't quite parse what he was hearing. Was she saying she wanted to get back with him? Retiring out to Spain – yes, he could understand that; this was something she'd often talked about, joking about how she would probably spend most of her time trying to dodge her ex. But things had obviously moved on. Now her retirement was imminent and her relationship with her ex wasn't quite as extinguished as she'd always implied. 'So this is why Kane is able to call in favours? One phone call to you and you get me to back off. If Kane goes down, he takes your ex, and quite possibly you, with him.'

'Kane would never willingly drop himself in it, but if he were ever backed into a corner, there's no knowing what he might start saying. Kane's first instinct is to protect himself.'

'So, we can't go after him. Even though he's clearly involved in this up to his neck.'

'Not the murders,' she said. 'I believe he's very likely involved in the attack on Andrea Bowden – that's his way of making sure Malcolm Carver keeps his mouth shut about any possible involvement in the property scam. But I honestly don't think he's behind the murders of Ray Bowden or Corey Gates. That's just not his style.'

'What about the others who were rumoured to have been involved in the property scam? Adam Tanner and the rest? How do we know he wasn't involved with what happened to them?'

'Nothing happened to them, Matt. It was either an accident or suicide or nothing at all. There's no conspiracy. And even if there were, there's nothing to suggest Kane was in any way involved. You have to let that drop.'

He was beginning to come to that conclusion, albeit reluctantly. They were still looking at a distinct lack of evidence, and without support from above it was going to be hard to find any. And as DCI, McKenna had ultimate responsibility for what happened with this case. She had made her views clear: Kane was off limits. If he wanted to pursue that angle, he would have to go over her head.

Was that something he really wanted to do?

He tried to put the thought out of his head, for the time being at least it would have to simmer on the back-burner. Any action involving Alfie Kane would have to be handled with great care.

# Chapter Forty-Five

Molly felt like she was pissing into a hurricane for all the progress she was making.

According to the phone call to the pathologist, there was no watch, expensive or otherwise, found on Corey's body.

It was possible the watch had been stolen. But who could have had the opportunity? The paramedics and police who attended Corey's murder? The CSIs? The pathologist's office…?

It all seemed unlikely.

There was also the possibility Zella had lied about the watch. But why would she lie?

It niggled away at Molly. Zella had been so insistent about the watch. Someone had given it to Corey and he'd treasured it. But she couldn't think why anyone would have taken it.

Corey's family had finally been traced in Sheffield. The pub she named had been demolished about seven years ago, but Corey's dad and stepmother – the previous land-lords – had been easy enough to trace. Zella had been right about him not giving a damn about Corey. According to the officer who had spoken to them, his family seemed more relieved than upset. Corey Gates had led a short and troubled life. Whilst he had never actually been in trouble with the police, he'd had a few near misses. It seemed he'd fallen in with the wrong crowd at an early age, skipping school, staying out late and doing drugs. After his mother's death, his father had struggled to look after him; endless arguments had ensued, culminating in Corey being asked to leave the family home. He was sixteen at the time. The inevitable drift to London had quickly exposed the reality of life in an anonymous city: the streets really weren't paved with gold.

Molly had read the emailed report from Sheffield CID with a heavy heart. Corey's life story wasn't so totally different from her own: an awkward relationship with parents, pressurised into leaving home at an early age, drifting without direction. Her life had been saved by joining the police. She wasn't sure where she'd be now if she hadn't made that decision.

Corey, it seemed, hadn't be so lucky.

At her request, the family had been asked about the missing watch. However, it seemed they knew nothing about it.

She checked her phone again. There had been no further anonymous phone calls since she had spoken to Jon the other night. It could be a coincidence, but she couldn't help thinking she'd resolved that particular thorny problem by creating another one. Jon had got her back in his life, which was exactly what he'd wanted all along. She hadn't had time to think about her plans for Christmas, but she was pretty certain they weren't going to involve her ex-boyfriend.

The subject of relationships made her think about Alison Harvey. It was amazing how two people could have totally different opinions on the same person. When she'd been talking about Ray, it was with warmth and affection. Andrea Bowden and Malcolm Carver could barely conceal their dislike of the man. Had Andrea known about his secret life all along, despite claiming otherwise?

Molly felt there were still unanswered questions here, and the best person to try and answer them was Alison herself. She checked her watch. It was time to pay her another a call.

–

Alison was in the kitchen this time, making soup. Molly sat at the cluttered kitchen table sipping a mug of herbal tea. It tasted of blackberry and something else... mint, possibly...

She'd told Alison about Andrea Bowden being knocked down and almost killed by a car, and was surprised to find a note of sympathy in her response.

'I've never borne Andrea any malice,' she said, chopping some carrots and adding them to the large pot that was bubbling away on the stove. The kitchen was untidy, but clean: bits of things cluttering worksurfaces, and shelves full of jars and containers. 'We both loved Ray in our own ways.' She wiped her hands on a tea towel, then turned to face Molly. 'Do you think the accident is suspicious?'

'I can't really comment on procedural matters,' Molly said. 'But we think there may be a connection between that and Ray's murder.'

'Of course. I wasn't prying.'

She sipped her tea. Alison had a mug of tea beside her on the worktop, which she was mostly ignoring. 'I really wanted to ask you about Leon,' Molly said. 'Well, to be more specific, his relationship with his dad. How did they get on?'

'Like I said the other day, fine.' Alison turned the heat down under the pot. 'For the most part anyway.'

'Really?'

She sighed and sat down opposite Molly. 'When he was young, he got on fine with his dad – he just accepted the situation for being what it was. It wasn't like he didn't have a dad, and plenty of friends at school had parents who were divorced and rarely if ever saw their fathers. It was only when he reached his teenage years that things started to change. He wanted to have his father in his life more. Perhaps it was understandable. It was the only time Leon and I argued, really.'

'Go on.'

'He told me I should find someone else. He said Ray was never going to leave his other family for me and I was being a fool for sticking with him and thinking he would. OK, he didn't exactly use the word "fool" but you get the gist.'

'So he resented Ray for the way he treated you?'

'It wasn't like that. Not really. He resented the situation, I suppose. The fact his father had two other children that had him more or less full time. At least, that was how Leon saw it.'

'The two of you fell out?'

Alison gave a dry laugh. 'I wouldn't say we fell out. Leon and I were always close and it would take a lot for us to have seriously fallen out. It was more a case of Leon venting his frustration at the situation. He was a teenager and he was testing boundaries, I suppose. And that was more about how the situation affected me rather than him. He felt Ray was being unfair to me.'

'Did Leon ever meet his half-siblings? He must have been curious about them.'

'Not as far as I know. Obviously he knew about them, but I don't think he was all that interested.'

'He must have resented them?'

She shook her head. 'Leon wasn't like that. He under-stood the situation. He knew he had to share his father with another family. He was cool with it all. That was his exact word – "cool".'

'Except when the two of you argued?'

'That was different.'

'Was he angry?'

There was a pause before she answered. 'No. Not angry exactly.' She sighed, stood up and stirred the soup, then sat back down at the kitchen table. 'Leon was going through a difficult time. He was lashing out, as all teenagers do. But if you're asking, "Did he hate his father?", then no, he didn't. He wasn't that kind of person.'

'What about Ray? He must have been devasted by Leon's death. Did you notice any changes in his behaviour afterwards?'

Alison stared into her mug of tea for a moment before answering. 'Ray blamed himself for a while. He seemed to think that if he'd left Andrea and moved in with us, then it wouldn't have happened. I told him that was a ridiculous thing to believe. Then he blamed himself for being a bad parent. To be honest with you, we were both in such a mess at the time. I needed Ray to be there and help me through it, but equally I didn't want him around. In the end I found it easier to cope on my own. I suppose I pushed Ray away. It was shortly after that he was arrested and it all came out about the fraud.'

'And you never tried to visit him when he was in prison?'

'I wrote to him, asking him why he'd done it. He just said he was sorry about everything that had happened, said we'd all be better off without him. He finished the letter by saying he didn't want to see any of us – either me or Andrea and his other children. I wrote another letter after that but he never replied. That was it. The next time I heard about Ray was when I was told he was dead.'

'I'm sorry,' Molly said. 'In spite of everything, it must have come as an awful shock for you.'

A sad look washed over Alison. 'Maybe if I'd tried harder. Insisted on visiting him when he was in prison, or not pushed him away when Leon died. Perhaps things might have been different.'

'You can't change what happened. And it was Ray's decision to cut himself off from his family. Both of them.' Molly couldn't stop thinking about Ray Bowden's closeness to Corey. It wasn't, as Kinsella had hinted, anything sordid; he was simply looking out for someone who reminded him of his own son. A son he clearly wished he'd spent more time with in his formative years.

# Chapter Forty-Six

Malcolm Carver wasn't happy to see Denning. The thunderous look on his face, combined with the heavy sigh that greeted Denning when Carver had opened his front door, told Denning his presence was not welcome.

'If you hadn't been harassing my wife none of this would have happened,' he said. 'She was obviously distracted when she was hit by that car.' He knocked back what looked like a large gin and tonic. 'That's all she's been able to talk about for the past week – Ray's bloody murder. It's not like they were still married for Christ's sake!'

As soon as he'd paused for breath, Denning jumped in. 'I'm sorry you feel this has been harassment, but we are investigating a murder. Two murders, which are more than likely related. We have reason to believe that there's a good chance what happened to your wife is somehow connected to the ongoing investigation into Ray Bowden's death. I think, maybe, you should sit down, Mr Carver, and start telling me the truth.'

Carver had dismissed the idea of an Osman Warning almost as soon as Denning had suggested it. He saw no reason why he should be in any danger, sticking to his claim the incident involving his wife was an accident and had nothing to do with Ray Bowden's murder.

He looked indignantly at Denning and went to take another sip of his G&T before realising his glass was empty. Grumbling to himself, he marched over to the drinks tray on the sideboard and poured himself another generous helping of gin, to which he added a token splash of tonic.

'I've told you everything I know. Andrea has told you everything *she* knows, which is very little. You've even spoken to our children. You still don't seem to have a clue who killed Ray, and yet you seem to think my wife's accident has something to do with it. When are you going to actually start making some sodding progress in this investigation?'

It was a question Denning had been asking himself for some time. 'The best way we can make progress here is if you start being honest with me.'

Carver shot Denning a filthy look. He stared at the gin and tonic in his cut-crystal glass, whirled it around a bit and took another sip. 'I'm being honest. I've told you what I know.'

'When was the last time you saw Ray Bowden?' Denning asked.

'I told you – I haven't seen him since before he was sent down, over five years ago. Why would I want to see him? He nearly destroyed my company, and left Andrea and the kids high and dry. Frankly, I wanted nothing more to do with him.'

'So you didn't visit him at the former Shoreditch station site a few days before he was killed and offer him a large sum of money?'

'Of course I didn't.' Carver's indignation was reaching a peak now. He was eyeing the drinks tray on the sideboard, clearly tempted to go up for a refill. 'Whoever told you that is lying.'

'We have a witness who claims they saw a man fitting your description talking to Ray Bowden and offering him what looked like an envelope full of money. We're currently checking through any CCTV in the surrounding streets from the day in question. We may also need to examine your mobile phone to see if it was in the vicinity at the time.'

'You're wasting your time, Inspector. I had nothing to do with Ray's death. And you won't find anything that proves I did.'

Denning tried a different direction. 'OK, Mr Carver. Another question to which I'd like an honest answer: have you been threatened by Alfie Kane?'

The slight twitch Carver's left eye gave told Denning what he needed to know. But Carver was determined not to make it too easy for him. 'I've never heard of him,' he said quickly.

'What if I were to say he's heard of you?' Denning was taking a punt here. He only had the most circumstantial of evidence to link the two of them, but if the mention of Kane's name was enough to rattle Carver, then it was a card worth playing.

'Lots of people have heard of me, Denning. Not least because of all the negative publicity that stemmed from the bloody court case my former business partner dragged me into.'

'Alfie Kane's name came up in connection with the investment fraud for which Ray Bowden was convicted.'

'No one ever mentioned his name to me at the time. And I repeat: I've never heard of him.'

'But you have been threatened? A phone call shortly before Andrea was hit by that car? Someone phoned you and threatened you to keep quiet, presumably about the fraud and the names of the others who were involved.'

Carver gave a dry chuckle. 'Sophie telling tales. My stepdaughter has a great imagination, but I'm afraid she's got entirely the wrong end of the stick.'

Denning wanted to push things further, but he was reluctant to make things difficult for Sophie at home. This family was already damaged enough without him adding to their toxic dynamic. But he was running out of options. He could arrest Carver, formally question him and demand he tells them about Kane. Possibly offer immunity from prosecution, that was assuming Carver wasn't their killer. But that would take time and manpower, and there was no guarantee Carver would tell them anything, especially with a good brief covering his back. He decided on a different approach. 'What about Adam Tanner, Keith Prideaux or Terry Benson? Do you recognise any of these names?'

Carver knocked back more of his G&T. 'I've never heard of any of them. This is all nonsense, Denning. You're wasting time asking me all these dumbass questions. You should be out there trying to find out who nearly killed my wife.' His eyes narrowed as he looked at Denning. 'You know, it's almost like you couldn't care less about what happened to Andrea. All you're interested in is this obsession with Ray bloody Bowden and that damned fraud case. I think you need a wake-up call. Round up those bloody homeless losers Ray was shacked up with. One of them killed him. That's where I'd be looking if I were you.'

'Thanks for the advice, Mr Carver,' Denning said with a smile. 'In the meantime, if you do suddenly remember anything about Alfie Kane and threatening phone calls, or decide that you did actually visit Ray Bowden just before he was murdered, then please do give me a call.'

As Denning left the house, he could sense Malcolm Carver's stare burning into his back.

# Chapter Forty-Seven

Ever since Molly had texted Jon to let him know she wouldn't be spending Christmas with him after all, she had the unsettling feeling that her problems were about to start up again. She didn't have to wait long.

Another strange phone call, no message and from an unknown number. There was someone there, she was certain of that, but they wouldn't speak. Just like before, after a few moments whoever it was hung up. She also had the feeling someone had been outside her flat when she left for work that morning. There were a couple of plant pots in the scrap of frosted lawn that passed for a front garden. One of them had been knocked over, a trail of earth scattered across the path. It was possible a cat or a fox could have done it, but it felt deliberate. The pot had been next to the living room window. If she'd had more time she would have spoken to her neighbours, asked if any of them had seen anything.

She'd decided she would mention it to Denning; not in any official capacity, just tell him what had been happening and hear what he had to say. A rational and objective mind might help her see things more clearly. In the meantime, she'd focus on work. If nothing else it would serve as a welcome distraction.

She'd already checked the Register of Births and Deaths to confirm Leon Harvey had died when Alison claimed he had. Of course Alison had been telling the truth. She had struck Molly as an honest, *decent* person, not the sort to invent stories about her child dying. Molly had only been poking at a vague theory: if Leon was still alive he might have a motive for wanting Ray Bowden dead. Despite Alison's words about him being 'cool' with the situation, Molly suspected there had more than likely been some brooding resentment there. The older Leon had got, the more he would have realised his father was clearly someone who wanted to have his cake and eat it, as her grandmother would have said.

But Leon Harvey was dead. As was his father, and Corey.

They were going to have to look elsewhere for the answers.

She watched Denning enter the office. He looked glum faced. This was proving a tricky, twisty case. There was a good chance Denning was regretting throwing everything they had at it.

Denning was a good detective, if sometimes blinkered. He had a strong sense of right and wrong, which wasn't necessarily a bad thing for a police officer, but it did mean he tended to overlook the grey areas that often accompanied a murder investigation.

She got on well with Denning. She wouldn't have gone as far as to say they had a friendship, but he was – as Jon had pointed out – her line manager, and she felt she had to talk to someone about her problems.

'Have you got a minute?' she asked once he was sitting at his desk.

He glanced at the clock on his screen. 'Yes, sure. Grab a chair.'

Denning's desk was at the front of the office, slightly separate from the others, meaning their conversation wouldn't be overheard. She grabbed a chair from one of the empty desks next to Denning's and wheeled it over.

'What's on your mind?'

She wasn't sure how to start the conversation. Perhaps it was best just to jump straight in. 'I don't want to make things official just yet,' she said. 'But I think there's someone after me.'

'After you?' He looked confused. 'In what way?'

'Harassing me.'

'Have you been threatened?'

'No, not threatened. Not exactly.' She was beginning to regret telling him what could still be nothing. Sharing her paranoia with a senior officer only made it feel worse. 'I've had a feeling someone's been following me. Watching me… I can't explain it.'

'Someone involved in the recent murders?' Denning asked.

'No. Well, I don't think so. In fact, I'm certain it's not connected to that. The first one happened before Ray Bowden was murdered, so I don't think there is a connection.'

Denning looked even more puzzled. 'The first one?'

'Phone call.' She felt embarrassed. 'I've been receiving silent phone calls. They come at random times. Evenings usually. There's someone there but they don't speak or leave a message.'

'How many times has this happened?'

She rubbed her hand over her forehead. She felt awkward bringing this up; uncomfortable at discussing her private life with a colleague. But it wasn't like that. This was impacting on her professional life too now, and that made it his responsibility as her superior officer. 'Three,' she said. 'Well, four actually. Always the same. I'm certain there's someone there but they never speak.'

'How many people have your number?'

'Well, it's on my business card, so anyone I've handed it out to.'

Denning appeared to be thinking over what she was telling him, weighing up whether or not she was expecting him to take things further. 'But you're certain this has nothing to do with the case? This couldn't be someone like Zella trying to get in touch but getting cold feet at the last moment?'

'I did think that might be a possibility, but like I said, this first call happened before Ray Bowden was murdered.'

'OK... Is there someone you've upset recently?'

'No. I don't think this is someone I've upset, Matt. I think it could be someone I've arrested or somebody close to someone I've arrested. I'm worried. Whoever it is knows where I live.'

Denning looked at her sympathetically, but she got the impression he wasn't taking it very seriously, or at least not as seriously as she would have liked. 'Have you mentioned any of this to DCI McKenna?'

She looked over at their boss's office. 'I don't really want to bother McKenna with this. At least, not yet.'

'Then I'm not sure what to suggest.' He smiled at her, but she could tell by the look on his face that his mind was elsewhere. 'Maybe you could move back in with Trudi and Charys for a while. Or have a word with your ex?'

She didn't like to say that neither option was ideal: Trudi and Charys had only just got their flat back to themselves after she'd moved out, and bringing Jon into things had only served to add further complications to an already complicated situation.

Despite having been no help, she thanked him and returned to her desk.

*Was* she being paranoid? It wasn't as if she had received any actual threats? But as much as she wanted to put the whole thing out of her mind, she couldn't. If Denning was too preoccupied to help, and she certainly didn't want to approach Betty Taggart with this, then it was up to her to sort it out. She would confront her stalker head on. She was a police officer so she was trained in how to deal with difficult situations and potentially dangerous people. The only problem was that the situations and people she usually dealt with didn't directly involve her.

## Chapter Forty-Eight

Denning glanced over at Molly Fisher's desk. He felt bad that he hadn't been able to offer her much beyond bland reassurances regarding what she'd told him. It was obvious from the tone in her voice that she was worried, with a real fear that she was being stalked. He *should* have been able to handle his colleagues better: be a sympathetic ear as well as a motivator. He'd always told them he was there for them to talk to any time they wanted to share something. That was the sign of a good manager.

But the truth was he was currently too absorbed in his own problems. McKenna's words were still ringing in his head. The Metropolitan Police was such a thorny place to work right now. McKenna was right when she said it was all about politics if you wanted to progress, and he wasn't sure he did want to progress. The more he thought about it, the more the prospect of joining the NCA appealed.

It was a fairly straightforward application form. He could easily get a couple of solid references, and Steve Marsh would put in a good word for him.

Meanwhile, Andrea Bowden's 'accident' was raising more questions than answers at the moment. There was still no trace of the mystery BMW, let alone any indication of who was driving it. But if his theory was right, then the person who was ultimately responsible would have made sure any evidence had been well and truly destroyed. It was likely the driver of the car was out the country now and would never be located. People like Alfie Kane didn't leave loose ends.

Then there was the matter of the threats: Malcolm Carver had been threatened, with the incident with Andrea Bowden proof that Kane wasn't bluffing. And could what was happening to Molly be somehow linked to Kane, too? It seemed unlikely. Would Kane even know who Molly Fisher was?

There were so many things about this case that didn't make sense.

He glanced over at Molly Fisher's desk again. It was clear he hadn't handled the situation as well as he could have. His gut feeling told him he should hand this over to McKenna, but that would be nothing more than passing the buck. He probably knew Molly Fisher better than their DCI did, and besides, if he did apply for the DCI's job, then he was going to have to come to terms with every aspect of staff management, even the trickier ones.

'Sorry,' he said. 'I didn't handle that well.' He pulled a chair over and sat beside her. 'I've been so focussed on our current investigation, I'm not thinking clearly. Obviously, this is serious. You were right to talk to me about it.'

She smiled at him, which made him feel worse. 'Forget about it. I shouldn't have put you in an awkward situation by mentioning it. I suppose I just wanted a bit of advice really.' She sighed. 'The biggest problem is that I just don't want to see myself as a victim. I've tried hard to put this whole ordeal out of my mind, but it keeps coming back to the same thing: I don't feel safe. And I don't like that – I should be able to look after myself.'

'Our professional lives are never a good barometer for our personal ones. The job is about other people

– where we can be objective and impersonal. In fact, the job calls for it most of the time. But when it comes to our lives away from the job, it's almost impossible to be objective.' He looked at his hands, trying not to feel uncomfortable. 'You should report this, make it official. Your local CID will have someone with specialist knowledge. They can access CCTV, ask for witnesses. If you were followed on the train, they can ask the British Transport Police for CCTV footage. It should be easy to identify this individual. In the meantime, to put your mind at ease we can arrange to have a panic button installed in your flat.'

Denning knew Molly well enough to know this would probably make her feel like a victim, something she would be determined to avoid. But sometimes pragmatism had to take priority over pride.

'OK,' she said. 'Let me think about it.' There was a pause before her next question. 'I was wondering… Anna Klein… Have you heard from her recently?'

'Anna?' He couldn't keep the surprise from his voice. 'You don't think she's got something to do with this?' He had to admit, the same thought had occurred to him, but that wasn't Anna's style: she would have confronted Molly directly, thrown half-baked accusations at her and demanded they thrash it out together. 'I mean I could speak to her, but I don't think Anna's behind this.'

'No.' She didn't sound convinced. 'In a way, I hoped it might be her. At least then we could sort things out. I can understand why she would hate me…' She trailed off.

Denning could sense the guilt she seemed to be carrying around with her, and all for just doing her job well: Corey's death and Anna Klein's disciplinary hearing.

Neither of which were her fault. 'Make it official. I'll support you. You can have time off if you need it.'

'Thanks. That's good to know.'

# Chapter Forty-Nine

Molly had decided to speak to Steven Hodge again. The mystery of the drugs raid had bothered her. She'd spoken to someone she knew who worked in regular CID to get some further background on the raid and the reasons for it. The tip-off had been anonymous, that much she already knew, but why would the police take an anonymous tip-off so seriously. There would have had to have been something more for them to have taken action.

Hodge was the most likely person to have manipulated this. According to her CID contact, it turned out he had a friend who knew the Deputy Assistant Commissioner. He also had a strong motive for wanting the squatters out of the station building. It had been assumed Corey was right and it was Malcolm Carver who had offered Ray Bowden the money. Perhaps it had been Hodge in an attempt to persuade Bowden to pressure the squatters to move.

'DS Fisher.' Hodge offered Molly his hand. 'Would you like something to drink?'

She declined and followed him into his office. They sat on a smart leather sofa with an impressive view beyond the window. 'How can I help you?' he asked.

'It's about the squatters in the old Shoreditch station,' she said.

'I have already spoken to someone about that,' Hodge said calmly. 'A DI Denning, I believe.'

'These are just some follow-up questions.'

'Fire away. It's not like I've got anything to hide.' He smiled at her. While it should have felt reassuring it actually felt disconcerting.

'How often did you visit the station both prior to purchasing it and after the sale was completed?'

He made a great effort of having to think about this. 'Oh, about two or three occasions. There were no squatters there when I first viewed the site, which would have been around eighteen months ago. Immediately prior to the completion date I arranged for a team of surveyors to check the place over. That was when I discovered there had been a break-in. I checked the place over and contacted the police.'

'What happened then?'

'To be honest, the police weren't much use. They said I would need to apply for a court order to have them forcefully evicted.'

'And did you see or speak to Ray Bowden at that point?'

He looked confused. 'No. Why would I? I didn't know he was there.'

'So you didn't offer him money to try and persuade the squatters to move out?'

'No. I didn't speak to Ray Bowden. I didn't speak to any of them. Look, I'm not sure where you're going with this line of questioning, but I can assure you I did not kill Ray Bowden or anyone else.'

'What about the drugs, Mr Hodge? Did you plant them? Or pay someone to do it?'

His voice raised half an octave. 'No. I'm starting to think I should have my lawyer present while you make these baseless accusations.'

'If you feel you need a lawyer, then by all means call one. At this stage all I'm trying to do is ascertain your involvement in what happened.' She wanted to shout at him; tell him that the building he owned had been home to some people. It may not have been perfect but it was somewhere they felt safe.

'I'm very sorry about what happened. But these people were occupying my property illegally. They had no right to be there, either legally or morally. And if that's all, then I really have to get back to work.'

'That's all for now, Mr Hodge. I'll be in touch if there are any further questions.'

She was about to leave when she heard the door to the outer office open and a voice that sounded familiar spoke to Hodge's secretary. A moment later there was a knock on Hodge's office door.

She was slightly taken aback to discover Finn Bowden standing there, looking as shocked to see her as she was to see him.

# Chapter Fifty

Claire had sent Denning a message saying she wanted to talk. He could sense this was going to turn out to be one of those protracted conversations that would inevitably culminate in some kind of argument. He was tired and still smarting from his bruising encounter with McKenna and not in the mood for another confrontation, but if this concerned Jake then it was important.

He pulled up outside the house in Surrey Quays. There was another car parked outside: a new Toyota. Denning pulled up behind and it and got out of the car. It was already dark, with flecks of snow fluttering in the air.

He rang the doorbell and waited. Claire opened the door and let him in. There was a smartly dressed man in the living room, helping Jake to decorate the Christmas tree. He turned to look at Denning. 'Hi, Matt. How's it going.' It was George, Claire's new partner. He smiled when he saw Denning.

Denning smiled back. 'Good, George. Busy with work, but otherwise all is well.'

He hadn't banked on George being here, and was slightly taken aback to see him getting on so well with Jake. 'Hello, Little Fella,' he said, reaching out to hug Jake.

His son looked up at him, a momentary wrinkle of confusion on his face at seeing his daddy in the same room as the man he would soon be calling his stepdaddy. A second later recognition switched in and he ran towards Denning with his arms outstretched, giving his daddy a big hug. 'Will you be here on Christmas?' he asked. 'Uncle George has bought us a Christmas tree. A proper one. Do you like it?'

Claire usually hauled the ancient artificial tree down from the attic every year as she hated the mess a real tree made, but this year she'd bought a real Nordmann fir. Already it had thick glittering snakes of tinsel draped around it, along with a new set of lights that twinkled cheerily on the tree.

Denning looked over at Claire, who was now standing next to George; a picture of unity that said 'this is how it's going to be from now on'.

'Yes, Little Fella.' Denning rubbed his son's head in an affectionate gesture. 'I'll be here on Christmas morning. And, yes, I like the tree.'

Jake gave a little cheer then returned to his decorating.

'Maybe we should talk in the kitchen,' Claire said.

They sat round the kitchen table. Claire had made a cafetiere of coffee, and poured the contents into three mugs.

'Jake would love to see you on Christmas morning,' George said, making clear the invitation was for only part of the day. This suited Denning as he wanted to spend as much time with Sarah as possible over Christmas. It was the one time they could actually spend a bit of decent time together without work getting in the way.

'Well, he's my son. Naturally I want to see him on Christmas Day.' Denning liked George. Or rather, he couldn't find a good enough reason to actively dislike him. However, Jake was his son and not George's; something he felt inclined to remind everyone of whenever possible.

Claire finished pouring the coffees and sat down. 'That isn't why we asked you here, Matt. Though obviously you're still very welcome at Christmas.'

Denning wasn't sure why he had been asked by both of them. Had things moved on so far in their relationship that Claire was now thinking in terms of 'we' rather than just herself? 'OK…?'

'George and I are buying a place together,' she said, looking at her new partner. 'He's already put his flat in Islington on the market and I've had a couple of estate agents round to value this place. Naturally I wouldn't take matters any further until I'd spoken to you.'

'Selling?' They'd bought the house together shortly after he'd been promoted to detective sergeant nearly ten years ago. Claire had been expecting Jake at the time and they wanted a house with a garden. When they'd split up they'd both agreed that Claire and Jake would stay on in the house to give Jake continuity and stability. He thought about his son playing in the next room, unaware decisions were being made about his future.

'Both the agents I spoke to reckoned we'd get a good price for this place. It's a very desirable area. Of course, I'd split any profit with you.'

'What about Jake?' Denning asked. 'This is his home.'

She looked at George. 'Wherever we move to, we'll make sure Jake is happy first. But it would be nice to move somewhere with a bigger garden. Maybe even out of London and into the countryside.'

'The further out of London you go,' George added, 'the more you get for your money.'

'We wouldn't be moving far,' Claire added. 'You would still be able to see Jake as you do now.'

Denning sipped his coffee. He didn't know what to say. It felt very much like a done deal. In many ways it made sense for them to move. Despite paying half the mortgage, the house hadn't felt like his for a long time. Freeing up the monthly commitment would give him and Sarah greater flexibility when it came to buying their own place. But it felt like he was severing further ties with the past. 'When were you thinking about moving?'

Claire was still looking at George, as though she felt like they should be talking as one. 'I thought we could put the house on the market in the New Year. There's no point doing it now as it's a dead time of the year for selling, and we wouldn't want people traipsing through here at Christmas.'

What she said made sense. There was little point in arguing against this. 'OK,' Denning said. 'Just let me know what I have to sign.'

# Chapter Fifty-One

Molly was surprised to get a phone call from Joanne Owen. Joanne's daughter, Bex, had been Molly's best friend at school. She hadn't spoken to or even seen Joanne for over a decade. Not since the court case.

Molly had been in a bad place at the time: her mental health was suffering and the anti-depressants her GP had prescribed seemed to be doing her more harm than good. Joanne Owen had been in an even worse state. Even when the guilty verdict was read out she had barely reacted, knowing that a prison sentence would never bring her daughter back.

'I'm actually Joanne Brooks now,' she told Molly as she stirred her caramel latte and tried not to look awkward. 'I remarried a few years back. I needed a fresh start and everything about my old life reminded me of Bex.' She stopped stirring her coffee and looked up at Molly. 'So I left Phil, moved out of the old house in Finsbury Park and got a job in another school. It was very cathartic.' She smiled as she spoke, but the empty look in her eyes told another story to the one she was currently sharing with Molly: a truer one. No matter how much you tried to run away from the horrible events in your life, they somehow found a way of tracking you down and living rent-free in your head forever. Years of therapy had helped Molly reach that realisation, and even then she felt like she was only able to deal with what had happened by blocking out the finer details. For while Joanne Brooks only had to live with the pain of her daughter's murder, Molly had had to live with the guilt too.

'How is Phil?' she asked, partially by way of conversation, but also because she genuinely wondered how her murdered best friend's dad was. He was having to live with the pain of what happened too. Perhaps he hadn't been as ready to move on as Joanne had.

'He's OK, from what I hear. Remarried too, so I gather, though it didn't work out.' She offered another watery smile. 'And you... joined the police, your mum told me. She and your stepdad must be proud. I often wonder what Bex would have ended up doing for a job. Hairdresser, or something like that. Course, she always wanted to be a model, but then her head was in the clouds most of the time. My old mum always said she was a flibbertigibbet...'

Molly didn't realise her mum was still in touch with Joanne, but then they hadn't spoken much in recent years.

She could tell that Joanne wanted to talk about Bex: bring her out into the open and remember her as a person and not as a murder victim. Someone real with dreams and hopes and a zest for life. A life that was cut short before it had much of a chance to get going.

'We got the guy,' Molly said. There had been two of them: depraved monsters working as a pair, murdering women for some kind of sadistic pleasure. One of them, Anthony Ferguson, dubbed the Bermondsey Ripper by the press, had been arrested shortly after Bex's murder. Initially, they assumed he'd been working alone and, as the MO fitted Bex's murder, he'd been found guilty of killing her along with the others. Only Ferguson hadn't been responsible. His accomplice, Daniel Placzek, had killed Bex and had got away with it for over a decade, reinventing himself and changing his name. Justice had finally caught up with him just over a year ago, thanks in no small part to Molly's determination. 'He's serving a thirty-year sentence in Whitemoor. Even if he does ever get parole, he'll be an old man by the time he gets out.'

'I read about that,' Joanne said. 'I did think about attending the court case, but what would be the point? We already lived through one when that other bastard went down. I don't know if I had the heart to sit through another one.'

Molly nodded her agreement. They sat in silence for a while, drinking their coffees. Molly wasn't sure why Joanne had got in touch after all these years. When Daniel Placzek had been arrested last year, Molly had thought about contacting Joanne and Phil and telling them, but she wasn't sure how they would react hearing from her after such a long time of no communication. But she imagined Joanne had a reason for getting in touch now.

'It's Tom,' Joanne said after a moment. 'I'm worried about him. I was wondering if you'd heard from him?'

Molly shook her head. She hadn't seen or spoken to Bex's brother for years. She didn't even remember seeing him at court during Ferguson's trial. Of course, she'd been so out of it that it was entirely possible he'd been there and she'd just never noticed. 'No,' she said. 'Is everything alright?'

Joanne stirred her latte again, then said, 'He hasn't been well. He was discharged from the army a couple of months ago, and, well, things haven't been easy for him. He's been staying with me – he and his father had a big falling out years back and they don't speak – but I could never turn my back on him.'

'What happened?'

'I don't know. Not exactly. Something happened in the army. He'd been in the Middle East – Afghanistan – and I think it just all got too much for him.' She lifted her latte to her lips, but placed the tumbler back on the table without taking a sip. 'It's just he's become obsessed with what happened to Bex. He keeps talking about her… going over what happened. I thought he might want to talk to you about it. I mean, you were Bex's closest friend…' She let the rest of the sentence hang in mid-air, knowing how the friendship ended, and why.

'I haven't heard from him,' Molly said, and the truth was, she didn't expect to hear from him, even assuming he knew how to get in touch with her. She had never really got to know Tom when he was around. He'd joined the army when they were still in sixth form, and had always been a bit too laddish for Molly. Bex had never been especially close to her brother as far as Molly was aware, but it was hard to tell with families. Molly would never have said she was all that close to her own brother, but when he'd found himself in trouble not very long ago, she'd tried her best to help him.

'I'm just worried that he might do something stupid,' Joanne said. 'He's never been right since Bex died.'

Molly thought about Tom. He was always slightly odd as a teenager. Maybe *odd* wasn't the right word. He had struck Molly as being something of a lost soul when she knew him: always trying a bit too hard to fit in. Perhaps the army had been the best place for him. Perhaps he'd changed and was now more comfortable in his own skin.

Right now, however, he was low down on her list of concerns.

She told Joanne she'd let her know if Tom did get in touch. She felt a pang of sympathy for Joanne. Life had dealt her the cruellest of blows when Bex had been killed and now she was in danger of possibly losing her son too.

# Chapter Fifty-Two

Molly wasn't sure if she was doing the right thing. The problem wasn't going to go away on its own, no matter how much she wanted it to. Denning had been about as much use as she'd expected him to be, if she was being honest with herself. But she had to talk to someone about it, and now that she was certain Jon wasn't involved, he seemed the obvious person to turn to.

After the silent phone calls had resumed, she'd persuaded herself she now had to start being more proactive. She would take direct action: confront the person who was stalking her. Find out who they were and front it out. A face-to-face meeting. She would listen to what they had to say. Ask them why they were doing what they were doing.

She knew this was the only way to end the nightmare situation she had found herself in, through no fault of her own. She knew all about victim blaming and guilt and having to live with consequences. But she also knew that hiding from a problem never made it go away.

Jon was now sitting opposite her, sipping an Americano and shaking his head. Perhaps unsurprisingly, he didn't agree with her. He thought she was taking an unnecessary risk, but she'd persuaded him that she was going to do this. She needed closure. She needed to draw a line under this whole sorry saga and move on. She did and her stalker did.

'You should tell Denning about this,' Jon said. 'He needs to know what you're planning.'

They'd agreed to meet on neutral territory. Well, it was almost neutral. Babushka had been their favourite coffee shop all the time they'd been together. Sunday mornings would be spent sitting in the window seats browsing the papers and people-watching. Sometimes breakfast would stretch itself into lunch. Easy, lazy days that were now behind them.

'I've already mentioned this to Denning. Well, not what I'm going to do, but he's got the backstory. He wanted me to talk to McKenna.'

Jon placed his cup back in the saucer. 'Maybe that's not such a bad idea. She's senior and she's a woman. She might take this whole thing more seriously.'

Molly doubted Betty Taggart would give any more shits than Denning had. She could sense their DCI was winding down before her upcoming retirement, counting the days until the gold clock came her way. Though to be fair, she probably wouldn't have given too much of a toss even if she wasn't on the brink of leaving the job for good. When it came to work issues, McKenna was totally behind her team: she had your back and you knew it. She'd fight your corner no matter what. But when it came to personal matters, she tended to hide behind formality. You left your personal life at the door when you came into work every day and the job instantly became your focus.

'I don't want to involve McKenna,' she said. 'I don't really want to involve you. I just need someone to be, well – I suppose I need someone to be around in case I've called this wrong and it all goes tits up.'

'Then let me confront them. I'll speak to them. I won't hurt them, I promise.'

'I don't want that, Jon. I want you to stay in the background. Don't make your presence known, unless I need help. In which case...' She didn't know. She still wasn't convinced she was doing the right thing.

He raised his hands in mock surrender. 'OK, OK. I'm happy to go with whatever you want. This is your call.' He finished his Americano and indicated to the young lad behind the counter that he'd like another one, offering Molly the same again. He shook his head again. 'I just don't see why you won't make this official. Stalking is a crime – you're a victim. I know you don't want to think of yourself as one, but the fact is there's someone out there who wants to harm you. You have to protect yourself.'

'I've told you – I don't want to make things official. Not now.'

'I don't understand why not.'

She waited until the barista had brought their drinks over and cleared the dirty ones from the table.

'Because,' she said, 'I think I know who's doing it. And more importantly, if it is who I think it is, then I know why they're doing it.'

## Chapter Fifty-Three

Next day, Denning gathered the team together to establish what they'd discovered so far. He could sense they were beginning to lose momentum here. They hadn't wanted this case in the first place. He'd been the one who'd insisted they pursue it to its ultimate conclusion. What they'd ended up with was messy and disconnected, like a children's puzzle with too many pieces missing for it to make any real sense.

But he *would* make sense of it. He'd find the pieces and make them fit.

'Molly,' he said, starting with DS Fisher, the brightest and most committed of his team, 'have we confirmed what happened to Corey's watch?'

She shook her head. 'I'm not sure this sodding watch even existed in the first place. Zella seemed to think it was some kind of family heirloom, but I've heard from Corey's family in Sheffield – who weren't particularly helpful incidentally – and they know nothing about any watch. They certainly didn't seem to think it was any sort of family heirloom, or if it had been then they didn't know how Corey had got hold of it. And then there's the mystery man in the Parka jacket that was seen hanging around. We haven't been able to trace him, and CCTV hasn't come up with anything.'

'OK.' Denning had written 'watch' on the whiteboard and put a question mark after it. He still wasn't sure what, if anything, the relevance was with the watch. From what Molly was saying, it sounded like it was a dead end anyway. 'Right now, we need to trace the man. Keep going over CCTV, extend the search area if need be. Let's speak to him and eliminate him if necessary. As for the watch... I'm still not convinced of its relevance. If we knew what happened to it, that might give us something.'

'It's possible he could have sold the watch,' Neeraj suggested. 'If it was worth something then it would have brought in a bit of useful cash.'

'To buy drugs?' Kinsella added drolly.

The others ignored his comment.

'Where would he have stolen a watch from?' Molly asked. 'It's not like he and Zella used to spend their days targeting jewellers' shops. The main reason they went shoplifting was to get food.'

'He could have mugged someone,' Neeraj added. 'Or just taken it from them.'

'I don't think so,' Molly said. 'I don't think he was lying when he said someone gave it to him.'

'Right,' Denning said, 'we keep the watch in mind. If it turns up, or if Zella suddenly remembers where it is, then great. But let's not focus too much on it. It may yet turn out to be of no real relevance to this investigation.' He looked around the team. They were tired. Tired and fed up, waiting for the case to be over and for Christmas to offer the chance for some much-needed cheer. But there would be no Christmas cheer for Ray Bowden or Corey Gates: the least they could get was justice.

'Has anyone got anything else they think might be relevant at this stage?' he asked.

He spotted Molly's hand in the air. Always Molly Fisher doing the heavy lifting… 'Molly?'

'Finn Bowden works for Steven Hodge's property company. It's a strange coincidence.'

'Why did we not know this?' Denning wrote Finn Bowden on the board, with an arrow connecting him to Steven Hodge.

'I guess we didn't think to ask him where he worked when we first interviewed him,' Molly said.

Denning realised by 'we' she meant him; he'd conducted the original interview at the Bowden/Carver home and should have ascertained where Finlay Bowden worked. Thinking back, Andrea Bowden had never offered that information, which should have rung an alarm bell with him at the time. But he was still regarding the Bowdens as victims then; he wouldn't have thought it relevant.

'There's more,' Molly said. 'I've done a search on the Companies House website. It seems Carver Investments have invested a considerable sum of money into Hodge's property development company.'

'So Carver has as much of a vested interest in ensuring this project goes ahead as Hodge does.' Denning considered the significance of this. Could it be a coincidence? This was a connection they couldn't ignore. He kept thinking about what Kane had said about looking at the family for the answers to this. Was Kane just trying to distract him or was there something else here? Everything seemed to keep coming back to Malcolm Carver. 'Do we know how long Finn's worked for Hodge, and in what capacity?'

Molly shrugged. 'He didn't say how long he's worked there for, but I don't think it's been very long. I think he's mostly some kind of glorified office boy. I get the impression the job was likely some kind of favour to Carver.'

'Carver is the obvious connection,' Denning said. 'He knows Hodge, and he has a direct link with the others. If Corey Gates was right, then it was Carver who gave the envelope full of money to Bowden. I think we need to have another word with him.'

'But he has a solid alibi for the night Bowden was murdered,' Kinsella said. 'And the other lad too.'

'Alibied by his wife,' Trudi said. 'It's possible she's covering for him. Wouldn't be the first time that kind of thing has happened.'

'Right, we check and double-check his alibi for both nights. See if someone other than Andrea Bowden can vouch for his whereabouts. What about CCTV Trudi? Has anyone fitting Carver's description been spotted near the station?'

Trudi shook her head. 'No. I've checked the surrounding streets, the ones that have CCTV coverage anyway. It *is* possible he could have approached the station from a side street, or via the park that runs alongside the railway line, neither of which have any coverage.'

'It's also possible he could have paid someone to do it,' Neeraj said. 'Carver strikes me as the kind of person who doesn't like to get his hands dirty.'

'A hitman?' Kinsella said. 'He'd have to be certain he got the right person. A load of homeless guys all dossing down together. It would have been easy to get the wrong person.'

'Bowden was always separate from the other rough sleepers,' Molly said. 'He might have been easy to identify if he was by himself.'

Denning wasn't sure. Somehow this felt personal. They couldn't rule anything out just yet. There was something that still bothered him though... 'Molly, you spoke to Ray Bowden's other family – the mistress, for want of a better word. What about Bowden's other son? Any contact with him yet?'

'No.' She explained about Leon Harvey having died from a brain tumour. 'I reckon it was Leon's death that knocked the stuffing out of Ray Bowden,' she said. 'Apparently his personality changed after that. I mean, it must have been tough on him – his son dies and he's unable to properly grieve for him. It would be enough to drive anyone to the edge.'

'It would help to explain why he allowed Malcolm Carver to manipulate him over the fraud case. Initially buy his silence then force him into taking the blame for everything.'

'You're certain Malcolm Carver's our man?' Kinsella asked.

'I'm not certain of anything, Dave,' Denning said. 'But I think he's our most credible suspect right now. But in the meantime, Molly, I think you should speak to both Steven Hodge and Finn Bowden again. Find out how long Finn has worked for Hodge, and if either of them knew of Ray Bowden's presence at the station site. Carver must have found out Bowden was there somehow.'

'There's more,' Trudi said, raising her voice to make sure she had everyone's full attention. 'I sent some CCTV footage over to the tech guys to get it enhanced. It was taken the day of the drugs raid. They've just got back to me with something interesting.'

The team gathered round Trudi's desk to look at the footage on her monitor. The screen showed the junction between the alleyway leading from the old station and Brick Lane. A figure could be seen standing by some trees roughly halfway along the alleyway, wearing a Parka jacket with a distinctive logo on the lapel. The moment the local CID arrived to search the station, he turned and headed back down the alley in the direction of Brick Lane. His face was partly hidden by the hood of his jacket, but just for a brief second he glanced up and his face was caught by the camera. It was somebody they all recognised.

# Chapter Fifty-Four

Molly thought Steven Hodge's secretary wasn't going to let her speak to Hodge. She stood defiantly in the outer office while his secretary tried to fob her off with a stream of excuses. In the end, Molly threatened to arrest her and march into Hodge's office unannounced if she didn't inform her boss she was there to speak to him.

She finally relented and phoned through to tell Hodge DS Fisher was there to see him.

'There really is nothing further to add,' he said once she was in his office. 'Finn isn't here at the moment, so you can't speak to him and I've already been over the whole thing with you.'

'Where exactly is Finn Bowden?' Molly asked.

Hodge sighed. 'He phoned in sick this morning. I imagine he's at home.' He looked at Molly. 'What is this about? Finn had nothing to do with anything. He didn't know his father was living in that old station. How would he?'

'What exactly is Finn Bowden's job here, Mr Hodge?' Molly asked.

'He's my office manager. I'm training him up in the business.'

'At Malcolm Carver's request?'

'OK, I initially agreed to take Finn on as a favour to Malcolm, but he's a bright lad. He's keen to learn and he's got a nose for property.'

'So his job was mostly office-based?'

There was a pause before he answered. 'Mostly, yes.'

'Mostly, but not exclusively?'

Another pause. 'Well, OK, he did do the occasional site visit, but it was rare. That kind of thing was mostly down to myself or one of the senior partners.'

'Did he ever visit Shoreditch station?'

Hodge looked awkward now. He shuffled uncomfortably in his chair, dodging eye contact. 'I'm not sure.' Another fidget. 'It's possible.'

Molly was whirling things over in her head. Finn Bowden was an angry young man and a lot of that anger was directed at his father. A father who had let him down on so many levels. 'In which case he could have come into contact with his father?'

'Nobody knew Ray Bowden was sleeping rough in the old station. How could we? I was only interested in the building's commercial potential. That was all any of us were interested in. Once we convert that derelict site we can start making some good money on it.' He let out a breathy sigh. 'You know, I'm beginning to regret ever having set eyes on that bloody place. It's been nothing but trouble from the start. They now think there might be a sodding bat colony living there. If it wasn't bad enough we had those homeless deadbeats to contend with, now we've got sodding bats. You know what that means? We won't be allowed to touch the place as long as the bats are living there.'

Molly hoped he wasn't trying to elicit sympathy from her, because he was going to be very disappointed if he was. 'Finn Bowden, Mr Hodge, did he ever visit the station site?'

He nodded, wiping a hand over a sweaty forehead. 'Yes. A couple of times. Once to accompany a structural engineer on a site visit, another time to check the site was secure. But how were any of us to know? Finn hadn't seen his father for years. How would he have recognised him?'

But supposing he had, Molly thought. It was just possible Finn had recognised his father, and... Resented him? For what? If anyone had had a reason for resenting Ray Bowden, it would have been Leon Harvey.

'So, to confirm,' Molly concluded, 'Finn Bowden visited the station site on at least two occasions?'

Hodge nodded sheepishly. 'Yes,' he said quietly. 'Like I said, he had to show the structural engineer around. The builders were due to start work in the New Year and needed to check the building was still structurally sound.'

'And on the second occasion?'

'Second occasion?'

'You said he visited the station twice. Why did he go back a second time?'

Hodge was refusing eye contact, sensing he was treading on dangerously thin ice and potentially dropping himself and an employee in the shit. 'It was a work-related matter. It had nothing to do with his father being there.'

Molly was beginning to lose patience with Hodge. 'This is a murder investigation, Mr Hodge. You've already deliberately misled us by failing to mention Finn Bowden worked for you. Not only that, we have CCTV footage from the day the station was raided after an "anonymous" tip-off and just before Ray Bowden's body was discovered. Finn Bowden can be seen in the vicinity of the station. It raises the obvious question of what he was doing there the day of a police raid. So, unless you start telling us the truth, we will have no option but to arrest you.'

'Arrest me for what? If you had any evidence, you'd have taken me in by now.' He splayed his hands on his desk. 'Look, I didn't kill Ray Bowden. That's all you need to know. I didn't do it and I have no idea who did. So Bowden's son works for me. Finn's stepdad has invested both his and his clients' money into this project. And we're talking millions, potentially. The least I can do is return the favour by offering his son a job, even if he is virtually unemployable. I didn't know Ray Bowden was sleeping rough in the bloody place with those losers. And neither did Finn.'

'But Finn was there the day the place was raided. Why was he there?' She stood in front of Hodge's desk, hands on her hips. 'I'm not going anywhere until you answer the question, Mr Hodge, so you might as well tell me.'

Hodge shook his head, almost as though he could sense that the game was up. 'He was the one who planted the drugs.'

'Why did he do that?'

'You would need to ask Finn that.'

'He isn't here, Mr Hodge, so I'm asking you.' He didn't answer. She waited for a moment, then repeated the question.

Hodge looked up at Molly, and slightly shook his head. 'I asked Finn Bowden to plant drugs. He slipped into the station the night before and planted them, then I notified the police. Anonymously. Finn went round on the day of the raid to make sure the drugs were found. It was the only way I could get those homeless people out of there. Your lot were no use and the investors were beginning to run out of patience at the lack of progress.' He looked pleadingly at Molly. 'I was desperate, OK. I potentially stand to lose a lot of money if this deal goes pear-shaped. Not to mention the people who've put money into this project. I didn't have much choice...'

Molly looked at him. Hodge had just confessed to having committed a serious crime. She would pass the information, along with Hodge's confession, on to DI Jephcott and let him deal with Hodge. She'd be surprised if even Hodge's smooth tongue could talk him out of a custodial sentence if it were to get as far as court, but at least it proved Corey, Zella and the others had had nothing to do with the drugs.

'So, it is possible Finn Bowden could have seen his father and recognised him?' she asked.

'Yes,' Hodge conceded. 'I suppose it's possible.'

As Molly left the office, she could hear Hodge shouting after her, asking what was going to happen next. But she didn't care. She tore past the bemused-looking secretary and out of the reception area, heading towards the lifts. As she waited for the lift doors to open, she thought back to what Zella had said about the man she'd seen arguing with Corey the day before he was killed. Something made Molly think Zella had known exactly who he was.

She had to phone Denning, and speak to him before it was too late.

# Chapter Fifty-Five

Denning could hear raised voices as soon as he got out of the car. There was shouting coming from the Carvers' house, which was audible halfway down the elegant street. He ran up the short pathway and banged on the front door. When there was no answer he turned the door handle and discovered the door wasn't locked. He pushed it open and entered the hallway.

Molly Fisher had phoned to tell him about Finn Bowden, and suddenly a lot of things were making sense.

Neeraj followed him into the house. The shouting was coming from the sitting room off to the left. Denning stopped in the doorway: Sophie Bowden was arguing with Malcolm Carver, while her mother sat on the sofa, her hands over her ears, yelling at them both to shut up.

Sophie Bowden stopped shouting as soon as she spotted Denning and Neeraj standing there. Carver stopped too, though it took Andrea Bowden a moment to realise what was going on. She was shouting, 'Shut up' over and over again, before she noticed everyone had done exactly that.

She looked at Denning with cold fury on her face. 'What the hell are you doing here? This is a family matter.'

'I did try to make myself heard at the front door,' Denning said, 'but you seemed to have other things on your minds.'

Sophie Bowden stepped forward, her hands raised in a conciliatory gesture. 'This isn't a good time, Inspector,' she said calmly. She glanced towards Malcolm Carver, a look of disgust on her face. 'We're having a bit of a family discussion.'

'So I heard.' Denning took in the three family members. He wondered what would have happened if he hadn't arrived when he did. Would things have turned violent? Despite the raised voices, Sophie Bowden came across as a calm and together person, but he wasn't so sure about Malcolm Carver. 'I need to speak to Finn. Is he here?'

His question was met by silence. 'If he isn't here, then you need to tell me where he is.' Denning was still standing in the sitting room doorway, Neeraj immediately behind him. Neither of them was going to budge until someone in this damaged family told him what he needed to know.

'I don't know,' Sophie said after a moment. 'I've tried phoning him, but it's going straight to voicemail.'

'Finn didn't do anything,' Andrea said unprompted.

'I didn't say he had,' Denning added. 'But we do need to speak with him. Fairly urgently.'

Malcolm Carver made to push past Denning and Neeraj. Denning put a hand out to stop him. 'I would prefer it if you stayed here, Mr Carver. I believe you might be able to answers some questions for me.'

'I need to get back to the office,' Carver said. 'You can't keep me here. This is my house.'

Denning remained where he was. 'Now, maybe. But it *was* Ray Bowden's house, which you took over, along with his family and his share of the business. You successfully convinced Andrea that Ray had been planning to leave them all for his other family. Only that wasn't quite how you put it, was it?'

'You might as well be honest, Malcolm,' Sophie said. 'Mum will find out anyway.'

'I saved this family just as I saved the company. Ray would have happily destroyed both just so he could live with that other woman and his bastard kid. *That*,' Carver insisted, 'is the truth.'

'You told us Dad was going to throw us out this of house,' Sophie said. 'You told Mum he planned to move that other woman and their son in here and we'd be the ones who were homeless. But that was a lie. Dad never planned to chuck us out of here. Even if he did eventually decide he wanted to live with Alison, he would have made sure we had a roof over our heads and money to go on living here.'

'Don't mention that woman's name,' Andrea yelled. 'This whole mess is her fault. If she'd just kept out of our lives, we'd have been alright.'

'Well, we'll never know now,' Sophie shouted, 'because Malcolm saw to it that she was never given that chance.'

'This is all lies,' Carver said. 'Ray was hopeless. Hopeless as a business partner and hopeless as a parent. The truth is he was plodding along until I bought into the business. The only reason he was able to afford this house is because I was the one who turned that company into a success. He would have spent his entire life just bumping along. It was me who chased after the rich clients and took the company to the next level.'

'By lying and cheating,' Sophie said. 'Dad never wanted that. I mean, OK, he liked having money, but that was mostly because Mum wanted the best of everything – best house, best schools for us. He did it to keep her happy.'

'And you,' Andrea Bowden spat. 'You were never shy in asking Ray for handouts – skiing trips at that posh school, latest designer clothes. Everything you wanted was handed to you on a plate.'

Sophie sat on the arm of the sofa. 'Maybe I did when I was younger. At school these were the kind of stupid things that mattered if you wanted to fit in, especially in a school full of shallow airheads. Now I'm older and I've lived a bit, I realise how selfish I was. But none of that excuses the lies you told, Malcolm. Lies that you were happy to go along with, Mum.' She looked at Denning. 'They planned it together – OK, it was mostly Malcolm's idea and he was very successful at persuading Mum to go along with it, but she was a willing accomplice.'

'And you're only admitting it now?' Denning wondered why the truth had taken so long to come to light.

'I wanted to give them the chance to do the right thing and turn themselves in. Besides, it's taken me until now to fully admit the truth to myself. We always knew what really happened, or at the very least suspected it. It was just easier to pretend that wasn't the case. But I think we all need to start being honest with each other.'

'Sophie,' Andrea said, 'you need to think carefully about what you're about to say…'

Sophie ignored her mum and continued. 'They framed Dad. Accessed his computer at home as well as his files at work and made it look as though he'd planned that stupid property fraud all along. Dad denied it, naturally, though he was savvy enough to know he was being set up. That was why he didn't want to see any of us when he went to prison. He thought we were all against him. That's probably why he chose to live rough with a bunch of strangers in an abandoned Tube station rather than try to make things up with his family when he was released. We let him down. All of us. But you most of all, Malcolm. He trusted you and thought you were his friend.'

Silence fell upon the room again. Andrea Bowden opened her mouth to speak, but nothing came out. There was probably very little she could convincingly say to contradict the accusations her daughter had just made.

Malcolm Carver wasn't having any of it, though. He barged past Denning and Neeraj and made for the front door. 'Deep, arrest Mr Carver. Conspiracy to commit fraud.'

Neeraj chased after Carver and grabbed him as he tried to open the front door. As Neeraj read Carver his rights, Denning turned to Sophie Bowden. 'Sophie, I need you to find Finn for me. I need to stop him before he does anything else stupid.'

'Finn has nothing to do with this,' Andrea Bowden shouted into the room. 'Leave him alone.'

'What's he done…?' Sophie Bowden looked at her mother, and then at Carver. 'What have you two ghouls driven him to?'

'He hasn't done anything,' Andrea repeated. 'Finn is just a confused, unhappy young man.' She looked at Denning. 'He's had his problems. He was bullied at school after it all came out about his dad. He's always found life difficult.' She looked over at Sophie. 'It's alright for you. It's always been alright for you. You were Daddy's Little Princess. You could do no wrong: clever, pretty. Always able to say the right things. Finn struggled. People have never given him a chance.'

'That's rubbish, Mum. Finn's always been difficult,' she said, looking at Denning. 'Even before my dad was sent down, he never fitted in. He used to get into trouble at school. Stealing, lying to teachers. He's never had a proper job. He only got the job with Hodge because Malcolm pulled some strings.' She looked accusingly at her stepfather as though all Finn's problems lay at his door. 'Mum used to cover for him. When Dad went to prison, he just lost the plot completely. He used to stay out all night, or come home drunk.'

'It's lies,' Andrea was saying to no one in particular. 'He hasn't done anything…'

'Sophie,' Denning said firmly, trying to bring some order to the chaos that was descending on the room. 'Where is Finn?'

'I don't know…'

'It's up to you, Sophie. You can stop him before he commits another murder.'

'Murder?' Andrea put her hand to her mouth. 'What are you talking about?'

'Finn murdered his father.' Denning kept his voice calm. There was enough anger in the room without him adding to it. 'He recognised him when he visited the old station a couple of weeks ago along with an engineer who was assessing the site. When Steven Hodge told Finn to plant the drugs, Finn saw it as the opportunity to kill his father. He resented Ray for treating him like he was a constant disappointment. It was bad enough that Ray made no secret of the fact he preferred Leon over Finn, but when Finn discovered Ray treated Corey – a complete stranger – like he was his son, he really snapped. Zella saw Corey arguing with someone we now know was Finn, only she didn't appreciate the significance of it at the time. But at some point she worked it all out eventually.'

Sophie looked at her mum. 'And we know why Finn felt the way he did about Dad, don't we?'

Andrea Bowden didn't speak. She looked like she was in the middle of a nightmare and just wanted to wake up.

'Mum?' Sophie prompted.

'That's because he always thought Ray wasn't his dad.' She looked at everyone in the room, defiant yet sheepish. Another silence fell upon the room. As it grew, Andrea knew she had to continue. 'There's no truth in that. He's Ray's son.' She looked over at Carver. 'Even if Ray never believed it.'

'You were having an affair with him at the time.' Sophie pointed at Carver. 'Is it any surprise that they were never close when they spent most of their lives believing they weren't father and son?'

'We need to speak to Finn,' Denning said.

'I don't know where he is,' Sophie said. 'But I do know that Finn will want to tidy up any loose ends.'

'Meaning?' Denning looked round the dysfunctional family unit, wondering if any of them realised the problems they had caused.

'If this girl, this Zella, had recognised him, then he'll want to confront her. Make sure she doesn't talk.' She looked at her mother for a reaction, but Andrea Bowden was still looking at Carver; mother and daughter each looking to someone for support which they were never going to get.

'He's already killed two people, Mum. It's not going to take much for him to kill for a third time.'

But Andrea Bowden didn't answer. She turned to look at her daughter and just shook her head slowly.

## Chapter Fifty-Six

Zella was screaming for help. Finn Bowden was standing in front of her holding a knife, presumably the same knife he had used to kill both his father and Corey Gates.

Denning had raced straight to the squat, though he couldn't guarantee Zella would still be there. Denning had taken a chance and headed there. Molly had texted him earlier that morning to tell him that Zella must have figured it all out and knew who their killer was. The only possible reason she would have kept this information to herself is she thought there was something to be gained from buying her silence. She would have put two and two together and realised he worked for the property developers. CCTV footage had confirmed the person who was seen loitering in the alleyway the morning of the police raid, dressed in the Parka jacket with the distinctive logo, had also been spotted in the area the evening Zella said she saw someone arguing with Corey.

All she had succeeded in doing was placing herself in even greater danger.

Neeraj was taking Carver to a nearby police station, where he would be interviewed under caution for his part in the investment scam that had seen Ray Bowden sent down for a crime he hadn't committed.

But it was Finn Bowden that had concerned Denning, and suddenly it had all made sense to him. He hadn't been at the station that morning to make sure the drugs raid went according to plan: he wanted to be there when his father's body was discovered. Guilt, maybe, or perhaps he just wanted to make sure he really was dead.

Zella was standing by a window in a smoke-damaged sitting room, trying not to look as scared as she must have been feeling. Her eyes were dancing between Denning and Finn.

'Let her go, Finn,' Denning said quietly.

Finn Bowden turned to look at Denning. 'It's too late,' he said. 'It's too late for anything now.'

Zella tried to make a break for it. She jerked to one side and made to dodge past Finn. She was too slow. He grabbed her and threw her to the floor.

Denning took a step closer. He saw the knife in Finn's hand, the blade flashing in the filtered winter light.

'Give me the knife, Finn, and let Zella go.'

Finn looked at Zella then at Denning, his mind clearly racing through the limited options that were open to him. Denning watched as he gripped the handle of the knife, raising it, about to bring it down. Zella lying on the floor, kicked her leg out and the heel of her boot connected with Finn's shin. He gave a sharp cry of pain and cursed. The distraction was enough. Denning lunged at him, grabbing his arm as Zella clambered onto her knees and frantically crawled out of danger.

Denning used all his strength to push Finn's arm as far away from him as possible. Finn punched Denning in the face with his free hand. Despite the wincing blow, Denning launched himself onto Finn, throwing him to the ground, using his knees to pin the young lad to the floor. He bashed the hand with his knife against the floor until Finn dropped the knife.

As Denning pulled him to his feet, he saw there was a dejected look on Finn's face, as though he knew his luck had just run out; as though he'd known it the moment Denning had entered the squat.

In some weird, pathetic way, Denning felt sorry for him. He'd killed two men: one of them a lad barely older than himself, the other one his father, but he was clearly damaged rather than deranged. He'd grown up in a family where lies were commonplace. But his sister had turned out alright, so maybe there was no excuse after all.

'Why did you do it?' Zella asked. 'Why did you kill Corey?'

She was standing by the doorway, anger having replaced the fear she'd felt before.

Denning heard the sounds of police sirens approaching. He'd naturally called for back-up before he'd entered the building, in total breach of police procedure, but with a life potentially in danger…

'Why?' Zella repeated the question. 'What had he ever done to you?'

Finn couldn't look at her. His eyes were fixed on the floor. 'The watch,' he mumbled after a moment.

'The watch?' Zella looked at Denning. 'It wasn't worth anything. Not really. Only in Corey's stupid head. Why kill him for that?'

'Because it was mine,' he said. 'My dad had promised it to me. It belonged to my grandfather. He always said I could have it. When I asked him about it, he told me he'd given it to Leon. I thought he meant Alison's kid.' He looked over at Zella, his face a mixture of hatred and guilt. 'He meant *her* boyfriend. Corey. He thought he was Leon.'

Zella was crying. 'He wasn't my boyfriend.' She wiped a hand over her eyes. 'I loved him. But he wasn't my boyfriend.'

Finn just shook his head and stared at his feet.

Denning could hear footsteps running along the narrow hallway. A moment later half a dozen uniformed officers in body armour ran in, followed by Molly Fisher and DCI McKenna.

Denning handed Finn over to one of the officers and pointed to the knife lying on the floor. Another officer picked it up with a gloved hand and placed it in a plastic evidence bag.

Molly was speaking to Zella, asking her if she was alright and if she needed medical treatment. Zella shook her head.

McKenna came to Denning. 'That was foolish. You should have waited for back-up. He was armed and potentially dangerous. I should be giving you a right bollocking.'

'Then why don't you? If you really think that's what I deserve.'

She just shot him a withering look. She jerked her head at Molly, who was still comforting Zella prior to taking a formal statement. 'The pair of you are as bad as each other. I'd be wasting my breath. And do you really want to know something? I don't think I care anymore.'

Despite himself, Denning smiled. Zella had wiped away the tears now and nodded at him. 'Thanks,' she said with a slight quaver in her voice. 'You saved my life.'

'You were pretty brave yourself,' Denning said. 'Kicking him like that.'

She gave a watery smile. 'He deserved that and more for what he did to Corey. Corey never even wanted that stupid watch. He was going to sell it to some bloke he knew, but then the stupid prat lost it.'

'The watch?' Molly said. 'That's what this was about?'

Denning shook his head. 'I think it was about more than just the watch, Molly. It's about a damaged family that couldn't bring itself to be honest with each other. At least not until it was too late.' He was thinking about Sophie; her father murdered by her brother. She didn't deserve that.

As Zella was led outside by one of the female officers, McKenna asked, 'Why come after Zella? Unless he thought Corey had given her the watch?'

'Perhaps she recognised him,' Denning said. 'From that first time he came round to look at the old station with the structural engineer.'

'I suspect it's more likely she made Corey tell her who he really was. After she saw them arguing that time. I think Corey was slightly scared of Zella. I suspect if she went on at him enough he would have given in eventually. It wouldn't have been difficult to track him down through his work. She would have figured out what really happened that night, assumed he was responsible for Corey's murder too, and blackmailed him. She obviously didn't realise just how disturbed he was. Very nearly got more than she bargained for.'

'Technically, we should charge her with blackmail,' McKenna said. 'But I'm not sure that would help anyone right now. And I'd say she's learned her lesson when it comes to messing with the wrong people.'

They headed out into the street as a flurry of early December snow started to fall. Denning watched as Finn was driven off in the back of a police car. Zella was standing by the side of the road. 'All my stuff's in there,' she said. 'When can I go back in?'

'It's a crime scene at the moment,' McKenna said. Denning could see the forensics van pulling up to fill the space where the police car had been. 'I can't say how long they'll be.'

Zella looked crestfallen. 'What is it with you bastards…?'

'Look,' Molly said, 'I still need you to give me a full statement, not just about what happened in there, but everything you know. From the start.' She looked at McKenna. 'We could find the nearest police station. Or we could see if that café's open. It's not far from here. And I could murder a mug of hot, stewed tea.'

The look on Zella's face suggested she was going to tell Molly where to go. After a second, her face changed and she said, 'OK, but you're paying.'

'I'm pretty certain that's against police procedure,' McKenna said.

Denning smiled. 'We *could* arrest her for blackmail and withholding information about a murder. Or we could give the kid a break. It is Christmas.'

'Hmm…' McKenna didn't look convinced. 'We will need to formally interview her at some stage. But right now, I think I could do with a cup of tea, too. Though preferably not stewed.'

'Well that's good,' Denning said, 'because I've got a favour to ask you.'

# Chapter Fifty-Seven

They were back in McKenna's office. As far as Denning was aware, Molly wasn't back yet. She'd asked if she could finish early today as there was something she had to do. The case was pretty much wrapped up now, so he didn't see any reason why she shouldn't leave early.

Malcolm Carver had been charged with his part in the property fraud. He would keep Kane's name out it. Kane had made sure of that. They would hand him over to the NCA, and good luck if they could get him to talk. Steve Marsh had pointed Denning in the direction of one of the investigating officers who had handled the original fraud case: there was nothing to prove there was anything suspicious in the deaths of the men involved. If anything came to light to suggest otherwise, he would inform Denning straightaway. But he was told not to build his hopes up. Denning realised he was going to have to let this one go.

One a more positive note, Finn Bowden had been charged with two counts of murder and one of attempted murder. In reality, the latter charge would more than likely be reduced to threatening behaviour, and even then it depended on how forthcoming Zella was likely to be when it came to making a formal statement.

'Forensics found a Parka jacket in his wardrobe that matches the one worn by the figure spotted on CCTV.

OK, it's not enough to convict him, but taken along with all the other evidence, we have a pretty strong case against Finlay Bowden. So, job well done,' McKenna said. She'd dug out the bottle of single malt whisky she kept in the bottom drawer of her desk and had poured herself a generous glassful, then waved the bottle in Denning's direction.

Denning declined the offer. He wanted to keep a clear head.

'Perhaps not the outcome I would have liked,' he said. 'There's a strong chance Finn will argue diminished responsibility, but whatever happens, you can't help feeling sorry for him.'

'Not our problem, Matt. He's off the streets, that's what matters.'

She took a slug of whisky. 'Are you sure you don't want a glass? This is good stuff – a twelve-year-old Macallan.'

'I'll pass, if you don't mind.' He waited until she placed the glass on her desk. 'I really wanted to talk to you about my future.'

She gave him one of her wry smiles. 'You're going to go after the DCI's job? Brilliant news.'

'Actually, I'm not.' He waited for his words to sink in. 'I'd like to apply for a post that's come up with the NCA. Nothing's been confirmed yet, and I still need to talk it over with my family, but I think I'm in with a chance. I'd like to go for it.'

For a moment, it looked like he'd caught her on the back foot. She opened her mouth to speak, but nothing came out. She quickly regained her composure. 'Wow, that's a bit left field, but it's your life. If you really feel that's where you want to take your career, then go for it.'

'I'd need a reference. A good one.'

She continued eyeing him, lifted the whisky from her desk and swirled the amber liquid around the glass. 'You're a dark horse, Matthew Denning. When you first pitched up here with your flashy degree and condescending attitude, I'd put money on you being after my job. I reckoned as soon as you got a whiff that I wanted to retire, you'd have had your CV into senior management before my arse was even halfway out that door.' She took another sip of whisky. 'I obviously got you wrong, which is not like me. I'm generally pretty shrewd at guessing people right.'

He wanted to tell her she wasn't a million miles off the truth. He *had* wanted her job when he'd first pitched up there as DI. But things had changed. He liked the cut and thrust of a police investigation; the sense of knowing you were in the job to make a difference. He'd quickly discovered the higher you went in this job the more detached you became from actual policing.

'I've never hidden my ambition,' he said. 'It's just that it looks like it's taking me in a different direction now.'

'The NCA? A lot of it's routine. Yes, it has its moments, but you'll never get the same buzz you get from a murder investigation.'

'Maybe that's a good thing. Maybe I'm not cut out for the "buzz" that goes with a murder investigation. I got it wrong about the fraud case being the key to all this. I allowed myself to be blindsided by Kane and his involvement in the murders. I missed the obvious. A damaged family trying its best to keep its secrets buried in the past.'

McKenna looked like she was about to say she'd told him so. Instead, she drained the last of the whisky and smiled. 'You weren't entirely on the wrong track. Perhaps if Ray Bowden hadn't been framed for something he hadn't done and had stayed out of prison, none of this would have happened. On the other hand, we caught the person responsible, so it doesn't matter. Look, if you want to leave Major Crimes and seek another adventure somewhere else, then that's fine with me – I'll happily recommend you. But at least think about it first. Make sure it's what you really want to do. Don't base your decision on one case.'

He promised he'd think about it, but he knew, in his heart, that he'd made the right decision.

'One more thing, Matt,' she said, as he got up to head back to his desk. 'The attack on Placzek. They got the two men responsible. Apparently he'd got on the wrong side of a couple of cons. A bit of verbals in the dinner queue, or some stupid piece of nothing. They've admitted it, and Placzek is expected to make a full recovery, unfortunately. Case closed.'

'So I'm off the hook?'

She didn't bother to reply, just shot him another withering look, which he took as his cue to leave her office.

## Chapter Fifty-Eight

Molly waited in the pub as she'd said she would. She'd been here a couple of times with Jon, but only when they'd been meeting friends who lived nearby. There were two exits either side of a long, central bar, and several booths where people could talk undisturbed.

Jon was sitting at the bar, looking at his phone, but also glancing over often enough to make sure she was OK. She was now having second thoughts about asking him to come along. She should have asked Trudi, or even Denning. Someone neutral who wasn't involved and wouldn't take the request as a sign of something else.

She sipped her gin and tonic. Not her usual drink, but a pint of Kronenbourg felt wrong somehow, as if this was a social event, which it wasn't. She went to take another sip, but put the drink back down, realising she had to control her nerves and the alcohol probably wasn't helping.

She glanced at her phone for the third time in five minutes. She was early, and she wasn't even sure he would turn up. Her insides were churning, and part of her was still convinced this wasn't a good idea, despite the reassurance of knowing Jon was within sight, should anything go wrong.

She took her mind off it by thinking about Zella, or Zoe Jeffers, to give her her real name. She'd been quite chatty when Molly had taken her out for tea and something to eat. She'd admitted she'd been stupid to try and blackmail Finn Bowden after she'd recognised him. She told Molly it had all been part of an elaborate ruse to get Finn to reveal himself as the killer: lure him out into the open and get him to confess.

Molly had suspected that was a lie to try and cover up the fact that she'd wanted to extort money from him in return for her silence. She could never prove it, and arresting Zella would have been counterproductive. She'd reluctantly agreed to make a full statement and even go to court as a witness when the time came. Probably in return for Molly not taking the blackmail claim any further. She'd told Zella about a homeless hostel near Paddington where her brother had stayed briefly when he'd found himself homeless. It had been a bit of a dive, but it was warm and clean and might just offer her the chance to get herself sorted over Christmas. She assured Zella that there would be no questions, or hassle or pressure to speak to anyone she didn't want to. Zella had said she'd think about it. Molly had left her at the café, promising to keep in touch, and had headed to the pub, contacting Jon en route to confirm she was sticking to her 'crazy plan', as he'd called it.

She was about to take another sip of her gin and tonic when she was suddenly aware of a figure standing next to the booth. For a brief second she thought it was Jon coming over to try and persuade her to change her mind again.

But it wasn't.

It was someone she hadn't seen for a long time. Not in over a decade; not since they'd all stood on the steps of the court after the guilty verdict had been delivered. They'd lost touch after that. Until now.

'Molly?'

She glanced over at Jon to tell him everything was OK. He glanced back, a frown wrinkling his forehead. She quickly shook her head and he seemed to relax a little.

The man sat down opposite her. He was a few years younger than her. He'd filled out quite a bit since they'd last met, when he was a scrawny sixteen-year-old with floppy hair and a sulky attitude. He was broader now, shorter hair and tattoos on his arms, and a Celtic symbol on his neck.

'Can I get you something to drink?'

Tom Owen shook his head. 'I don't want to stay. I'm not sure why I came. I don't even know what to say to you.'

'I am glad you came though.'

'I hated you for so long. Part of me still hates you. But...'

His face dropped. She thought he was going to cry. He'd been invalided out of the army having been diagnosed with PTSD, he told her, confirming what his mum had told Molly. A young girl, the same age as Bex, had been killed one evening, shot by a stray bullet fired by a sniper from an abandoned building; either Tom or one of his comrades had been the intended target. She'd died at his feet, looking at him with cold empty eyes, the way Bex would have looked when her body had been found that summer's evening over a decade ago.

Molly found it impossible not to feel sorry for him. Their shared grief should have bound them together, but it was more complicated than that.

Tom's sister Bex had been Molly's best friend all through school. When they had turned eighteen and left school to face the big bad world, they had gone out to celebrate. Only Bex hadn't come home.

Molly had tried to persuade Bex to get into a taxi with her. But Bex had had too much to drink, wouldn't see reason and had refused to get in. Her body was found the following morning beside a railway line. She'd been murdered by a maniac who'd been targeting women. He was behind bars now, but it had torn apart so many people. The damage and pain was still being felt all these years later.

Molly had lived with the guilt ever since.

'Is that why you've been stalking me? Hanging round outside my flat? Following me on the Tube?'

'I never followed you on the Tube...'

So she *had* been wrong about the guy on the Tube. Paranoia had made her jump at shadows. 'OK, but everything else. The graffiti on my front door. Why did you do it?'

'I wanted to scare you. I wanted you to feel scared like Bex would have felt. That night... the night it happened...'

The night of the murder. The night all their lives changed forever.

'I was scared out of my wits. I thought someone was trying to harm me.' As he sat opposite her, looking twitchy, she wasn't convinced he didn't want to harm her. Not now anyway. Something must have changed. Something must have kicked in to prevent him from taking things further.

'How did you find out where I lived? Come to that, how did you manage to get my phone number?'

'My mum. She's still in touch with your mum. She mentioned that you'd recently moved. She gave my mum your phone number in case she wanted to get in touch with you.'

'Why did you do it, Tom?'

'At first I wanted to scare you. Then I don't know… I still hated you. You'd got on with your life like nothing had happened. I just keep thinking about Bex. About what happened to her. For so long, I blamed you for what happened. If you'd stayed with her that night. If you hadn't let her out of your sight.' He shook his head.

'I never forgot about Bex, Tom. I think about her every day. I replayed that night in my head every day for years, wishing I could have done something else. Wishing I could have forced her to get in the taxi with me that night… I tortured myself over what happened. Over and over until I thought I was cracking up. That's one of the reasons I joined the police – to try and save women like Bex.'

He nodded. 'I googled you. I know you helped catch that man, the one who really killed Bex.' He blushed, avoiding eye contact. 'That's when I thought about what I'd done. I wanted to talk to you, but I didn't know what to say.'

'You should have said something. Put my mind at rest that there wasn't someone out to harm me.'

'I know. I'm sorry.'

Molly wanted to shout at him. Arrest him for what he'd put her through. But she couldn't stop feeling sorry for him, despite her anger. 'I spoke to your mum. She told me what happened. The army… It can't have been easy for you.'

She leaned over and touched his arm affectionately. 'However much you blame me for what happened that night, it could never be as much as I blame myself. It took me a long time to accept that it wasn't my fault. There was only one person to blame and he's rotting in prison, where he belongs.' She'd heard about the attack on Daniel Placzek: Denning had mentioned it in passing, almost as though he was deliberately trying to underplay the incident and distance himself from its implications. Part of her was sorry Placzek hadn't died, but another part of her had felt nothing. Placzek was a nobody as far as she was concerned. A mythical monster who had been slain long ago. She refused to let him dominate her thoughts more than he already had.

'What are you going to do?' Tom asked.

There was no point in reporting him, making it official and adding to his pain. 'I think you need to talk to someone, Tom. I think you need to get support and find a way of working through what happened. Not just in the army but with Bex. Believe me, I've tried running away and blaming others, but it just adds to your pain.'

He nodded. She could see he was fighting to hold back tears. A moment later, Jon came over. He sat down next to Molly. 'Is everything alright?'

Molly looked at Tom. 'Yes,' she said. 'I think it is now.'

## Chapter Fifty-Nine

The restaurant was busy. There was a staff Christmas party taking place in a far corner: loud chatter and ribald laughter that echoed across the tight space. Uniformed waiters dashed between tables juggling food and drinks orders. Behind the noisy chatter, soothing jazz music played over hidden speakers.

Denning and Sarah, Claire and George. A table for four, laid out with smart linen napkins and grey ceramic tableware. Jake was being looked after by his favourite neighbour, the elderly lady with the wiry Jack Russell. He was probably tiring himself out playing with the dog and filling his neighbour's head with his hopes for Christmas.

The grown-ups were there to talk about the future.

It was Denning and Claire's favourite restaurant: over-priced but with a kind of kitsch charm that stopped it from being too pretentious.

A waiter arrived with the drinks order: beer for Denning and George; white wine; gin and tonic for Sarah and a brandy and a rum and coke for Claire. They were still trying to agree on a wine for the main course.

'I feel like some kind of toast is in order,' Sarah said.

'That might be a bit premature,' Claire offered, assuming Sarah was referring to her impending nuptials. 'We haven't even set a date yet.'

'Well, how about we just say here's to a lovely Christmas.' Sarah raised her glass and the others followed suit. 'And, well, to the future in general.'

They clinked glasses, and to the outside world must have seemed like nothing more than two couples enjoying a pre-Christmas dinner.

Denning hadn't told Claire about the attack on Daniel Placzek. So far, it had still been kept out of the media. There was always the danger word would get out and Placzek would become newsworthy again. The spotlight would be on Denning and Claire too, and Jake by association. But Denning would jump headfirst off that bridge when he came to it. For now, he just wanted them to enjoy themselves and at least appear normal.

'I think I've finally managed to dissuade Jake from wanting a puppy,' Claire said.

Denning smiled. Every Christmas, it was the same: Jake wanted a puppy, and every year they said the same thing, that he was too young. Perhaps once Claire and George had settled into their new home things might be different.

'Is he looking forward to moving house?' Sarah asked.

'You know Jake,' Claire said. 'He's always resistant to any kind of change. But he'll be alright once we've moved and he's settled in.'

'We might be moving too.' Sarah looked over at Denning. Although he hadn't agreed to move, he had said it was something they should give serious consideration to in the new year.

'Anywhere in mind?' Claire asked.

'I'm not too fussy,' Sarah lied. 'Though it would be nice to have a garden.'

There was a general clatter of consensus about the benefits of a garden, and Denning took the opportunity

322

to think back to his earlier conversation with McKenna. She'd agreed to support his application for the NCA, but had asked him to seriously think about putting in for her job when she retired.

He'd discussed the possibilities with Sarah earlier that evening. As always with Sarah when it came to his career, she made it clear the decision was down to him, adding that she would support him whatever he decided.

He still wasn't sure where his future lay. But as he looked around the table at his extended family, he was certain that whatever happened, things would somehow work out for the best.

# Chapter Sixty

Jon had offered to see Molly home. He'd kept insisting she should report Tom, and make it official. Men like that, he claimed, didn't change. She thanked Jon for his help and promised she'd be in touch, hoping he'd take the hint and back off.

Tom wasn't a threat anymore. In truth, he probably never really was. He'd scared her, which was what he wanted at first, then he'd realised she was as hurt as he was. Adding to her pain wasn't going to help him or anyone.

The truth was, she wanted to be by herself. She wanted the chance to spend a bit of time thinking about Bex and how what had happened all those years ago had shaped the person she'd ultimately become.

She'd blamed herself for so long until the guilt had eaten away at her and threatened to consume whatever remained of her life. In the end, she'd joined the police, both for a sense of closure and for the opportunity to bring justice to women like Bex. Or to help people like Zella, whose family had turned their back on her just because she'd dared to be her own person.

It had been harder for Bex's family. Her parents had split up after the court case. Tom had never got over it, clearly hoping the army would give him the answers to life's complex questions.

Molly often wondered what would have become of Bex if she was still around today. Which direction her life would have taken. Bex was always the lively one; the one who would drink too much, never afraid to make a fool of herself and then laugh it off the next day. The one who had sat next to Molly on her first day at school when no one else in her class would speak to her because she was new and spoke with a strange accent. Bex had been her best friend. Her death had left a gaping hole that she'd tried to fill with booze and men and craziness. She had been in danger of going off the rails until her stepfather, a solicitor, had helped her join the Met. She'd worked her way up from uniform to CID to Major Crimes. She knew Bex would have been proud of her.

She walked along the road towards the cemetery. She found Bex's grave easily enough. Sleet was drifting in the air and it was cold.

She hadn't brought any flowers this time. She recalled that summer's evening nearly fifteen years earlier. Warm and sunny. Now it was cold and winter.

Molly traced the letters on the gravestone with her finger. Granite that was cold to the touch.

She kissed her fingers and pressed them against the cold, grey stone as sleet began to turn to snow.

# A letter from Graeme

Thank you for choosing to read *Truth Lies Dying*, the sixth outing for Met detectives Matthew Denning and Molly Fisher. The joy of writing a serial crime series like Denning and Fisher is that by now I feel as though I really know my main characters; the challenge is finding something new and fresh for them to face. This book sees Molly finally coming to terms with her past, while Denning is thinking about his future.

*Truth Lies Dying* tackles the difficult issue of homelessness, something which is sadly on the rise as accommodation becomes less and less affordable for many people, especially in London. Warming Up the Homeless (WUTH) is a real-life charity based in the South East: https://wuth.org/. I hope they don't mind me borrowing their name – hopefully it will help to highlight the amazing work they do.

If you've enjoyed reading *Truth Lies Dying*, please mention it to your friends and family, as a word-of-mouth recommendation can really help make a book. And do please leave a review – it can be as long or as short as you like, it all helps new readers to find my books.

I love hearing from readers, so feel free to get in touch, either via my website: www.graemehampton.com, or you can say hello on Twitter (@gham001) or Instagram (@graeme_hampton). I have recently joined the ranks of

TikTok (which I'm still struggling to get the hang of...), and can be found @graemehamptonauthor.

Best wishes,
Graeme